Another Way Home

Other books in the Chicory Inn series

ANOTHER WAY HOME

HOME

A Chicory Inn Novel

Deborah Raney

Abingdon Press
Nashville

Published in association with the Steve Laube Literary Agency.

Macro Editor: Jamie Chavez

Scripture quotations are from the Common English Bible. Copyright
© 2011 by the Common English Bible. All rights reserved. Used by
permission. www.CommonEnglishBible.com.

Library of Congress Cataloging-in-Publication Data

Raney, Deborah.
Another way home : a Chicory Inn novel / Deborah Raney.
pages ; cm
ISBN 978-1-4267-7045-6 (binding: soft back : alk. paper) 1. Domestic fiction. I. Title.
PS3568.A562A82 2015
813'.54—dc23

2015011546

Printed in the United States of America

15 16 17 18 19 20—10 9 8 7 6 5 4 3 2 1

For my wise and wonderful parents,
Max and Winnie Teeter,
who've given all of their children
such a wonderful heritage of faith.

Sing to God! Sing praises to his name!
Exalt the one who rides the clouds!
The Lord is his name.
Celebrate before him!
Father of orphans
and defender of widows
is God in his holy habitation.
God settles the lonely in their homes;
he sets prisoners free with happiness.

—Psalm 68:4-6a

1

Danae Brooks buttoned her shirt and slipped on her shoes, trying desperately not to get her hopes up. The dressing rooms in her doctor's office were more like something in an upscale spa—heavy fringed drapes curtained private alcoves decorated with framed art prints, and flameless candles flickered on tiny side tables. Soft strains of Mozart wafted through the building. Of course, for the fees her obstetrician charged—or rather, her "reproductive endocrinologist," as his nameplate declared—the luxuries felt well deserved.

She gathered her purse and continued to the window at the nurse's station.

Marilyn—she was on a first-name basis with most of the nurses by now—looked up with a practiced smiled. "You can go on down. Dr. Gwinn will be with you in just a minute."

Danae had quit trying to decipher the nurses' demeanor. So far, month after month, every smile, every quirk of an eyebrow, every wink, had meant the same thing: she wasn't pregnant. Again. Still.

She walked down the hall to the doctor's sparse office and was surprised to find him already sitting behind his desk. She forced herself not to get her hopes up, but she'd always had to wait for a consult before. Sometimes twenty minutes or more. Could it be?

"Come on in, Danae." He looked past her expectantly.

"Oh. Um . . . Dallas isn't with me today. He . . . couldn't get off work." Of course he could have if he'd really wanted to.

"I understand. No problem. Come on in and have a seat." She took one of the duo of armchairs in front of his desk, feeling a bit adrift without Dallas beside her.

Dr. Gwinn scribbled something on the sheaf of papers in front of him, then slipped them into a folder before looking up at her. She knew immediately that there was no baby.

"Well . . ." He pulled a sheet of paper from the folder he'd just closed and slid it across the desk, pointing with his pen at an all-too-familiar graph. "Nothing has changed from last time. Your levels are still not quite where we'd like to see them, but we're getting there. I'm going to adjust the dosage just a bit. Nothing drastic, but you might notice an increase in the side effects you've experienced in the past."

"It hasn't been too bad."

He steepled his fingers in front of him and frowned. "That's good, but don't be surprised if the symptoms are a little more marked with this increase."

Dr. Gwinn wrapped up the consultation quickly and suggested she call his office if she experienced any problems on the new dosage.

For some reason, his warning encouraged her. Maybe this boost in meds would be the thing that finally worked. As quickly as the thought came, she tried to put her hope in check. Almost every week there was something that got her hopes up only to have them dashed again.

But Dr. Gwinn sounded so hopeful this time. Of course, they'd all been hopeful. For more than three years now, a string of clinics had offered endless hope—and had happily accepted their checks for one fertility treatment after another. But despite test after test, a string of doctors in a string of clinics could not seem to find any reason she and Dallas could not have a baby together. "Unexplained infertility" was the frustrating diagnosis. They'd done just about everything but in vitro. Or adoption. And though

Dallas was adamant they would not take that route, Danae was beginning to think it might be the answer. The only answer.

At the reception desk, Danae slid her debit card across the counter. Another three hundred dollars. She dreaded Dallas seeing the amount in the check register. She wasn't sure how long they could keep draining their bank account this way before her husband said, "Enough."

The woman handed her a receipt. "We'll see you in two weeks, Mrs. Brooks."

"Thank you." She forced a smile and sent up a prayer that next time she wouldn't have to endure the shots and medication—because she'd be pregnant. But it was getting harder and harder to be optimistic. And she wasn't sure how long she could hold up under repeated disappointment.

She shoved open the door as if shoving away the discouraging thoughts. Or trying to. The late September air finally held a hint of autumn, and she inhaled deeply. As she unlocked the car door, her phone chirped from her purse. Dallas's ring. She fished it out of the side pocket. "Hey, babe."

"Hey yourself. How'd it go?" The caution in his voice made her sad.

"Same ol,' same ol'. But he upped my dosage a little."

An overlong pause. "It's not going to make you bonkers like the last time they did that, is it?"

"No." She hadn't meant to sound so irritated. She'd kind of forgotten the incident Dallas referred to—like the worst PMS in the history of the world according to her husband. Which was funny given she'd never really experienced PMS, so how would he know? It was probably an apt description though. "That wasn't even the same drug I'm on now, Dallas. And even if it was, everything went back to normal as soon as they cut my dosage back again. Remember?"

"I know . . . I know." His tone said he was tiptoeing lightly, trying not to start something—and trying too hard to make up

11

for not coming with her to today's appointment. "So, do you want me to pick up something for supper on my way home?"

"No, I'm making something." No sense adding expensive take-out to the financial "discussion" that was likely to happen after he saw the checkbook. "Maybe scalloped potatoes? It actually feels like fall out here today." She held up a hand, as if he could see her testing the crisp air.

"I need to go, Danae. We'll talk tonight, OK? But you did remember I'm going to the gym with Drew after work, right? Can I invite him to eat with us?"

"Dallas . . ." She gave a little growl. "It's Tuesday. You know we're going to my folks tonight."

"Oh, yeah. Sorry, I forgot."

"Did you think we were only having scalloped potatoes for supper?"

"I didn't think about it. Sorry. Well, I'll invite Drew another night then. We can—" A familiar click on the line—the office call waiting signal—clipped his words. "Hey, I've got to take this. See you tonight."

"Sure." She spoke into the silence, feeling dismissed. Sometimes she thought Dallas preferred his brother's company to hers.

She climbed into the car and buckled up, imagining the day when she'd be buckling a precious baby into a car seat first. *Please, God. Please.* After three years, this shorthand had become the extent of her prayers.

. Pulling out of the parking lot, she was tempted to come up with an excuse to get out of going to the inn tonight. She'd almost come to dread these weekly family dinners for fear of all the questions about their quest to have a baby. But the truth was, her family had grown weary of the subject and had mostly quit asking. Maybe that was just as well.

She rarely volunteered information to her parents and her sisters now that it had become obvious they'd run out of encouraging things to say month after month.

For the first year after they'd started seeking medical treatment, Dallas hadn't even wanted to tell anyone. But she convinced him that she needed someone else to confide in. Once tests had confirmed that the fault was hers alone, and that Dallas was fully capable of fathering a child, he had been more willing to talk with friends and family about their issues. Now she sensed he was losing interest in the whole subject as well.

She turned toward home. *Home.* It still felt a little odd to turn into the new neighborhood. The divided, stone entrance was an elegant introduction to the upscale development. She and Dallas had traded houses with her sister in August—almost two months ago now—and she still felt like she was going to visit Corinne and Jesse whenever she pulled into the driveway. She and Dallas had traded a paid-off mortgage for a house payment. They'd put a nice down payment on the house, and they could afford it, but it had definitely made things a little tighter than they were used to. And made writing checks for the fertility treatments even more painful.

She pulled into the garage and pressed the remote to lower the door. She loved this house and was slowly adding her own touches to the decor. The trade of homes had been a real blessing to Corinne and Jesse at a time when they needed to downsize quickly, and Danae had no regrets. She and Dallas had been looking for a house big enough for the family they hoped to have, and this place was perfect.

Corinne had given up a lot to make it possible for Jesse to go back to school and get a teaching degree. Danae felt for her sister. She couldn't imagine Dallas suddenly deciding to switch careers after almost a decade of marriage—and three kids. Now the Penningtons' family of five was crammed into the little two-bedroom house she and Dallas had owned. And yet, they seemed happy. She sensed it was still hard for Corinne to see someone else in the house that had once been her dream home, and it had strained the sisters' relationship, but Danae thought time would take care of that. Hopefully Jesse would have a teaching job in a couple of years and things would get back to normal for all of them.

And hopefully, *hopefully*, she and Dallas would have a baby by then. Because if they didn't, she wasn't sure she could go on believing in a loving, caring, *fair* God.

∼◦∞◦∼

It was only nine thirty when the last of the kids pulled out of the driveway, the taillights of the minivan casting a red glow on the new sign Grant Whitman had just erected in front of the Chicory Inn. Watching the vehicle disappear down Chicory Lane, he patted the head of the chocolate Labrador panting at his side, and inhaled the crisp night air.

He caught the scent of wood smoke from their nearest neighbor's chimney half a mile up the lane. Tonight was probably the last time the weather would allow them to eat outdoors, although Audrey usually managed to talk him into one last wiener roast before they stored away the lawn furniture and put the gardens to bed for the winter.

He sighed. "Come on, Huck. Let's call it a day." He bent to scoop up the last of the stray paper cups that had blown off the tables and caught in the corners of the vine-covered pergola. The trumpet vine enveloping the structure was beginning to turn a rainbow of autumn colors.

Grant had instituted these Tuesday family dinners more than a year ago, and he still wasn't sure whether the kids truly enjoyed them or merely tolerated them. The evenings had gone well throughout the summer, but already, now that Jesse and Corinne's oldest was in school—and Jesse too—Grant saw the handwriting on the wall. Now there would be early bedtimes to worry about, and at least during the school year, his kids would understandably want to cut the evenings short.

Chase and Landyn's twins were starting to be a handful, too, now that they were semi-mobile. He smiled, thinking of little

14

Emma and Grace. The babies were growing faster than he could keep up with. Born nearly bald, they'd both quickly turned into carbon copies of their curly-headed mother. And speaking of growing . . .

Landyn had done some growing up since the twins were born. Watching his daughter with the babies tonight, Grant had been so proud of her. She'd turned in to a devoted, conscientious mother. He suspected a lot of people thought Landyn was his favorite because she was the baby of their family. But like any father, he had a soft spot in his heart for each of his daughters—and for his daughter-in-law, Bree.

And the truth was, that soft spot was reserved for whichever daughter was hurting. And right now, it was Danae who clutched at his sympathies. Their second child—"my second favorite daughter" he always teased her—Danae was the one with the tender heart. And so pretty he'd wanted to lock her up and throw away the key when she turned ten.

Danae was pretty still. She wore her distinctive pale blonde hair shorter now, but always sleek and stylish. But it just about killed him to see the premature lines creasing her forehead, the spark gone from her lively blue eyes. He still saw glimpses of that spark when she looked at her husband—*thank the Lord for that*—and when she played with her nieces. But even then, he detected pain. He knew God had a purpose in all this . . . He always did. "But please don't wait too long to give them children, Lord," he whispered.

"What'd you say, Grant?"

Audrey's voice startled him. He hadn't realized she was still out here. "Nothing . . ." He reached for her and drew her close. "Just thinking out loud." He planted a kiss on the top of her head. "We've had a pretty good life, haven't we?"

She pulled back to study him. "We have. But . . . um, it's not over yet, dear."

"No, but it could be. It could all be over in the blink of an eye. A kumquat could fall off the shelf at the grocery store and bingo, I'm history."

She cracked up, which, of course, had been his goal. He did so love making her laugh.

She gave him a dismissive kiss and wriggled out of his arms. "You go ahead and stand there with that smug grin on your face. I'm going in to load the dishwasher."

"I'll be there in a few minutes." He squatted to pull Huckleberry close. If he couldn't hug his wife, there was always the dog. Despite making Audrey laugh, he felt the melancholy creep over him again. Huck seemed to sense it and leaned heavily against him.

Eyeing the dark sky, the ache of sadness—one that autumn always seemed to bring—grew heavier. It would pass. It always did. But something about the death of everything in nature, and the long winter to come, caused his heart to be heavy.

Before heading in to help Audrey with the dishes, he checked the yard one last time for the usual Tuesday night detritus of errant paper plates and the occasional pink sock. Five granddaughters now. That ought to be enough to lighten any man's heart. But still . . . Danae . . .

He walked slowly toward the house, watching his wife silhouetted through the kitchen windows. As much as Audrey loved these family nights, they were a lot of work for her.

When he opened the back door a few minutes later, she looked up from a sink full of pots and pans. "Everything OK?" The question in her eyes said he must be wearing his worry on his sleeve.

He didn't want to open a can of worms, but he didn't think he was imagining things either. "Did you think Danae seemed a little . . . *off* tonight?"

"How so?"

"I don't know. It just seemed like she was distracted, kind of off in her own world."

"Why? What happened?"

"I don't know that anything happened . . . she just seemed a little down. And she was short with Corinne. That's not like her."

Audrey winced. "I think it's hard for her to be around the babies. Especially the twins. But I hope she's not taking it out on

16

her sisters. They can't help it that they have kids." The way she said it made him wonder if she knew more than she was saying.

"I know, but it's got to be hard seeing them both having babies left and right when she wants one so badly. I just hope she's the next one to get pregnant."

Audrey stilled. Then sighed. "Too late for that."

"What? What are you talking about?"

She turned and leaned back against the sink, pressing her palms on the counter ledge behind her. "Corinne's pregnant again."

"What?" He put his dish towel on the counter. "How did I miss that announcement?"

"Oh, there hasn't been an announcement yet. At least not that I know of."

"When did she tell you?"

"She didn't. A mother knows these things."

He cocked his head. "That's a pretty serious . . . accusation, Audrey."

"*Prediction.* A mother knows," she repeated.

"You think a sister knows, too?"

Audrey shook her head. "I don't think so. But Corinne is probably waiting as long as possible, knowing it will be hard news for Danae to hear. Especially in public."

"Well, that might explain the tension between them. But why wouldn't she tell us?" Grant frowned. "Has Danae said anything about how they're doing on that front?"

"The baby front?" Audrey shrugged. "I haven't asked in a while. Lately it seems like she'd rather not talk about it." She took the damp dish towel from his hand and replaced it with a fresh one.

He had to admit to being disappointed. A person would have thought there's-a-baby-on-the-way news would have been celebrated in this family, but if Corinne and Jesse's news was rife with tension, it would mean that exactly half of the new grandbaby announcements in their family had come with trepidation. It just wasn't right.

2

The first week of October had brought Indian summer to Cape Girardeau, and Dallas Brooks was actually looking forward to a good workout, which was something after the workday he'd had. He pulled in to the parking lot to find his brother already waiting outside the gym.

Andrew jogged over to the driver's side.

Dallas rolled down his window. "Hey, Drew. What's up?"

"It's packed in there." He hooked a thumb over his shoulder toward the fitness center, then glanced up at the cloudless sky. "We could do the Cape LaCroix trail. Weather's great."

"Sounds good. Hop in. I'll drive."

Drew went around and climbed into the passenger seat. Ten minutes later the brothers were jogging along the scenic trail that connected several of the parks in Cape. They ran hard, concentrating on breathing instead of talking for the first fifteen minutes, but when they ducked beneath a tree-canopied section of the trail the dusky shadows forced them to slow their pace.

"So how's everything with you?" Drew asked, still breathing hard.

"Good . . . good." It wasn't a lie, but it wasn't the whole truth either.

"Danae doing OK? How's the fertility stuff going?"

The encroaching darkness made Dallas braver. He needed someone to talk to, and he couldn't very well confide in Danae, since she was the problem. In a sense, anyway. "It's . . . going. And going and going and going. I'm about sick to death of it. I tell you, I never thought I'd see the day that I dreaded . . . *sleeping* with my wife." He laughed but he knew his brother wasn't fooled.

"Bro?" Drew looked askance at him. "That doesn't sound good."

"I'm exaggerating, but not by much. She's a slave to that thermometer, and every month I can pretty much mark my calendar to be miserable when she starts her period and—"

"Whoa!" Drew formed a cross with his index fingers. "TMI, bro. You forget I'm a bachelor ignorant of the ways of the fairer sex."

"Sex?" Dallas slugged his arm. "We're not allowed to use that word, remember? Mom would have washed your mouth out with soap."

Drew's laughter made Dallas grateful to have and to be a brother.

"Anyway, as I was saying when I was so rudely interrupted . . . this black cloud descends on the house and God forbid I should say anything hopeful or positive."

Drew's expression turned serious. "How long have you guys been at this anyway?"

"You mean the fertility stuff?"

Drew nodded.

"Too long," he said, too quickly. "I don't know. More than two years, I guess. Probably closer to three."

His brother shook his head. "That's a long time with no hope. Do the doctors think there's still a chance?"

"So they say. Hope springs eternal and all that. They do keep saying there's no reason she shouldn't be able to conceive. Sometimes I think they just have us on a hook, and want to keep us there as long as we pony up another three hundred dollars. Shoot, at the rate we're going we won't be able to afford a kid if we *do* get pregnant."

Which wasn't true. He made good money as a plant manager at Troyfield & Sons. Maybe he wasn't exactly changing the world one high-efficiency particulate absorbing air filter at a time, but he didn't mind his job. Somehow he'd acquired the knack for placing workers in the position that best utilized their talents and skills. He had a gift for managing people. Except, apparently, people he was married to.

"Have you thought about adopting?"

Drew's question jarred Dallas from his thoughts. He clenched his jaw and sped up. His brother matched his pace but didn't press for an answer, jogging in silence alongside him.

"That's not an option," Dallas said finally.

"Man . . ." Drew shook his head. "You of all people should be able to convince Danae to at least give it a try."

He ground to a stop, planting his hands on his waist, his breath more labored than their easy jog warranted. "It's not her that has a problem with it."

"What? Then why aren't you pursuing it?"

"You really have to ask that?"

Drew jogged in place, facing him. "I don't get it. Why wouldn't you consider it?"

"Are you serious?" This was the second time his brother had brought up the subject, and it was seriously ticking him off. "You've apparently forgotten a few things."

"I haven't forgotten that adoption got me a great brother." Drew clapped him awkwardly on the shoulder.

"I appreciate the mushy sentiment, but I wouldn't put a kid through that for anything."

"Through what?" Drew seemed genuinely puzzled.

"You know. What I went through. Wouldn't be fair."

"Your circumstances weren't the norm, Dal. Nothing says it would be the same if you adopted a kid."

"Yeah, and nothing says it wouldn't."

His brother shrugged and took off at a slow jog.

Dallas followed suit, but stayed half a step behind Drew to avoid being scrutinized. So far, in this journey with infertility, he'd mostly managed to avoid the adoption subject, but the more time that went on without Danae conceiving, the closer he got to being forced to examine, again, all the issues entwined with his own adoption.

It was no secret he'd been adopted as an infant after his parents had been married for ten childless years. Then, miracle of miracles, when he was three, his mom conceived. Andrew Wayne Brooks had been born in time to be his Christmas gift. Dallas had loved his baby brother from the start, and not until his teens had he really understood or felt the differences between them.

As far back as he could remember, his parents spoke matter-of-factly about his adoption, so there'd never been a day of shocking revelation for him, or even a time of wondering where he'd come from, since they'd shown him his adoption papers and told him his story from the beginning.

He and Drew looked enough alike that they could have been blood brothers. In fact, Drew had been a strapping four-year-old, and at seven, Dallas had been on the scrawny side, so for a while they'd often been mistaken for twins. A fact Drew had relished and Dallas pretended to despise. But looking back, it had made him feel like they were *real* brothers. Not *half*-brothers, as one of Drew's former girlfriends had labeled them after finding out they were adopted. Which, as Drew had quickly pointed out, wasn't even accurate. "Maybe we don't share any blood, but we're as much brothers as any—and that's by law."

Dallas had clung to his brother's declaration. They'd had the same fights and competition and brotherly hugs that turned into wrestling matches as he imagined most blood brothers shared. All in all, they'd had a great childhood, and he'd never felt like less of a son to Wayne and Marsha Brooks than Drew.

Until he turned eighteen.

Then everything hit the fan. Their dad had a seizure, and two weeks later, a stroke that felled him. Their mother was distraught and, like an idiot, Dallas had chosen that time to go through a world-class identity crisis. One for which he would likely never forgive himself. One he'd cried bitter tears over at their mom's funeral three years later. Sometimes he still wondered if he'd been responsible for her death—even though the coroner's report said it was heart failure that killed her. At fifty-eight.

Nine years ago now. He and Drew had been orphans for nine years. It didn't seem possible. And even though now, at thirty, while he'd mostly worked through things, his reaction to his brother's question told him it wouldn't take much to send him plunging back into the abyss he'd fallen into on that long-ago October day. A day he'd tried hard to forget.

"Hey, man . . ." Drew surged ahead of him on the trail, then turned around and ran backwards, making it impossible to avoid his eyes. "I'm sorry if I was out of line. I know that was a hard thing and I—"

Dallas waved him off. "Don't worry about it." Desperate to change the subject, he dug his phone out of the pocket of his running shorts and checked the time. "I'd better get home. Danae has supper in the Crock-Pot."

They came to the spot along the trail where they usually looped around again. "You going another lap?" he asked Drew.

His brother hesitated for a millisecond. "Yeah, I think I will. You have time? Got to get rid of this gut." He patted his flat belly.

Dallas rolled his eyes, looking for a note of levity to exit on. "I don't even want to hear it, you big stud, you."

That won the smile he was hoping for from his younger brother, and they jogged on in silence.

But driving home later, he couldn't quit thinking about his brother's comments, and when he pulled into the garage, he struggled to put it out of his mind, knowing Danae would be able to tell something was wrong. Her radar always pinged his moods with annoying accuracy.

He caught a whiff of supper and hollered for her in the kitchen. Getting no answer, he did a quick sweep of the counters and her desk in the keeping room where she usually left notes for him if she was going to be gone when he got home. Finding nothing, he checked the calendar on the refrigerator. Nothing there either. She must have gone out to her parents' or to see one of her sisters. Her family had a way of always keeping her longer than she expected.

Which was fine tonight. He'd have time to get his act together before he had to face her. He was trying to trust God with all this—his past, and his future with Danae. But it was easy to say and a whole lot harder to do.

He lifted the lid on the Crock-Pot and inhaled the spicy barbecue before heading for the shower. He found the Cardinals game already in progress on the Bose in the bathroom and turned it up loud enough to hear from the shower in their master bath. As the warm water from the rain showerhead pelted him, he mentally switched gears to the barbecue waiting in the Crock-Pot and found escape from the troubling thoughts Drew had stirred. Squeezing the shower gel harder than necessary, he made a mental note to steer clear of the subject next time he was with his brother.

Danae hiked her purse up on her shoulder and rearranged the bulky items she'd been juggling for the past half hour. The store would close in ten minutes but she'd changed her mind about this bedding three times, and now, as she headed for the checkout counter, she was feeling a little guilty for how much it cost. Especially when Dallas would be home when she brought her packages in from the car. Not that he ever cared when she spent money—and they did need bedding for the second guest room.

When they'd first bought the house, she'd had a blast redecorating the rooms to suit her taste. And Dallas's, of course, although he didn't have many strong opinions when it came to home decor. At the time, she'd been glad she wasn't working, since getting settled in the house was pretty much a full-time job, especially if she factored in her frequent doctors appointments. But the house had come together quickly and she was starting to regret giving up her part-time position with an accounting firm. Maybe next spring—if she wasn't pregnant by then—she'd pick up some hours during tax season.

She looked at the price tags on the bedding again and did the math. It was even more than they'd spent on the bedding for their master bedroom. Still, it would last forever. Or at least until she grew tired of it. Mind made up, she secured the items in her arms and started for the cash register.

"Danae?"

She turned at the uncertain voice behind her and saw Heather March hurrying her way.

"Danae Whitman! It *is* you!"

"It's Brooks now, but yes, it's me." She laughed, genuinely glad to see an old friend. Heather and her family had attended Langhorne Community's youth group back when they were in high school, and she and Heather had been quite close their sophomore year. "How are *you*? It's been forever!"

"I know. Can you believe it? I'm married too." Heather held out her left hand, showing off a huge diamond.

"Congratulations. Anyone I know?"

"Probably not. I met Jake in college. He's from Chicago. How about your hubby?"

"Remember Dallas Brooks? He was a senior when we were sophomores."

"Oh. My. Gosh. You married *him*?"

Danae giggled. "I did. Four years now."

"Wow, four years? Do you have kids?"

And there it was. "Not yet." She pasted on a smile that felt uncomfortably familiar and groped for the routine deflection. "How are your parents?"

"They're good. Still in Langhorne. And yours?"

"They're doing well. They opened a bed and breakfast about a year ago and it keeps them hopping."

"Really? A B&B? Where?"

"At our house out on Chicory Lane, where I grew up."

"Oh! I always loved that house."

"You wouldn't recognize it now. They totally redid it. Named it the Chicory Inn. Dad did almost all the renovations himself after he retired, and now he helps Mom run the place, but it's mostly her baby."

"How about the rest of your family? Did those handsome brothers of yours ever get married?"

She swallowed. The second hardest question she got asked. "Link's still single. Tim was married. You probably didn't hear, but . . . he was killed in Afghanistan—"

Heather gasped. "Oh, Danae. I'm so sorry! I didn't know."

"Four years ago. Almost five now, I guess." She was surprised at the math.

"I'm so sorry," Heather whispered again. "I didn't know."

"No, of course not." She patted her friend's arm. So often it seemed like her family ended up doing the comforting where Tim's death was concerned. "It's been hard, but in some ways it's brought us even closer. Even with Tim's wife, Bree."

Still visibly shaken, Heather nodded. "You guys were always so close. All you Whitman kids."

"Yeah, we still are. Corinne and I both live in Cape, and everybody else is in Langhorne or nearby." She shifted the bundles of bedding in her arms and tried to read the watch on Heather's left wrist. Dallas was probably wondering where she was.

"Oh, you know, I ran into Corinne a couple weeks ago at my obstetrician's office." A blush crept up her neck and painted her cheeks. "I thought I was pregnant, but it was a false alarm."

"Oh . . . I'm sorry." Maybe she'd found a kindred spir—

"Oh, gosh! Don't be sorry! We are so not ready for that yet. Scared us to death!" She clutched her throat dramatically. "But your sister seemed really happy. What does this make for them, four?"

"No. Just three. They have three little girls."

25

"All girls? I bet they're dying for a boy this time. Or does she already know what it is?"

"This time? Um . . . yeah," she finished lamely, rewinding Heather's words, trying to make sense of them.

"Well, whenever we are ready for a baby, I hope Dr. Pharr is still delivering. I really liked him, and everyone says he's the best."

"It was . . . Dr. Pharr's office? Where you saw Corinne?"

"Yes. She said he delivered her girls too." She hesitated, looking puzzled.

"Yes. Yes, he did." Despite the store's twenty-foot ceilings, the room was closing in on her. She looked pointedly at her wrist, even though she wasn't wearing a watch. "I really need to run. But it was so good to see you, Heather."

"You too." Heather reached around her for an awkward hug, given the bulky packages in Danae's arms. "Maybe we can do coffee sometime?"

"Yeah . . . sure." She carried the bedding around a corner, desperate to get out of there. Looking around to make sure no one was watching, she deposited the carefully chosen merchandise in a sale bin like so many rags. Casting about for an exit, she hurried toward the nearest one and pushed open the doors, drinking in the brisk autumn air.

Struggling to remember where she'd left the car, she pointed her keys in the general direction of where she usually parked and gave a little gasp of relief when taillights flashed and a familiar short blast of the horn sounded. She managed to hold it together until she was inside the car.

She forced herself to take deep breaths, and tried to remember exactly what Heather had said. Maybe she was confused. Maybe it hadn't been Corinne she had spoken to at the obstetrician's office at all. Or maybe it was much longer ago than she thought. Maybe it had been when Corinne was pregnant with Simone.

But Heather had said "a couple weeks ago," and she'd known Corinne had three girls. She'd said "this time."

She held her hands in front of her and watched her fingers tremble, as if they had a life of their own. She dug her phone out of her purse and punched in Corinne's number.

"Hey, sister. What's up?" Corinne's cheery, matter-of-fact greeting gave Danae hope that it was all just a huge misunderstanding.

"Hi. Do you have a minute?"

"Sure." Now Corinne sounded wary. "Is everything OK?"

"I just ran into Heather March at the mall. Remember her?"

"Sure. She used to go to youth group at Langhorne Community, right?"

"Heather said she ran into you a couple weeks ago."

Silence.

"Corinne? She said she saw you in Dr. Pharr's office."

"Oh, Danae . . ."

"Is that true?" Her grip tightened on the phone.

"I'm sorry, Danae. I was going to tell you. I just . . . I knew it would be—"

"Are you *pregnant*, Corinne?" The trembling started again only this time it wasn't just her hands.

"I was going to tell you. I swear."

She let out a breath. "It's true then. You're pregnant. And I find out from someone on the street. I made a complete fool of myself." She really hadn't meant for it to come out with such bitterness. But there it was. "Does everybody else know?"

"No, of course not. We haven't told *anyone* yet. We—"

"Anyone except Heather March."

"Danae, I would have told her not to say anything, if I thought there was any chance you'd run into each other, but I . . . ." Corinne's soft sigh came over the line. "I'm so sorry, sis. Really, I am. I was planning to tell you. Soon. But . . . where are you now? Are you at home?"

"No. I'm in the car. I'm still at the mall." She willed her voice not to break.

"Do you want to come over and talk? I'd offer to come there, but the girls are already in bed and Jesse has class tonight."

"So, when are you due?"

"In May. Or maybe early June."

Danae did the math—something she was good at, having calculated an imaginary due date every month for the past three years of her life. "So you're already almost two months along?" She couldn't keep the hurt from her voice.

"We didn't plan this, Danae. Please come by the house so we can talk about it in person," Corinne pled. "I know you're angry, but—"

"I'm not angry!" She knew it was a lie the minute the words were out. But it wasn't Corinne she was mad at.

"Will you please come by?"

"Let me call home first. Dallas doesn't know where I am."

"OK. I'll see you in a few minutes."

Danae hung up and started to call home, but the tears were too close. He'd think something was wrong and freak out if he heard her crying. She put the phone back in her purse, leaned her head on the steering wheel, and let the tears come.

It wasn't fair. Three beautiful, healthy daughters wasn't enough for Corinne? She had to rub it in and make it an even four? The way God had been operating lately, it'd probably be twins. Maybe triplets. Even as the thoughts came, she knew she wasn't being fair. Jesse and Corinne had every right to have as many kids as they desired.

But it didn't seem fair that even though her sister was older than her by two years, she would soon have a four-kid jump on Danae. Corinne said they hadn't planned this baby. But that was exactly what made it all the more unfair. Why would God do that? Why did he give children to people who didn't even want them, hadn't even planned them, while those who would give anything for a baby were denied month after month, year after year?

And if it wasn't bad enough that her sister was having another baby, now she and Dallas would feel even guiltier that they lived in Corinne and Jesse's big new house, while the family of soon-to-be-six was crammed into the little house.

The truth struck her now like a slap in the face. It wasn't really her sister's *house* that had been her dream. It was Corinne's *life*.

The evening had grown cool so she started the car and turned on the heater. Fine then. She'd go talk to her sister and hear all about the new little niece or nephew who was on the way. And when Corinne and Jesse told the family, she would smile and pretend to be happy for her sister. She would bury her pain and go on with her life. But another little piece of hope had crumbled from the thin veneer she'd covered herself in. She formed her fists into knots. She wasn't sure how much more that veneer could crumble without being fatal.

And she wasn't sure who her fury was directed at—unless it was God.

3

Corinne's car was the only one in the driveway when Danae pulled in a few minutes later. That meant Jesse had already left for class. He and Corinne had to park outside since their garage was full of furniture and other items that wouldn't fit into this much smaller house.

Danae eyed the silhouette of stacked boxes through the windows in the garage door, wondering which ones contained all the baby clothes Corinne had packed up during the move. She tried not to think about the carefully folded stacks of baby clothes in the closet of the nursery at her house. Clothes she'd collected through years of waiting. And longing.

It still felt strange to ring the doorbell on the house she and Dallas had called home for five of their first six years of marriage.

Corinne answered and immediately pulled her into a hug. "Come in, sis."

"Congratulations, Corinne," she said over her sister's shoulder, working to keep her voice cheerful.

"Thank you." Corinne hugged her again before releasing her.

"I'm happy for you guys. I really am." She couldn't seem to keep her gaze from traveling to her sister's belly.

Corinne seemed not to notice and opened the door wider. "Come on in. I'll make you some of that tea you liked so much last time you were here."

Danae took a step back. This was awkward enough. She really didn't want to stay. "Thanks, but—I probably shouldn't stay too long. Dallas will be getting antsy."

Corinne set her lips in a thin line and stepped over the threshold, nudging the welcome mat on the porch. Finally she looked up. "I'm sorry, Danae. I really am. I don't know what else to say." She shrugged.

"I just . . . I wonder when it's going to be my turn. You know?"

"I do know. And I *don't* understand why you're having to wait so long for your dream. I know it must seem totally unfair that we weren't even planning this baby, and . . . here we are."

"Yes. If you want to know the truth, it does seem unfair. And I don't understand. Not at all. I—" Her voice broke and she shook her head, at a loss for words.

"I'm so sorry, Danae. But I hope you appreciate what you *do* have. I don't mean to be making comparisons here. I really don't, but it's not like *I've* gotten everything I ever wanted in the world. It's not exactly easy to see you living in my dream house while we try to figure out where to squeeze a new baby."

Danae bit her lip against words she knew she'd regret, and said instead, "Well, I'd trade you places in a heartbeat."

"I know you would. I know that." Corinne laid a hand on her arm.

"So, when are you going to tell the rest of them?"

"Probably next Tuesday night. But we haven't told the girls yet, and you know once we do it will be all over town, so . . ." She shrugged.

"So is this going to be your boy?"

"I'm sure Jesse is hoping so. Poor guy is so outnumbered there's really no hope." Corinne led the way through the house and they sat in the corner of the tiny eat-in kitchen.

"Where *are* you going to put a baby?" The question hadn't sounded so bitter before she spoke it.

Corinne's eyes filled with pained tears.

It tugged at Danae's heart. "I'm sure everything will work out fine." But that came out all wrong too. She hated the tone in her own voice, hated what she was feeling toward her sister right now, but she couldn't seem to make her words cooperate.

"Danae—" It came out in a sob. "I'm sorry I didn't tell you sooner. I'm so sorry you had to find out from someone else. I'm sorry I'm pregnant. We didn't plan this baby, and I don't *know* where we're going to put it. If I could somehow make this baby be yours, you know I'd do it in a heartbeat."

Danae stared. For a split second she wondered if Corinne was actually offering to . . . be a surrogate or something. She shuddered. That would just be too weird. And even if it wouldn't, she'd broached the subject of adopting with Dallas before and it was a closed door as far as he was concerned. She wanted their own baby too. She wanted to experience every awful and wonderful moment of pregnancy, of childbirth, of breastfeeding her baby. Things nearly every other woman she knew took for granted.

When she was six or seven and learned how babies came into the world, she'd spent hours stuffing her shirts with mounds of towels, pretending to be pregnant, then producing for her labor— after much groaning and panting—Cabbage Patch Kids or stuffed bears or otters, and later, full-grown American Girl dolls.

Still, if she were offered a baby for adoption tomorrow, she would take it and rejoice. "You said you're due in May?"

"We're not sure when I conceived. I think I must have skipped a couple of pills while we were in the middle of moving. I promise we weren't trying."

"Corinne, it doesn't matter if you were. You don't owe me an explanation, and it's none of my business if you have six kids." The words made more sense, sounded more true when she said them aloud than when she had tried to mentally convince herself earlier.

Her phone rang in her purse. Dallas's ringtone. "Oh, dear . . . I forgot to call and let Dallas know I was coming over. Hang on."

"Go ahead." Corinne gave a nod. "I need to go check on the kids anyway." She slid from her chair and went back to the bedroom where the girls all shared a room.

Danae answered, "Hey, babe. Sorry I didn't call. I'm at Corinne's."

"I wondered. Do you want me to wait on you for supper?"

"You haven't eaten yet?"

"No. I thought you'd be home any minute. I didn't see a note that said otherwise." He sounded irritated.

"I'm sorry. I'll explain later. Give me twenty minutes. And if you want to go ahead and eat, it's ready to dish up. Just turn the Crock-Pot—"

"Yeah, I got it. I'll see you whenever. If I'm not already in bed." The line went dead.

Great. Now she had a wounded husband to soothe when she got home. Sometimes she wasn't sure it was worth it to even stay on this dead-end track they seemed to be on. Dr. Gwinn still seemed optimistic, but was it realistic to keep on hoping after three years of trying—and failing?

She'd heard enough stories about people who finally gave up, and of course, that was when the miracle of life finally happened for them. She and Dallas had talked about it before, but she'd told him—and he agreed—she wasn't sure she could truly give up and not be thinking in the back of her mind that this would finally be the magic solution they'd been looking for.

Corinne appeared in the hallway with a sleepy toddler on one hip.

"Simone! Hey, sweetie. How are you?" Danae reached out to finger a blonde ringlet. Her heart melted—and then twisted—at the sight of her adorable niece.

"I'm sorry. Do you mind if I rock her while we talk?"

"It's OK. Dallas is waiting supper on me, so I probably should go anyway."

"I'm sorry," Corinne said again, and Danae felt personally responsible for the pain etched across her sister's forehead.

"There's nothing to be sorry about, sis. I'm happy for you." She pasted on a smile—one that was starting to feel oddly normal, if not genuine. "Please don't give it another thought. I'm excited for the rest of the family to find out."

Corinne gave her a grateful smile. Simone grinned at Danae from the safety of her mother's arms and stretched out one pudgy hand.

"Bye, sweetie." She took Simone's hand and leaned in and kissed the toddler's smooth cheek before looking up at Corinne. "Bye, sis. Tell Jesse and the big girls hi for me. See you guys Tuesday."

Corinne hiked the baby up on her hip and gave Danae a little wave.

Danae hurried to the car before the tears started again.

⸻

Gritting his teeth, Dallas paced the length of the kitchen that was three times the distance of the kitchen in their old house. The house they'd worked so hard to pay off. Each time he reached the front of the house, he parted the curtains and looked across the circle drive and down the street to see if he could spot Danae's headlights.

He didn't mind her going to visit her sisters. To tell the truth, he was glad she had them to talk to. He got enough of her angst as it was. If he'd had to listen to her moan and cry every time she got her period and mourn not being pregnant as if she'd lost an actual baby, he just might go mad.

He wanted children too. It wasn't that. Yet, if it didn't happen, he could be content. But it was starting to seem like Danae couldn't. It was starting to seem like he wasn't enough for her. Which didn't make a guy feel very confident in his marriage.

He heard a vehicle and turned on his heel in the middle of the kitchen. The car sped past, but before he turned away, he saw her headlights round the curve into their driveway. He exhaled, determined not to start a fight. It seemed like all they did lately was fight. But he wasn't sure he could go through the motions of comforting her one more time.

He dispensed ice into glasses and poured tea to go with their supper.

The minute she walked through the door, he could tell she'd been crying. "Hey . . . Everything OK?"

"Corinne's pregnant."

Uh-oh. "Seriously? Again?"

She nodded and shrugged out of her jacket.

"But everything's OK with the baby?"

"Of course. Everything's always OK with everybody *else's* baby."

"Danae . . ."

She glared at him. "Well, it's true, Dallas. I don't understand. Why is this so hard—so impossible—for us? I just don't understand."

He put the pitcher of tea down on the counter and went to take her in his arms. It was all he knew to do. He'd run out of words a long time ago.

"It'll be OK."

She tensed. "You don't know that."

He took a step back and stroked her cheek, then tucked a strand of blonde hair behind her ear. "Do you trust God with this or not?"

"I don't know. I want to. I really do, Dallas, but it feels like he's just toying with me. With us. Why would he let that happen?"

"What did *God* 'let happen'?"

She gave him a disgusted look. "Did you not hear what I just said?"

"You mean because of Corinne?"

"If God is trying to make me trust him, He has a funny way of going about it."

"I don't really think Jesse and Corinne's family planning has anything to do with our situation."

"Or lack thereof," she huffed. She grabbed a jar of applesauce from the refrigerator.

"What do you mean?"

"They didn't even mean to get pregnant. It was an accident."

"Ouch," he whispered. "But still, babe, it has nothing to do with us." Before the words were out, he knew they wouldn't sit well, but he couldn't seem to help himself.

She whirled to stare at him. "It sure feels like it has *everything* to do with us."

"No. It doesn't. Danae"—He pushed the air from his lungs—"I don't think you realize it, but this thing is consuming our lives. Our marriage. You can't make this your life. What if we never have a baby? You can't live every day, every month, as if that prayer is guaranteed to be answered. I mean, I'm praying for it too. You know I am. And I won't stop. I hope we have children. But you—*we*—have to find something else to focus on. Some other purpose to live for. Because frankly . . ." He looked away, then met her eyes again, not wanting this to be swept under the rug like too many similar conversations had been. "I love you, Danae, but I don't have the energy to do this anymore. To fight like this. To never know when you walk in the door if I'm going to have to walk on eggshells because something set you off."

Seconds ticked past, the soft trickle of water refilling the ice maker marking time.

She stared at him, then her eyes glazed over, the fight fading from her expression, replaced by a brokenness he knew only too well.

"You just don't understand." Her voice wavered. "It's not the same for you. You have your work. You have a purpose. You have—"

"Please." He held up a hand. "Danae . . . I love you, but we've been over this a thousand times. Yes, I have my work. I have a job I get to go to every day. But you've got plenty of stuff too. If you'd just—" He didn't mean for his sigh to sound so angry. But he *was* angry. And frustrated. "I'm tired of arguing about it. Besides, we're both tired and hungry. Let's just have dinner, OK?"

He went to her and drew her to him.

But she shrank from his touch. "Stop . . . Just stop." She turned on her heel and ran up the stairs.

He stood in the middle of the kitchen, biting his lip, half wishing he could take back the words, even though they'd needed saying. But sometimes it wasn't best to let it all hang out. He knew that. What he didn't know was how he could get his wife to accept this part of their lives that might never change.

4

Danae heard Dallas in the kitchen, presumably cleaning up after eating his supper alone. She was hungry, but she wasn't about to go down there and face him now.

She went to their bathroom and started water running in the whirlpool tub. Their master bathroom was larger than their entire bedroom had been in the old house—the house Corinne and Jesse were going to bring a fourth baby home to. *Stop. Quit being so negative. You're going to push Dallas to the brink.* He'd as much as said so.

She knew the thoughts were the truth. And maybe not merely her own thoughts, given the words from Scripture that floated to the surface now. Words she'd memorized as a child had a way of floating back into her memory just when she needed them: *all that is true, all that is holy, all that is just, all that is pure, all that is lovely, and all that is worthy of praise. Practice these things.*

"Please make my thoughts right and pure, Lord," she whispered. She tested the water, then undressed and slipped into the warm comfort of the tub full of bubbles. She had to admit—Dallas had a point. She'd never been a contrary person by nature, but lately she'd been anything but positive. Who would blame her husband if he was growing weary of her whining? She was growing weary of *herself.*

"I don't want to be this way, God," she whispered into the steamy silence. "Please help me to be patient. Help me to accept whatever your will is."

It was a prayer she'd prayed many times over the last few years—one she'd been sincere about to varying degrees. She wanted to mean it this time.

She soaked and prayed and wept for almost an hour before Dallas finally knocked on the door.

"You OK in there?"

She sat up in the tub, the bubbles long dissipated. "I'm just getting out. Sorry."

"No. Take your time. I was just . . . checking."

The slight tremor in his voice told her he was worried.

"I'll be out in a minute." She dried off quickly and put on her favorite flannel pajamas before going downstairs. She poked her head into the darkened media room and found Dallas punching the remote back and forth between ballgames. "Sorry. I didn't mean to take so long."

He shrugged. "I was going to watch a game, but . . . would you rather watch a movie?"

"No, you go ahead. I might bring my laptop in here and catch up on e-mail while the game's on."

"Great." He didn't like watching TV alone. He always wanted her beside him on the sofa. It hadn't been an issue in the old house, since there the TV room was also the living room, dining room, game room . . . Here, it was more of a challenge to find the togetherness he craved.

But her mom had reminded her that it was a privilege for her husband to feel that way about her, and she tried to honor that, even when sometimes she'd rather be cozied up by the fire in the keeping room, or on her laptop at the bar counter in the kitchen, rooms away from the media room.

"I'm going to make popcorn. You want some?" He smiled at her as if their earlier conversation hadn't happened.

"I'll make it," she said. "I have to go get my laptop anyway."

"Thanks, babe. Kettle corn, if we have it. Please."

They were both walking on eggshells, just like Dallas had said, trying to keep the peace, each sorry for the way they'd spoken to the other. It was a waltz that had become far too familiar, each of them just wanting to find the comfortable way they'd had with each other before all this baby stuff tilted their world on its axis.

She went out to the kitchen and put a bag of kettle corn in the microwave. Within seconds the rich sweet-and-salty aroma filled the kitchen.

It reminded her of when they'd first been married and popcorn was a staple. Made from "scratch" on the stovetop back then because that was all they could afford. Strange how a nice bank account, two fancy cars, and their dream house hadn't brought them any closer than they'd been in those lean years. If anything their wealth, and the privileges it had given them, had put a wedge between them.

Or maybe it was only the months of infertility that had created the wall. At first it had drawn them closer, and she'd felt like she and Dallas were in this together. But lately, it seemed like he was just along for the ride, like he'd given up and was only going along for her sake.

Well, maybe it was time to get off the train. For both of them.

She emptied the popcorn into two bowls and carried them into the media room. A commercial was on, and without having planned to say anything at all, she made a decision. Maybe it was wrought by desperation—as if she might lose him if she didn't. But she was going to voice it before she changed her mind.

"Hey, can I talk to you for a minute." Could she really do this and stick by it?

Dallas eyed her as if he was preparing for a battle. But he clicked the remote and the TV went silent. "What's up?"

"I'm sorry. I—" Her throat closed with emotion, but she pushed it back and continued. "I know I've been a real witch lately, and that's the last thing I want. I think . . . I think you're right. I need to find something else to focus on."

He studied her like he was waiting for the other shoe to drop.

She forced a smile. "I don't know exactly what it is, but I'm looking. I'm asking God to show me what it is. I'd like to finish out the rest of the year with the meds Dr. Gwinn has me on, but after that, I think we should take a break for a while."

"Are you sure?" He was frowning, but she read huge relief beneath his pasted-on expression.

Not knowing if she really was sure, she merely shrugged. "It's not like we can't go back and try again. And who knows, maybe they'll come out with something new, some big breakthrough. But I think we need a break. I need a break."

"Danae, if you're sure . . ." He closed the gap between them and wrapped her in the most genuine hug she could remember since the early months of keeping temperature charts, taking pills that made her bloated and cranky, and scheduling sex around her "fertile" days, which apparently were a joke.

She pulled away to look him in the eye. "I'm sure. Don't think I'm giving up. I just think we need a break and—"

"No. Of course not. We're not giving up," he parroted. "We'll keep trying. That's the fun part." He shot her a grin and wriggled his eyebrows at her. The old Dallas. That was all she needed.

She went back into his arms. "I love you. So much."

"I love you too, babe."

She wished she could feel as relieved as the husband in her arms obviously did.

Audrey carried the lasagna pan into the kitchen, keeping one ear tuned to the conversation floating up from the pergola in the backyard. The October weather had been warm and sunny and she'd convinced Grant to eat outside one last Tuesday before they stored away the lawn furniture for the winter.

Now she regretted it because she couldn't hear what was being said. She had a feeling the big announcement was about to come.

But surely Corinne and Jesse would wait for her to get back outside before they told the others about the coming baby. She hurriedly covered the pan and put it in the fridge. Grant could finish it off for lunch tomorrow.

She started outside with a trash bag for the paper plates but met Corinne on the back deck with Simone in tow.

"I hafta go potty, Gram." The little girl held herself and did a little dance.

Audrey laughed. "Looks like you'd better hurry."

"Potty training is not for the faint of heart. How did you do it five times, Mom?" Corinne rolled her eyes and hurried down the hall after her toddler.

"Just be thankful this is your last one," Audrey called after her. She felt a little guilty setting a trap like that, but if Corinne didn't hurry up and announce her news, Audrey was going to pull rank and ask her outright. Being a mother came with certain privileges, after all.

Either Corinne didn't hear her or she wasn't taking the bait.

She stopped to fold a small load of forgotten dish towels from the dryer. When she finished and opened the door to go outside, Simone dashed from the bathroom and beat her through the door.

"Where's your mommy?"

"Mommy hafta go potty."

That proved it! Corinne had excused herself to the bathroom not twenty minutes ago. If she wasn't pregnant, Audrey was going to recommend she see a urologist. "You wait here with Gram, sweetie. Mommy will be out in a minute."

As if on cue, the toilet flushed and the sound of water running in the sink preceded Corinne's exit. "Oh," she said, when she saw Audrey. "I thought you already went out."

"I was just waiting for you."

Corinne eyed her suspiciously. "Is everything OK?"

"You tell me. Are *you* OK?"

Corinne lifted Simone into her arms and gave Audrey a smile that told all.

"That's what I thought. You're pregnant."

"What's pwegnut?" Simone tilted her little blonde head to one side.

"You never mind," Corinne said, her eyes still smiling at Audrey.

And Audrey couldn't help but mirror her daughter's smile. A new grandbaby was the best news she could think of. It never got old. She put a hand on Corinne's shoulder. "Everything's OK? You guys are happy about this?"

Corinne sighed, but her smile didn't fade. "We are. It took a little while to get used to the idea. And I don't have a clue where we're going to put this kid. But we're happy about it. Maybe this will be Jesse's boy."

"Poppa would be thrilled if it was a boy." Audrey pressed a hand against Corinne's stomach. The swell that filled the space of her palm surprised her. "When are you due?"

"May or June. I'm not sure about my dates and we haven't had a sonogram yet. We're not sure what our new insurance will cover."

"Were you ever going to tell us?"

"Mom, I'm only six or seven weeks along." For the first time, Corinne's smile faded. "We're telling everyone tonight. But we want to keep it real low-key." Her face crumpled. "I feel so bad for Danae, Mom."

"I know. But she'll just have to accept it."

Corinne cringed. "She already knows."

"Oh?" Audrey's mouth slipped open. "You told her? When?"

"A couple days ago. But I didn't tell her. She heard it from a friend."

"What?"

Corinne explained, and Audrey winced inwardly, knowing how that must have hurt Danae.

"Oh, dear," Audrey said. "How'd she take it?"

"She was pretty upset. But she's been really sweet to me tonight. Honestly, it would almost be easier if she hated my guts for it."

"Corinne! You don't mean that. Besides, who could ever hate your guts?"

"Just pray please, Mom. We want to tell everyone, but I don't want it to be uncomfortable for Dallas and Danae."

"That's very sweet of you, honey, but you just tell it like it's the wonderful news that it is. God will take care of—"

The back door opened and Grant hollered in. "Audrey? Where are you guys?"

"Thanks, Mom," Corinne whispered. She took a deep breath and hiked Simone up on her hip. "OK . . . here goes."

Audrey gave her a quick hug around the toddler then took Simone from her. The three of them met Grant in the hallway. "We're coming, we're coming."

"Come on, Dad." Corinne playfully turned him back toward the door. "You're not going to want to miss this."

Grant gave Audrey a questioning look. She winked at him and hurried ahead.

Sari and Sadie were playing down by the creek under the climbing tree. "Do you want them here?" Audrey asked, angling her head in their direction.

"They don't know yet so we probably ought to get them in on this."

"Grant, go get the girls and bring them back up to the table."

Audrey looked down to the pergola where the lights Grant had strung through the trumpet vine twinkled. Link was holding court, telling one of his stories, and his brothers-in-law were laughing, egging him on. Danae and Landyn cleared away the last of the paper cups and napkins. Bree held one of Landyn's twins—Audrey still couldn't tell them apart from a distance—and the other one was playing with Huckleberry at Bree's feet. She couldn't help imagining what it might have been like if Tim and Bree could've had children before he'd lost his life in that desolate desert in Afghanistan. Oh, to have a flesh-and-blood legacy for their son.

She shook the thoughts away. How much more difficult it would have been if Bree had been left with a child to raise by herself. They were so blessed that Bree was still a part of their lives, their family. *She* was the legacy Tim had left to them. And tonight was a happy night. Good news was about to be delivered and celebrated.

Jesse looked up and saw Corinne coming and quickly pushed back his chair and came to her. "Hey, guys," Jesse said. "Everybody gather around. We've got something to tell you."

"Whoa . . . whoa!" Link said. "Last time you made an announcement you were downsizing and trading houses with these two." He pointed to Dallas and Danae. "You can't be downsizing any more unless you're moving to Dad's shed."

Grant had just herded Sari and Sadie to the table. "Wait, wait. What did I miss? *Who's* moving into my shed? And over my dead body, I might add—whoever it is." He aimed his glare around the circle at each in turn.

That got a good laugh. Audrey watched Danae closely, sending up a prayer that she would handle what was coming well. And praying that it wouldn't be long before she and Dallas were sharing their own good news. They were laughing together right now, and if Audrey didn't know what was coming, she would never have guessed that they were hurting.

"Don't worry, Grant," Jesse said. "Your shed is safe. For a few more months anyway." He wrapped his arms around Corinne and kissed the top of her head. "But there's going to be another chair at our Tuesday night suppers this time next year. A high chair, that is."

Happy chaos broke out as everyone congratulated them and asked questions about when the baby was due. Audrey saw Bree slip over to where Danae was sitting. Still smiling, their dear, dear daughter-in-law put an arm around Danae, squeezed her close, and whispered something that looked to Audrey like, "You'll be next."

Oh, please. From Bree's lips to your ear, God.

45

5

Danae was quiet in the passenger seat beside him. Dallas reached over and squeezed her hand in the dark. "You OK?"

She nodded, but he sensed she was close to tears. He pressed her palm to his again, and she squeezed back.

"It really wasn't as bad as I feared," she said, surprising him. "Bree was so sweet about it. Did you hear what she said?"

"No. I saw her whisper something, but it was too noisy to hear."

"She just said, 'it'll be you guys next.'" She smiled up at him. "You know, I kind of think it will, Dallas."

He tensed and gripped the steering wheel tighter, not wanting to encourage what seemed a little superstitious and—after two years with no hope of a pregnancy—unrealistic. Still, he wanted to be supportive too.

He curbed a sigh. He'd be so glad when their marriage wasn't such a tightrope between saying the wrong thing and getting it right. "I'm praying for that," he said finally.

"I know. Me too." She settled into her seat. "Hey, what did you think of that new salad Mom made tonight?"

Where had *that* come from? "Um . . . the tomato one? It was OK. I wouldn't drive too many miles to eat it again."

She laughed, and he felt like he'd dodged a head-on collision.

But then she did a quick U-turn and they were right back on the subject. "I'm not giving up on this, Dallas. I'm just . . . taking a break."

"Woman, you're giving me conversational whiplash. Are we talking about salads or babies?"

She ignored his joke. "I just know too many people who finally got their baby after five years of trying. Or ten."

"Hey, I'm not asking you to give up on it."

"OK." A long pause, then, "Can I ask you something?"

He didn't like the change in her tone.

"Sure, what?" He kept his eyes on the white line at the edge of the curvy road.

"Would you just consider putting our name in with an adoption agency? It could be . . ."

His gut clenched. So much for dodging that collision. "Danae, please. We've talked about this. You know how I feel about that. It doesn't—"

"Would you just hear me out?" She adjusted her seat belt and shifted in her seat to face him. "Please. Just this once, and then I won't bring it up again."

He was sure she'd already made that promise in the past, but he kept that to himself. "OK. What?"

She took a deep breath. "Bill Presky at church was telling me about this place their daughter and her husband adopted from. It was a church organization. Non-denominational, I think, but I'm not sure. They have a huge waiting list so it's a long shot—I think Bill's daughter waited four years. But they only deal with healthy infants and their adoptions are open."

"Open? Meaning we'd meet the parents?"

"Well, the mother. I don't think they usually involve the birth father."

Figured. Maybe if his birth father had been involved, things wouldn't have gone the way they had. His collar felt too tight and he had to make an effort not to squirm in his chair. "Even if I was willing to consider adoption, I don't know if I'd be comfortable with an open adoption."

"But here's the thing, Dallas"—excitement animated her gestures—"we wouldn't have to make a commitment. It would just be to get our names on a waiting list. It's almost guaranteed we wouldn't be faced with a decision for years. And hopefully, I'll be pregnant long before that. But at least we'd have started the process if we end up having to go that route."

"A last resort kind of thing, huh?"

She tipped her head in question.

Against his better judgment, he engaged. "It sounds like you're saying, if worse comes to worst, we could at least take this last resort option of adopting. How's that supposed to make a kid feel?"

"Dallas, that's not what I meant. You're the one who's been so negative about adoption. I'm *not* saying it's a last resort. I only said *any* of that because I know you're so leery of the whole idea."

"Well, can you blame me?" He did not want to talk about this. Any of it. He looked at the speedometer and tapped the cruise control up a notch. They'd be home in five minutes and maybe he could wiggle out of this conversation. "I'm totally on board with you finishing out the meds to the end of this year. But I thought you were going to take a break after that."

"I am, but this whole adoption thing could be something we do in the background, while we take a break from the medical stuff."

Which made the chance of an adoption decision coming up all the greater. "I'll think about it. But in the meantime, I think maybe you need to find something else to pour your passions into. Aren't there still things you wanted to do to the house?"

He hated mentioning it. She'd already spent a small fortune on "necessities"—things she claimed they needed for the house just because they'd moved into a place three times the size of the one they'd lived in before.

She blew out a sigh. "I'm sick of the house. Besides, those empty bedrooms are just a big fat reminder that they *are* empty. Maybe I should look for a job. We could use the money."

"If you want to work, I'd totally support that." He made enough money that she didn't need to work. Yes, their bank account had taken a hit with the purchase of this house and the bills from her fertility treatments, but they were managing.

He felt her eyes on him.

"You really wouldn't care if I got a job?" she said, finally.

"Danae, if that's what you want, I think that would be great. It's not like I haven't wanted you to work before." Granted, he'd been proud that his wife didn't have to work, but if a job would take her mind off of the whole baby thing, then sign her up. Yesterday.

"What would I do?"

"Do you think Franklyn's would hire you again?" She'd worked part-time for an accountant before they moved.

"Maybe. But I think I'd rather find something different."

"Like?" He smiled in the darkness of the car, wanting to encourage this new tack.

"I don't know."

"What if you volunteered somewhere? Weren't they looking for someone at the church nursery?"

She looked at him like he'd just grown a second head. "Seriously?" She shook her head.

"What?"

"I don't think embedding myself among forty babies is a very wise solution."

"Oh. Sorry." Their neighborhood came into sight and he turned onto their street.

"But I'll think on it. You're right about one thing—*something* has to change." She was pensive as they wound through the streets, then pulled into their garage. He was encouraged to realize that the expression on her face was the closest he'd seen to a smile in a very long time.

He only hoped it wasn't because he'd given her a morsel of encouragement about the idea of adoption. Because he'd only tossed her the crumb to keep from having to discuss it.

———✎———

The worship team left the stage and Danae took her husband's hand. She hadn't wanted to come this morning, but as always, she was glad now that she had. There was something about singing and praising God surrounded by people she loved and cared for. Something about getting her mind off herself and her problems even if only for an hour.

Despite the conversation she'd had with Dallas after Corinne and Jesse had made their big announcement, she'd been in a funk all week. Worse, she'd avoided talking to her sisters or her parents for fear they'd put on their sympathetic faces and ask her how she was handling the news. She hated it. Hated the feeling that she'd somehow spoiled her sister's joyful announcement. Hated that infertility had put this invisible mark on her forehead that seemed to make her a target for pity—or even avoidance.

One of the elders took the podium for announcements, and she settled into the cushioned chair. Her mind wandered, but a moment later something turned her attention back to what the man was saying.

". . . might take you out of your comfort zone a little, but it's a wonderful cause and we need your help. Many of us don't realize this kind of need even exists in our state, let alone in our own county. But those who've already gotten involved will tell you that the need is, sadly, very real. While domestic violence is a reality that, thankfully, not many of us will ever have to face, that is all the more reason to get involved. These women need someone who cares. Someone who will take the time to make a difference. If you feel God tugging at your heart, we invite you to come to an informational meeting tonight here at the church. You'll find more details in your bulletin."

Did she feel God tugging at her heart? Or was it just Dallas's appeal making her feel obligated to find something else to occupy her energies? Something else to be passionate about.

Still, she couldn't quit thinking about it. After the service, while he talked to a couple of guys about a basketball league the church was trying to put together, she went into the foyer where there was an information table set up for the women's center. She waited until the woman at the table was occupied talking to another church member, then slipped one of the brochures into her purse. Cape Haven, the shelter was called. At least she could think and pray about it. Taking the pamphlet wasn't a commitment.

She came across it again that afternoon while rummaging in her purse for her phone. She fished out the brochure and put it on the kitchen counter. A few minutes later, Dallas picked it up while he waited for his popcorn in the microwave. "Where'd this come from?"

"It's what the elder at church was talking about this morning. Jason, I think his name is."

"Jason Felder?"

"Yeah. That's him. I thought I'd see what's involved in volunteering at the women's center."

He folded and unfolded the pamphlet, his frown deepening.

"What's wrong?"

"I just don't know that I want you getting mixed up in something so"—he shrugged—"so risky."

"Risky?" She gave a humorless laugh.

"I don't know how involved you were thinking of being. I guess if you're just helping them raise funds or making phone calls or something like that, it might be OK." He creased the brochure and tossed it back onto the counter. "But I sure wouldn't want you getting in the middle of a domestic dispute."

She arched an eyebrow at him. The man was about to have a domestic dispute of his own if he didn't watch it. "It was your idea, Dallas! You're the one who said I should find something else to focus on."

"I was thinking more along the lines of fundraising for the building committee, or maybe helping stock the food pantry."

"So you want me to volunteer for something just as long as it's completely risk-free and as long as I don't come in contact with any humans?"

"Don't be ridiculous."

"Well? That's what it sounds like you're saying. If I'm just going to be a fundraiser or stock boy, I'd rather get a job and do something halfway rewarding, not to mention get paid for it."

"Correction. You'd be a stock *girl*," he said.

She threw the dish towel at him, earning a tentative grin. She didn't return the smile. She knew he was only trying to smooth things over and avoid a fight, but he'd started it. And she didn't appreciate his condescending attitude. "I think I'd like to go to the informational meeting tonight."

"Have you thought about the fact that there might be kids there?"

"So?"

"So how is that different from working in the church nursery?"

"Dallas, I'm not going to join a monastery just so I don't ever have to come in contact with a child again."

"Hey, you're the one who jumped all over me for suggesting you volunteer in the church nursery."

She held up a hand. "I know. You're right. I'm sorry. Can we not argue, please?"

The microwave dinged. She removed the steaming bag and opened it, releasing a mouth-watering fragrance into the kitchen. She popped a few of the warm, fluffy kernels into her mouth before pouring the popcorn into the bowl he had waiting. She handed it to him.

"You want some?" He offered the bowl back to her.

"No thanks. I'm good."

"You sure? Last chance." He cradled the bowl in the crook of his elbow like a football and started for the keeping room where a game was on the TV.

"I'm sure. Hey . . ."

He turned to face her, cramming a fistful of popcorn in his mouth.

"Are you OK with me going to the meeting tonight?"

He started to say something, then glanced up at the ceiling looking thoughtful. "I guess it can't hurt anything just to find out what's involved."

"Do you want to go with me?"

"Babe." You'd have thought she'd asked him to wallpaper another bedroom. But he sighed. "What time is the meeting?"

"It starts at seven."

"Oh, man. That's right when my game starts." He gave her those puppy dog eyes that always made her smile.

"*Your* game? As opposed to the one that's on right now?"

He had the decency to look sheepish.

"It's OK. I really don't mind going by myself. I can report back."

"*Whew*." Relief dripped from his voice. "That was close. Thanks. But please don't join the Peace Corps or anything without at least saying good-bye first, OK?"

She rolled her eyes and waved him away, laughing.

But a frisson of excitement rose in her. She was committed to going to the meeting now. It had been a long time since she'd done anything outside her comfort zone. Anything unrelated to their infertility struggles anyway.

Maybe it was about time.

6

Audrey pulled the last load of sheets out of the dryer in the second-floor laundry room and carried them down the hall to the boys' room. She stopped herself. The plaque over the door read The Brunswick. It had taken them a full year after opening the inn to finally name the rooms. Landyn had come up with the loosely connected chicory theme. But even though they'd remodeled—and despite the plaques clearly spelling out The Brunswick, The Leroux, The Orleans, and so on—she still thought of each of the bedrooms by which of her children had last occupied it.

And The Brunswick was Link and Tim's room. *Tim.* It had been more than four years since that dreadful day when Marines in dress blues had knocked on their door and delivered the unthinkable news that Tim was gone.

She deposited the pile of warm sheets on the bed and flung the windows open to air the room. A wood thrush sang its heart out in the branches of a tall poplar just outside the window. Smoothing the expensive fitted sheets over the pillow-top queen mattress, she smiled, remembering *Sesame Street* sheets and *Star Wars* bedspreads on little secondhand twin beds. How many times had she changed sheets in this room? Tim and Link had both been bed-wetters well into their toddler years, long before big-boy "diapers" and Pull-Ups were staples in every grocery store. Young mothers today didn't realize how easy they had it.

And yet, she'd do it all over again if it meant getting another chance to hold her boy in her arms.

She wondered what the magic time marker was that would render the mere whisper of Timothy's name powerless to wound her. Five years? That anniversary was looming closer than she could believe, and she couldn't imagine *any* date on the calendar that might suddenly heal their pain. Couldn't imagine that it would ever again be easy to answer the innocent question, "How many children do you have?"

Because to name Tim meant reliving his death all over again through someone else's eyes. But to not name him was akin to treason.

Still, she was grateful for so many small things where Tim's death was concerned. That she and Grant had been the ones to answer the door instead of Tim's young wife. Bree had been staying with them while Tim was deployed and she'd been out with friends that night. Not that it had been easy to deliver the news, but at least she'd been spared that nightmare of the military vehicle rolling slowly up the driveway.

As if bringing the memory to life, the crunch of tires on the gravel drive sounded below her. Unexpected tears stung her eyes and she went to the window, almost afraid of what she would see. Before she saw the car, Huckleberry's friendly yips told her it was just Grant, home from a morning of running errands.

She gave the decorative pillows one last plump and hurried into the room's small bath to check her makeup. It wouldn't do for Grant to know she'd been crying. He worried about her too much as it was.

He met her on the stairs, loaded down with Walmart sacks. He kissed her over the pile of bags. "I think all this stuff goes up here."

"Thanks. Did you find out how to get rid of your little friends?"

He'd been to the county extension center on a mission to figure out how to eradicate a family of moles that had invaded the meadow and were, he felt sure, working their way up to the backyard.

"Well, for one thing, the agent said Huck here might be a deterrent." He patted Huckleberry's head. "You do your job, Huck, you hear? Don't you let those rascals tear up my lawn."

Huckleberry looked up at Grant with what looked for all the world like a smirk.

Audrey laughed.

Grant lifted a Walmart sack. "Where do you want these?"

Audrey had talked him into picking up a few supplies for the inn while he was in town since they were booked solid through the weekend starting tomorrow. And she'd agreed to cater a light supper for a group coming in on Thursday. All good for the inn's bottom line, but not so good for her stress level.

She took an armload of bags from him and started unpacking paper towels, toilet paper, and tissue boxes. "I think we are single-handedly keeping Kimberly-Clark in business," she grumbled. Stacking everything in the hall closet, she wondered—not for the first time—if recent guests had helped themselves to the closet supplies. Frustrating. Now they'd probably have to start keeping the closet locked. She emptied another sack and held up a four-pack of square tissue boxes. "Grant? What's this?"

"You said we needed Kleenex."

"Not like this." She gave a little growl, took off the outer wrapping, and handed him a box emblazoned with school buses and cartoon characters.

His shoulders slumped. "You said to get whatever was on sale."

"Honey, I don't think our guests will appreciate the addition of *SpongeBob SquarePants* to the decor." She let loose a sigh. "I guess I can hide them in the tissue holder in the hall bath. Or give them to Corinne."

But Grant had already disappeared downstairs. He returned a minute later with another load of department store bags. "I saved you the trouble of buying me new skivvies."

"That was thoughtful of you."

"But can you wash these for me?"

"Sure. Just pile them on top of the washer."

He inspected a wrapped bundle of briefs, frowning.

"What's the matter? Did you pick up the wrong size?"

"It's not that," he said, shaking his head. He held up the package and pointed at the muscular male model pictured on the front. "I just hate it when they put my picture on the front of these things."

She swatted his backside, laughing. "If that's your biggest problem, I can't feel too sorry for you, buster. I can send them a cease-and-desist letter, if you're that upset about it."

"No, I guess I'll just have to live with the fallout."

"No pun intended?" she said wryly, which earned her a chuckle.

Oh, how she loved this man. She could weather just about anything as long as Grant Whitman was by her side.

"Hey," he said, suddenly serious. "I ran into Dallas at Walmart, and he said Danae's planning to volunteer at some women's shelter. Do you know anything about that?"

She frowned. "It's news to me. But I do remember reading something about the shelter in the *Missourian*. I wonder what got her interested in that. I'm glad though. She needs something to think about besides all this fertility stuff."

Grant's eyebrows formed a V. "What do you think volunteering means?"

"I don't know. They probably just need people to man the shelter. Maybe prepare meals or at least supervise while the women fix meals. We'll have to ask her Tuesday." She gathered up the empty shopping bags and started down the stairs.

"I don't like it."

She stopped and turned from halfway down the stairs to look up at him. "What do you mean?"

"I don't think she should be getting involved with something like that."

"Why not?"

"Isn't that a place where women go to escape their abusive husbands?"

"Something like that. It might be for homeless women too. I'm not sure," she said as she slowly made her way back up the stairs. "What does Dallas say?"

"He's worried too. Rightly so. What if some desperate guy tracks down his wife and comes in with a gun? Do you want Danae involved in something like that?"

She sat down on the top step. "She's a big girl, Grant. I imagine the chances of her getting in a fatal car crash are a lot better than the chances of getting caught in the crosshairs of some lunatic husband."

"Why would she want to take a chance like that at all?"

"I'm sure Dallas will talk her out of this if he thinks for a minute that it would put her in danger."

"And this is our intake office." The social worker, Renee Marin, pulled one of about twenty keys from a lanyard around her neck and unlocked a door.

Danae followed Renee through the door along with two other women who, like her, were volunteers in training.

Once they were all inside the small office, the social worker locked the steel door behind them. "We keep this door locked at all times, whether we're in the office or out in the house. This may also serve as a safe room should you ever have need of one."

Dallas had ended up going with her to two training sessions besides the introductory meeting, but Danae was glad he hadn't come with her tonight. The mere mention of need of a safe room— that, and the fact that they'd met at the church and been driven to the secret location of the safe house—would be all Dallas needed to change his mind about her going through with this. And she had to admit she was still on the fence herself. There was so much to learn, and she felt very much out of her comfort zone—as the social worker had warned during the training sessions that she would.

And yet, there was something exciting in learning something new, in feeling that she might make a difference in a woman's life. Renee, though she was barely out of college, had done a good job of explaining what they could expect on a typical night, and being with the other volunteers, who were all as green as Danae, had given her more confidence that she could do this.

After the training sessions he'd attended, Dallas had reluctantly admitted that it seemed safe enough. But she knew he didn't have the time, nor the inclination, to continue with the training. Besides, most of the things male volunteers were involved in—maintenance and upkeep, or bookwork—would have had them working different schedules. She suspected he was mostly just glad she'd found something to keep her mind off the whole baby thing. She'd graciously given him an out tonight, which he grabbed onto so fast it made her head spin.

The first three training sessions had been held at the church. Not until they'd been given a chance to back out had they been allowed to come tonight to the actual address of the center. And Danae was ashamed to admit that she'd strongly considered backing out. Letting Dallas's earlier reluctance give her an excuse to say no to the next step.

She'd tried to imagine pouring her passion and focus into the poverty and tragedy that some people lived with every day. If she was honest, she wanted to pretend those people didn't exist. Wanted to hide out in her beautiful home and shop online for yet another three-hundred-dollar bedspread or a new lamp for the second nursery.

But then she looked around and began to see all she'd been blessed with—a loving husband, a luxurious home, good health despite no baby, her happy childhood, and loving parents. She had so much! And by the time she went through the litany of blessings, she would have felt guilty *not* agreeing to volunteer.

So here she was in this residential home in an older, middle-class neighborhood. On the outside, it looked like any other home on the street. No sign or awning marked it as the women's shelter. But inside, the house had been modified to create bedrooms for up to twelve women, two women to a room. Most shared the two large bathrooms, but there were two family rooms that had private baths. Those were reserved for women with children, and on rare occasions, for couples who were threatened by a third party. Right now there were only five women in residence at Cape Haven, each assigned her own room, but they expected to fill up quickly once they were fully staffed.

"No matter how many women we have, there must always be two volunteers here at any given time. And we work on the buddy system," Renee explained. "Depending on the threat level, you may be instructed to stay together at all times. In a few minutes I'll show you the safe room in the basement and we'll go over the procedures for using that room if necessary."

Two safe rooms? Danae wondered if her eyes reflected the fear she saw in the other two volunteers' eyes.

Renee must have noticed, too, because her voice quickly turned soothing. "Don't worry. The vast majority of the time, that won't be an issue. We expect to use the basement safe room more as a storm shelter than a haven from a spouse who goes 'postal,' but we wanted to guarantee the safety of not only our women but the volunteers too. Most of these women have made a clean break with the help of family members or friends, or sometimes clergy. When that's the case, their abuser rarely has a clue where they are. In many instances, the women have come from St. Louis or Kansas City, so they—and you—will be far removed, physically, from their abuser."

Renee looked at each of them in turn. "Unfortunately, the more difficult part is removing these women emotionally from the person who has abused them. It's difficult for those of us in healthy relationships to understand how any woman could allow a man to control her to that degree, and there are as many reasons as there are women why someone would go back to a man who has beaten her within an inch of her life or even put her children in danger."

Danae shuddered inwardly. It *was* hard to understand. And it made her angry that God allowed women like that to have children when she and Dallas had been denied. She brushed away the thought as if it were a cobweb. She was here to keep her mind *off* of that topic. And to help women with worse problems than her own. She was grateful that spousal abuse was an issue she'd never had to deal with. She didn't even know anyone who'd suffered abuse at the hands of a man who supposedly loved her. Of course, given the statistics she'd heard over the last week, maybe she did know such a woman and just hadn't recognized the signs.

"Many times, dealing with these women's emotions will be your challenge," Renee continued. "While we don't expect you to play psychologist or counselor, the sessions over the next six weeks will train you in helping women to break the cycle of abuse and gain the skills they need to be on their own. We help empower women to leave their pasts behind, not just for their own good, but for the sake of their children and other family members." She looked over the sheaf of papers in her hands. "The center is new and we're all still working through things and figuring out what works and what doesn't, but are there any questions so far?"

Megan, one of the volunteers, timidly held up a hand. "I assume we aren't allowed to talk about what goes on at the shelter with just anyone, but can I talk to my husband about things?" She gave a nervous laugh. "I get the feeling I'm going to need to vent to someone."

Renee frowned. "You'll each have to sign a confidentiality agreement and I can't stress enough how important it is that you not discuss anything that happens here outside of the center. As we said before, and as the agreement you signed affirms, it's especially important that you not disclose the location of the center. I'm not going to say you can't talk to your husbands about your experiences. I'm not one who believes it's healthy for a husband and wife to keep anything from each other, but we would prefer that you not use full names or specific details when you share with your spouse."

Dallas wouldn't be happy about that part either. Yet, Renee had seemed to leave a loophole so that they could use their judgment about how much to tell their spouses. She wouldn't feel right not telling Dallas where she was each time she came to volunteer. And she knew he would argue, rightfully so, that he would need to know where to find her if she had car trouble, if the weather turned bad . . . No, she would tell him. It wasn't like she couldn't trust him to keep a secret. She'd just make it clear he was not to pass along the information.

A cloud settled over her as she thought back to their conversation the other night, when she'd tried—unsuccessfully—to convince him to consider getting their names on the list with the new adoption agency she'd heard about.

Though she had no evidence, she couldn't jettison the feeling that Dallas was keeping a few secrets from *her* in that regard.

7

Audrey held her hands out over the fire pit and looked up into the night sky. "I can't believe we got another night nice enough for a fire."

"You call this nice?" Grant shivered and zipped the collar of his jacket as high as it would go. How he'd let her talk him into yet another outdoor Tuesday night dinner he didn't know. She was wily, his wife.

"Well, it was nice. I admit it's a little chilly now."

In the meadow below them, lit only by two camping lanterns hung from the climbing tree, their kids and grandkids—except for Chase and Landyn's twins who were asleep in the house—played a raucous game of King on the Mountain. Their playful shouts, punctuated by Huck's yipping, floated up on the night air. He and Audrey exchanged knowing smiles.

He shrugged. "They don't seem to be bothered by the cold."

The fire crackled and snapped in reply, and he followed Audrey's gaze to a jewel box of stars. He had to admit it was a beautiful night. Overhead, a canopy of deep blue served as a backdrop to the glitter of stars. And the waning light of a crescent moon illuminated a tracery of tree branches still valiantly clutching their leaves of yellow and gold.

"These Tuesday dinners were a good idea." She leaned back in her chair and tilted her head back, closing her eyes.

"They were, weren't they?"

A trio came trudging up from the meadow. Corinne with her two youngest girls, judging by the silhouettes.

But when they got close enough, Grant realized it was Danae with the girls.

"Can we leave these munchkins with you guys?" She hefted Simone onto Audrey's lap, not waiting for an answer.

"You guys have enough light down there?"

"Too much. I keep getting captured." Danae laughed. "I shouldn't have worn a white sweatshirt."

Grant pulled Sadie onto his lap. "Didn't you want to play?"

"It's too dark, Poppa. Can I have another s'more?" She snuggled into his coat, petting his head as if he were a cat.

"Gram? What do you think?" He lived in fear of breaking one of the new parenting rules, and always deferred to Audrey when it came to the grandkids. Who knew there would be so many newfangled devices and so much newfangled advice by the time his kids had kids?

"Better not this late, sweetie. But maybe we can send home all the stuff to make one in the microwave tomorrow. What would you think about that?"

Sadie pouted a little, but Audrey soon distracted her.

"Thanks, Poppa and Gram." Danae started back down to the meadow.

But Grant stopped her. "Did Dallas tell you I ran into him at Walmart last week?"

"He did."

"Said something about you volunteering at that homeless shelter."

"It's not a homeless shelter, Dad. It's a women's shelter. A safe house for women who are in abusive relationships"—she winked—"like Mom, for instance."

He ignored her joke. "You feel safe there?"

She eyed him suspiciously. "What did Dallas say? Did he put you up to this?"

"No. I put me up to this. What if some hostile husband comes to get his wife and you're in the middle of it?"

"Dad, the women are there in secret. That's the whole point. No one is supposed to know they're even there."

"What does Dallas think about you working there?"

"I don't actually work there. I'm just a volunteer . . . probably only one night a week—maybe two—once the training is over. And Dallas is the one who suggested it in the first place."

He couldn't tell for sure in the dim light, but he didn't think she was quite meeting his eyes. From the way his son-in-law had talked, Grant hadn't gotten the impression that Dallas had encouraged Danae. Quite the opposite, in fact.

Danae gave him a quick hug. "They're waiting on me for a game, Dad. Can we finish this conversation later?"

"Sure. You go on. Don't step in a hole on your way down to the meadow. I've got a stupid mole that's intent on turning my yard into Swiss cheese."

"Yeah, Mom told us. Don't worry, I'll be careful."

He was pretty sure she didn't just mean about the mole holes. Not that it made him feel any better about her getting involved with the safe house. But maybe he was making a mountain out of, well, a molehill.

⁂

A twinge of guilt pinched Danae. It hadn't been quite a lie, but if she were being totally honest with her dad, she would have revealed that Dallas had his qualms about her volunteering. And while it had been his idea for her to volunteer, it was a stretch to say the women's center gig was his idea. A long stretch.

"Hey, sister, you coming or not?" Link waved from the meadow below.

"Hurry up, Aunt Danae. You're on my team." Sari charged up the hill toward her.

"I'm going as fast as I can, squirt. How'd you manage to get us on the same team?"

"Daddy said it was OK."

"Good for him."

"Mommy's too tired. She's goin' up to help Gram."

Corinne came up the hill behind Sari, looking worn out.

"You think it's going to be more restful up there?" Danae gestured over her shoulder.

Corinne laughed. "Good point. Maybe I'll just sit here and watch you guys for a while." She plopped down on a slope and propped her elbows on her knees with a sigh.

Danae bent to look at her. "Are you OK?"

Corinne waved her off. "I'm fine. Just tired." She gave a crooked smile. "It'll go away in a couple of weeks."

Danae fought off the thought that seemed to come no matter how she resisted it. *Will I ever know what it's like to be pregnant? Will I ever get to be the one talking about morning sickness and trimesters and labor pains?*

She felt like she should say something else to Corinne, but she couldn't think of anything that wouldn't sound bitter or woe-is-me, so she gave her sister a clumsy pat on the shoulder, then pointed down the hill. "I'd better go. They're waiting on me."

"You go. Win one for the girls."

She nodded and jogged toward the meadow. But she felt like crying and was glad for the cover of darkness. She missed the days before this awkwardness had sprung up between them. She felt like it was her fault, and yet she didn't have a clue how to fix it. Worse, the way things were between her and Dallas lately, she didn't feel like she could even talk to him about it.

Great. She'd shut out her dad by not being fully honest with him. She'd made things awkward with her sister by not knowing how to talk to her about her pregnancy. And things were tentative with Dallas because he wasn't crazy about the new "passion" she was pursuing.

Interesting that *she* was the common denominator in all these relationship woes. Maybe she should take a hint.

"Hurry up, Aunt Danae." Sari grabbed her hand. "We're ahead, but we need you!"

"OK, I'm coming, sweetie." At least somebody still liked her.

8

Dallas and his brother had been running the Cape LaCroix trail every chance they could, taking advantage of the most perfect fall weather Dallas could remember. And that was saying a lot, given southeast Missouri's typical stunning autumns.

It had finally gotten colder, but he didn't mind what Danae fondly referred to as sweater weather.

They'd run about a mile along the curvy tree-lined trail, and Drew had hardly said two words. Sometimes that was OK, but Dallas got the distinct impression his brother had something on his mind. As they rounded a bend in the sidewalk, he gave Drew a brotherly slug on the bicep. "How's come you're so quiet today? You having girl problems?"

"Ha!" Drew rolled his eyes. "Don't I wish. I'm starting to think all the good ones are taken."

"Hey, you're too young to give up hope."

"Easy for you to say, buster, since you're married to one of the best ones out there."

He didn't know what to say to that. Danae definitely was one of the best—*the* best—but it wouldn't be honest if he didn't admit that things had been better between them. He knew they'd get through this, but they were definitely in a rough patch right now. But his brother didn't need to get involved. This was between him and Danae. "Hey, you know we've offered to play matchmaker.

We weren't just kidding. There are some very nice girls at our church."

Drew gave him a sideways look. "'Very nice' being a euphemism for 'ugly as mud'?"

"No. Not at all. I'm serious. Come to church with us Sunday. I'll point out a few and we'll go from there."

His brother looked like he might actually be thinking about it. Drew was a good guy, and Dallas knew his brother's faith had remained strong even through four years of state college and a sales job in a decidedly secular atmosphere. But he claimed he didn't have time for church. Maybe meeting chicks wasn't the best reason to convince someone to come to church, but Dallas thought the ends justified the means in this case.

Drew surprised him by reaching out and stopping him with a hand on his shoulder. "You might be surprised to know that I wasn't thinking about finding a woman, but about finding a kid for you and Danae."

"What? What are you talking about?"

"Hear me out, bro." He moved to the edge of the trail while a pair of coeds jogged past. Drew's eyes followed them, appraising for a few seconds before he turned to give Dallas the look that was brotherly shorthand for *hubba hubba.*

He shook his head. "Too young for you, man. And don't look at me. I'm a happily married man." He took off, jogging at a slower pace, wondering where his brother was going with this.

"I can't quit thinking about what we talked about a few weeks ago."

Dallas waited for him to go on. When he didn't, he begrudgingly took the bait. "We've talked about a hundred things in the last few weeks."

"I'm talking about the adoption thing," Drew said finally.

"Drew, I—"

He held up a hand. "Will you please just let me get this out? I feel like I've been supposed to say something for the last two weeks and it wasn't easy to get my courage up."

Not liking the direction this conversation was going, Dallas nudged up the pace. He'd see just how strong his little brother's *feeling* to say something was.

"I was only fifteen when that all went down with your mom . . . your birth mom. And we've never really talked about it. Mom told me a little bit, of course, but I guess maybe I don't know the whole story. I feel kind of bad that I said anything the other day, since I *don't* know what happened back then. But if it's nothing more than Mom—*our* mom—said, then I have a speech for that too." He looked sheepish. "I just don't like having what feels like a wedge between us because we haven't really talked about this."

"What did Mom tell you?" He couldn't look at Drew. Wasn't sure he even wanted to know the answer to that question. Except that if he didn't get an answer, the wondering would drive him crazy and force him to think about things he'd long tried to bury. Dread rose up in his throat, choking him the way it always did when he thought about that day.

"Just that you wanted to meet your birth mother and she . . . wasn't willing. Is that right?"

"That's about it."

"Did you ever try again—to get in touch with her?"

"She pretty much didn't leave that as an option."

"I can understand why that was hard. And I'm not trying to make light of it, I'm really not, Dal, but can I just say, *her loss.*"

He swallowed hard. "Thanks, man. I appreciate that. It . . . was a long time ago."

"I know. But it seems like maybe it still has a hold on you. I just think it'd be a shame if some woman's mistake affected you to the point that"—he slowed his pace—"it kept you from getting to be a dad. Because I think you'll make a great one."

The sun was going down fast, and a light mist moved in off the Mississippi. The humidity made it harder to breathe. Or maybe it was the lump in his throat. When he could speak over it, he croaked, "Thanks for saying what you did, Drew. I don't know if I'll be a good dad or not. I'm still kind of figuring out how to be a good husband. I feel like I'm bending over backwards to keep Danae happy. She's redecorated every room in the house. We're paying through the nose for these fertility treatments. But nothing is ever enough."

"She says that? Seriously? That everything you've made possible for her isn't enough?" Anger tinged Drew's voice.

"No, of course not. I don't mean to make her sound like an ingrate. It's not like that. She's just so obsessed with having kids, having a baby, that she can't see the forest for the trees right now. You know, we bought this huge house and filled it with furniture. She's got two kids' rooms set up, which seems a little ridiculous to me."

Drew's grimace said he agreed.

"She thinks she's fooling me by calling them guest rooms, but it's no coincidence that one's pink and one's blue. For a while it seemed to kind of settle her down to have the house to work on. And same with every time she finds a new doctor or hears about some new treatment. For a while it makes her happy." He ran a hand through sweat-damp hair. "But even when she doesn't say anything, I just get this feeling that it's never enough. That *I'm* never enough."

"That's just crazy," Drew said.

"Yeah. I know . . ."

But he didn't know. And he could barely voice his worst fear to himself, let alone to his brother. What if they *never* had kids? Would Danae blame him? He'd had all the tests, and the doctors had assured them that the medical issues were Danae's, but sometimes he got the feeling she didn't quite believe them. He sometimes worried that she wondered if things would have been different if she'd married someone else.

And when he let himself think about it too hard, he worried too, that if they *did* have children, Danae would love them more than she loved him. He knew it was childish to think that way, but hadn't Jesse and Chase joked about something to that effect just the other night, talking about how they were demoted to errand boys once the kids came along? *We're out of diapers, Chase. Can you take Simone to potty, Jesse?* They'd laughed about it, sure, but there must be some truth to it.

Drew slowed down, breathing hard. "Danae isn't like that, Dallas. She might be letting this make her a little . . . off-balance, but I think I know her well enough to know she's committed to you. She's not going to let this ruin what you guys have."

"I know. You're right. I'm letting it get to me. Sorry. Let's talk about something else."

"Listen, I know I said this before, but just because your birth mother had issues doesn't mean—if you guys adopted—that your kid would have the same experience, whatever it was. I don't know what exactly happened." Drew shrugged. "Don't need to know. But it's not fair to let it mess with your decision about adopting."

"It's kind of hard not to."

"I get that, but can't you separate yourself from the emotional part? You've always been all about being practical."

It was true. He prided himself on being pragmatic and no-nonsense. Danae gave him grief for it too.

They came back around to the parking lot and Dallas bent and put his hands on his knees, catching his breath. But he looked up at his brother. "I'll think about what you said, OK? I can't promise anything, but . . . I'll try."

They went in opposite directions to their cars. Dallas climbed behind the wheel and adjusted the mirror. Meeting his own eyes there, he had to ask himself hard questions. Why *couldn't* he get past the emotional angles with this issue? Why couldn't he separate what happened to him from what might happen if he and Danae adopted?

Because what happened to him was a deep wound that had never quite healed. He didn't know how to fix it. And he sure wasn't going to set some kid up for the pain he'd suffered.

"If you'll just fill this page out, then I can talk you through the other intake forms," Danae said, sliding the paper across the desk to the young woman. She was surprised to see her own hands were shaking and pulled them back quickly, hoping the woman wouldn't notice.

She still had several sessions to go before her training was complete, but because they were so shorthanded she was working as an official volunteer tonight. Of the three who had started in her training class, she was the only one who'd continued past the second week.

And there were three new women at the shelter tonight, counting the one sitting in front of her, reeking of stale cigarette smoke and recent garlic. An olive-skinned little boy sat on her lap, his mop of thick, dark hair the same color as his mother's. Danae thought he looked about three—the same age as Simone. And if anyone had reason to be trembling, it was him. His right eyebrow sported a gauze patch secured with superhero Band-Aids.

The wound still oozed red, and the front of his shirt was splotched with not-quite-dried blood. He kept his head down and picked at the bandage with ragged fingernails.

His mother—Misty, according to the intake forms—slapped his hand away. "Don't mess with it, Oz. You don't want it to start bleeding again. And hold still. Mama has to fill out this paper."

She would have been pretty—beautiful even—but her crystal blue eyes had a vacant quality that made Danae wonder if she was high on something. Of course, she'd been through a horrific ordeal tonight, escaping from an abusive husband who'd turned his venom on their child. Apparently the police had gotten involved, and a social worker had driven them here tonight from St. Louis. Danae shivered. She couldn't even imagine what that must be like.

"We can put a clean bandage on that as soon as we get you settled in a room. Did it just happen tonight?" Danae guessed the answer, judging by the blood on the boy's shirt. "Do you think it needs stitches?"

Misty didn't quite meet Danae's gaze. "It's not deep. Just bled a lot. Head wounds do." She said it like she knew.

"We'll get him cleaned up and we can check then."

Misty shook her head. "He never went this far before—his dad . . ." She angled her head toward her son, a sudden spark filling the vacancy in her eyes. "That's it for me. No more. He's not gonna mess with my baby and live to tell about it."

"You did the right thing," Danae said. "We'll get you two settled in a room and find some toys for this guy to play with tomorrow."

His dark eyes lit at the mention of toys.

"What's your name?" Danae asked, smiling at him.

His thumb went into his mouth.

"It's Austin," Misty answered for him. "His dad calls him Oz for short. I'm not crazy about it, but it kinda stuck."

"Austin's a cool name. My husband's name is Dallas. Texas cities must make good boy names."

Misty made a wry face. "Don't think I'll be naming my next one San Antonio."

Danae laughed. "How about Bug Tussel? Or Dripping Springs?"

Misty looked dubious. "Seriously?"

"Pinky swear. Those are real towns in Texas. My dad used to threaten to move us all to Dripping Springs when my brothers were little and wetting their beds almost every night. Except he called it Dripping Bedsprings."

That earned her a wan smile.

She felt almost guilty about the excitement that went through her as she finished filling out entry forms for Misty and Austin. They were on a first-name-only basis here, though of course the locked records would have full names should they ever be needed.

Not that she was happy there were new women in the shelter, but she *was* elated that she was here to help. She was proud of the fact that she'd stuck it out, and Misty's smile told her she was already making a small difference.

And what Dallas had said was true: it helped to get her mind off her own problems. In fact, she'd started her period this morning, and while she was disappointed, the dreaded sign she wasn't pregnant hadn't caused the emotional meltdown it usually did.

She was eager to tell Dallas about her evening. He was still on the fence about her volunteering, but he'd have to give her some credit about this victory. With each day she came to the shelter to work, she felt a little more confident, a little more invested. And a little less desperate about having a baby. Not that she wasn't still praying with everything in her that God would answer her prayers. How could he not? She prayed so hard for that blessing that she almost understood how Jesus could have sweat blood— she edited her thought immediately.

It was a ridiculous comparison and she was immediately sorry. As her grandmother CeeCee often said, there were always people worse off than you. You just had to find the right people to compare yourself to.

Tonight, for the first time in a long time, she believed it. And felt grateful.

9

Danae checked the time on her phone. Almost eleven fifteen. She was supposed to get off at eleven, when the next volunteer came in. But no one had showed up to replace her yet.

"You go ahead and go home." Berta Salmans waved the back of her hands across the table as if she were shooing a flock of chickens. The grandmotherly volunteer reminded Danae of a younger version of CeeCee, her dad's mother. "Sherry said she was running a few minutes late. I'm sure she'll be here any minute. I can handle things here."

She shook her head. "I wouldn't feel right about that. I don't mind staying. Just let me call my husband again and let him know what's going on." She punched in Dallas's number, hoping he hadn't gone to bed.

"He worries about you, doesn't he?"

"He does. I don't know why he thinks I—"

"Danae? Where are you?" Dallas sounded irked.

She held up a hand to Berta and turned away. She kept her voice low. "Hey, babe. Were you sleeping?"

"No. I'm still up."

"The next shift hasn't come in yet, and I don't want to leave Berta alone. It should only be a few more minutes."

"I'm not going to bed until I know you're home safe."

"You don't have to do that."

"I know I don't have to. Drive careful, OK? Have you looked outside? It's foggy out there, like zero visibility."

"Oh. No, I hadn't seen the weather. Maybe that's why Sherry's late."

The phone on the office desk rang, and Berta answered before it could ring again. She listened to Berta's end of the conversation, but couldn't tell what was going on.

"Hang on a minute, Dallas. I'll call you right back."

Berta hung up, frowning. "That was Sherry's husband. She got about two miles from home and went off the road. He said the fog's so bad you can't see ten feet in front of you. She's back home now and not coming in tonight, and I don't think you should try to go home either."

Danae went to the window and parted dusty venetian blinds. A dense mist hung in the air, forming halos around the street lamps and porch lights. "Wow. It's bad out there. When did that move in?" She turned to Berta. "Let me see what Dallas thinks."

"If he thinks anything other than you need to stay here till that lifts, then let me talk some sense into the man."

She smiled, but Berta didn't return the favor. "I'm serious, girl. There's no sense taking a chance when we have beds here. You can go home first thing in the morning. Tell your man you'll be home in time to cook him breakfast."

"Yeah . . . you're probably right." She sighed and dialed Dallas again.

"No probably about it," Berta said. She scooted back her chair and went to the linen closet where fresh sheets and blankets were stacked. "You want the bed in here?" She motioned to a daybed in the corner of the office. "Or one of the guest rooms?"

"You choose. It doesn't matter to—" Hearing the connection going through, she held up a hand. "Hey, Dallas."

"Have you left yet?"

She turned away again. "No, not yet. And Berta doesn't think I should. Sherry, the girl who was coming on after me, slid off the road. I guess the fog is pretty bad. I wouldn't feel right leaving Berta here alone anyway."

A heavy sigh. "OK. I understand."

But she could tell he didn't like it.

"So when do you think you'll be home?"

She glanced up at the clock. "The next shift comes in at seven in the morning. I'll leave as soon as they get here and we do report."

"OK. Sleep tight. Or will you get any sleep?"

"Oh, sure. They've got beds here for us. Things are pretty quiet tonight. I'll be fine."

"I know." His tone softened. "I love you."

"I love you too, babe. See you in the morning."

She hung up and tucked her phone in her purse, feeling Berta's eyes on her.

"See?" Berta gave her a smug grin. "That wasn't so hard now, was it?"

"He does worry about me. He wasn't crazy about me doing this in the first place, so—"

A noise near the office door made them both look up.

Berta started to push her chair back, but Danae waved her off. "I'll get it."

"Check the peephole first," Berta reminded her.

She did and looked down to see the top of little Austin's head. She opened the door and knelt to his eye level. "Hey, buddy."

He stood there in the same blood-stained clothes he'd arrived in. "Where's my mama?"

Danae threw a questioning glance back at Berta. "Isn't she in your room?"

He shook his head and rubbed sleepy eyes, looking like he wanted to cry.

"Come with me, and we'll find her." She grabbed a flashlight from the shelf near the door.

Berta followed her from the office, locking the door behind them.

"Shh." Danae put a finger over her lips, then took the bare-foot boy's hand, wondering why he was still fully dressed. Even though Misty had fled her apartment with only the clothes on their backs, Berta had found pajamas for both of them in the supply room, and Misty had been coaxing him to change when she and Berta left the room after helping them get settled. "Everyone is sleeping, so we need to be very quiet, OK?"

She cautiously opened the door to Misty's room and shined the light on the bed. It was empty.

She flipped on the light switch beside the door. No sign of Misty.

Berta reached for the flashlight. "You stay here with him, and I'll go check the dayroom."

"Is my daddy gonna come and find us?" Austin looked up at her with eyes that were far too hollow with sadness for so short a life. He picked at the soggy bandage over his brow.

She knelt beside him again. "Don't mess with that, buddy. Here, let me see if I can make it stick better."

He flinched, but let her lift the bandage. She was glad to see that the wound had quit bleeding and wasn't overly red or puffy. But he'd probably have a little scar there.

"It's looking pretty good under there." She gently pressed the adhesive back in place. "We'll need to put a clean Band-Aid on before you go back to bed."

"I don't wanna go to bed. Is he gonna come and find us?" the boy asked again.

She started to reassure him that he was safe from the man who'd inflicted the wounds on the boy's head and face, but remembering what she'd learned in the training, she changed her reply to a question. "It might be a while before you see your daddy again. Do you *want* to see him?" She would never understand how a child could continue to adore a parent who'd violated them, and yet statistics bore out the fact that it happened far too often.

She couldn't read Austin's expression. His thumb went to his mouth and he lowered his eyelids, a fringe of long, dark lashes resting on the curve of his cheeks.

She went to her knees and set him on the floor, then knelt beside him and placed her hands on his shoulders. "You're safe here, buddy. We won't let anything happen to you. You won't have to see your daddy until he learns how to be nice to you and your mommy, OK?" She hoped she could keep that promise. She'd heard too many horror stories about women who went back to their abusive relationships like a dog to its vomit.

"Let's get you back in your jammies, OK?"

He dropped his head and backed away. "I can't."

"Why not?"

"They're wet."

"Oh. Well, let's go find some clean ones. How does a nice warm bath sound?"

"Am I gonna get a spankin'?"

"Of course not. Why would you get a spanking?"

"'Cause I wetted the bed."

"Hey, I know it was an accident. Nobody is going to spank you."

"Uh-huh. My daddy is." He shrank into himself.

"No, he's not. Your daddy isn't here, and he doesn't know where you and Mommy are. Nobody is going to spank you." Again, she worried she was making a promise the boy's mother might break. But she took his hand. "Let's go run some bathwater, OK? Then I'll have your mom tuck you in."

She took a detour past the dayroom where the greenish glow of the television told her Misty probably had been found. Sure enough, Berta came from the room and met her in the hallway.

"We're going to take a quick bath," Danae explained.

Berta frowned. "You should let his mother do that."

"I don't mind."

"It's not that, Danae. It's her responsibility. Not ours. This isn't a babysitting service."

Feeling chastened, she nodded. "OK. I'll take him to her. Is it OK if I help? Since she doesn't know where things are yet?"

"Of course. She just doesn't need to be sitting on her butt in front of the TV while we play babysitter and laundress."

Berta had volunteered for many years at a homeless shelter in Kansas City before moving to Cape Girardeau, and while Danae had discovered that the woman had deep compassion for underdogs and for the down-and-out, she also had no sympathy for anyone who wasn't willing to better themselves when they'd been given an opportunity.

"I'll be back in a little bit." Danae picked up Austin, wrinkling her nose at the pungent odor, and asked Berta over his head, "Were there any more pajamas his size in the bins?"

"I'll see what I can find and bring them down."

"Thanks." She carried Austin down the hall to the dayroom. Misty seemed oblivious to them over the low drone of the TV.

"Mama?" He lurched from Danae's arms and stretched toward his mother.

Danae eased him to the floor.

Misty jerked around. "What are you doing up, Oz?" The look she shot Danae was *not* one of appreciation.

"I'm gonna take a baff."

"No, you're not. It's the middle of the night. You get back in bed."

"Misty." Danae moved behind Austin and waited until his mother looked at her, then mouthed, "He wet the bed."

She shrugged. "That happens almost every night."

"Why don't we run a warm bath? It'll help him sleep. Berta's looking for another clean pair of pjs, and I'll change the sheets while you bathe him."

For a minute Danae thought Misty was going to argue, but she crawled off the dayroom couch with a sigh and headed toward their room. Misty had been given one of the family rooms that had its own bath, and Danae went through the room to the bath and started water running in the low tub.

Misty turned Austin to face her and pulled off his blood-stained T-shirt and undershirt. She tossed them in a corner. "Take off your jeans, too, baby."

Danae gathered the clothes into a pile. "We can run these through the wash." She held up the shirt and undershirt and inspected them. "Might as well throw these out. That blood will be pretty well set—"

"No!" Misty snatched the shirt from her hand. "That's the only thing he's got to wear. I'll just wash them out in the sink here. Done it enough times when we couldn't get to the Laundromat."

"Oh, OK. Well . . . I guess we can put them to soak in the washing machine. I think there's some stain removal stuff in the laundry room. You finish up his bath and I'll go get a load started and make up his bed with fresh sheets," she said brightly.

"I hope the mattress didn't get wet. He clean ruined his one at home."

"It'll be OK. We have waterproof covers on all the beds here." *Didn't everyone have those?*

She didn't want to seem condescending to this young mother, but the woman seemed clueless. And oblivious to her responsibilities.

Of course she was. She'd just been through a nightmarish situation. And now she was in an unfamiliar house in a strange town, apparently with only the clothes on her back, and likely no idea how she was going to support herself and her son. *Give her a break*, Danae chided herself.

And still, the first thought that pressed in on her was that this woman had a child she could barely take care of, one she'd put in harm's way, whether intentionally or not. Meanwhile, she and Dallas waited and longed desperately for a baby.

It took all the willpower she had to force the thoughts from her mind. This volunteer gig would do her no good if she only used it as an excuse to whine and grow bitter. This was about getting her mind off her own troubles and making someone else's life a little better. It was about being a blessing instead of a burden. *Help me live that out, Lord. Please . . . I'm not doing so hot on my own.*

It was after midnight when they finally had the little boy settled back in bed. Misty insisted she wasn't tired and parked herself back in front of the TV in the dayroom. Danae seethed. It was obvious Austin was upset and frightened. Why didn't his mother go comfort him?

Still, the training had emphasized that the shelter wasn't a prison, and that the goal wasn't to try to impose their own ideas on the residents. They were free to come and go as they pleased and within limits, they were free to conduct themselves as they pleased. The only inviolable rule was that they keep the shelter location a secret for the security of all.

She went to the foyer and looked out the arched window in the front door. It was almost one a.m. and the fog wasn't as dense now, but since Sherry wasn't coming in, and Dallas wasn't expecting Danae home until morning, she relaxed and resigned herself to spending the night. She hadn't yet worked an early morning shift, and it would be a good experience to see how things went.

Berta insisted she take the empty bedroom in the basement. It felt odd to be sleeping here. She felt vulnerable and unsettled, but it struck her that what she was feeling was a fraction of what any of the women coming here must feel the first night they stayed overnight.

The economy sheets were scratchy against her skin, but they were clean and she buried her nose in them, trying to mask the dank odors of the basement. She drifted to sleep feeling grateful for the chance to experience this day and hopeful it would make her more sensitive to the women the shelter would serve in the future.

A gentle wave of—was it contentment?—washed over her. She let it lift her. There were thousands of hurting women in the world, and she would never be able to reach even a fraction of them. But tonight, just for a few minutes, she'd made a difference. She couldn't wait to share her experience with Dallas.

10

Dad, where are you setting up the apple-bobbing station?" Danae loosened the strings on her hood and buttoned the red cape. They'd skipped Tuesday night family night in lieu of a Harvest Open House at Chicory Inn, an alternative to Halloween for the kids of the community.

Her dad turned from where he was lighting lanterns on the front porch. "Well, don't you look cute," he said, tugging on one of her braids. "What are you supposed to be?"

"Dad! Duh . . ." She held out the picnic basket she carried and pulled her hood up. "I'll give you a clue: I came with a Big Bad Wolf."

"Ah! I get it now." He looked past her and started laughing. "And there's the big bad cheese."

Danae turned to see her brother-in-law in a Wisconsin cheese hat, yellow tights, and a sandwich board that looked like Swiss cheese. "Jesse! That's hilarious."

He rolled his eyes. "Talk to your sister. She's the one who coerced me into this."

She fished her camera out of the basket and snapped a picture.

He deflected the flash with an upheld palm. "That had better not show up on Facebook!"

"No promises," she said, still snickering. "Where's the rest of the family?"

He pointed toward the house, and at that moment, the door opened and Corinne herded out three little stair-step girls dressed in gray sweat suits. From their long tails and whiskers, Danae guessed they were mice. Then she saw the masks covering their eyes. "Three blind mice! How adorable!" She eyed her sister quizzically. "And you are?"

Corinne, wearing one of CeeCee's frumpy house dresses with a frilly apron tied at her waist, pulled a giant cardboard "carving knife" from behind her back. "The farmer's wife," she said, straight-faced. "Who else?"

Danae clapped and made them pose for a picture with the "big cheese." Jesse was a good sport and let the littlest mouse climb up on his cheese board. Simone's mask was askew so that one eye peeked over it. It made a darling photo.

And it made Danae long for the day she and Dallas would be dressing up little "mice" of their own for a harvest party. She steeled herself against the feelings that always came when the family gathered and she and Dallas were the only couple without kids.

"Have you seen the twins yet?" Corinne asked.

"Not yet. Are they dressed up?"

Corinne grinned. "Just wait till you see. But Landyn is going nuts trying to get everything perfect. If you want to go help her and Mom inside, I'm sure they'd appreciate it."

Tonight's party had been Landyn's idea, a safe way for the grandkids to celebrate Halloween, and a chance to get people to the inn with hopes that touring it would spur some new bookings for parties or guests. Business had been pretty good through the summer, but Mom confided that things had fallen off a little recently.

"Jesse, have you seen Dallas?"

"You mean that scraggly wolf that wandered through the yard?"

"That's the one."

"He's out back, getting the fire pit ready."

"Thanks."

She started up the steps to the front porch, but ran back to the driveway to snap a photo of the inn before it was completely dark. The place looked beautiful in the dusky autumn light, the woods making a perfect backdrop behind it. Dad had worked his holiday magic with lights strung all across the porch, and glowing lanterns nestled among mums and pumpkins along the sidewalks and fences. Even Huckleberry was dressed for the occasion with a pumpkin-colored bandana tied around his neck.

Watching the kids, Danae thought about little Austin at the women's shelter. Berta had told her the shelter didn't participate in Halloween because of safety concerns. Since the safe house, Cape Haven, was hidden away in a residential neighborhood, that meant they had to turn out the lights and pretend no one was home. "We'll have a movie night in the dayroom," Berta had said. "Make a party of it ourselves." But Danae doubted that would be much fun for Austin.

She hadn't worked since last Friday, but she hoped someone would think to take Austin trick-or-treating in the neighborhood, at least to a few houses. Of course, Misty probably wouldn't appreciate having her three-year-old on a sugar high. But still, it made her sad to think of him missing out on the festivities.

She opened the front door and her brother almost bowled her over on his way out. "Link! Where's your costume? Come on, get into the spirit, will you?" she teased.

"Thanks, but I think I'll pass. I don't want to show anybody up, you know?"

"Yeah, right. You just couldn't come up with anything clever enough. Rumor has it Dad has a prize for the best costume."

Link frowned, looking skeptical.

"A *cash* prize."

"Seriously? Man, that might be worth getting in on." He did an about face and led the way back into the house.

Danae laughed and gave him a brotherly shove.

He ignored her, but asked over his shoulder. "Have you seen the dice yet?"

"Dice?"

A big grin spread across his face. "Follow me. This is going to be a tough act to beat."

He led the way to the kitchen where Landyn and Chase stood wearing white cardboard boxes painted to look like dice, and feeding two smaller "dice"—the seven-month-old twins dressed in white Onesies with rows of black felt circles sewn on their fronts and backs.

"Would you look at that!" Danae crowed. "A full house!"

"Actually"—Link gave an exaggerated wink—"It's *paradise*. Get it? Pair. Of. Dice?"

Danae and Mom laughed at the puns, but Landyn just groaned and handed Danae a baby spoon. "Hey, Red, would you mind taking over here?"

"Sure. What are we eating?" Danae held up a jar and squinted at the label.

"Squash and peaches in the jars." Chase poked another spoon-ful of peaches into Emma's eager mouth.

"I want to put the girls down around eight before it gets too wild here," Landyn said.

"Too late." Link affected a droll smile.

Landyn fanned herself. "It's hot in here!"

Link sucked in a short breath. "Hey, that gives me an idea for a costume." He bounded for the basement stairs.

"You'll never outdo the Yahtzee family!" Danae hollered.

Her brother ignored her and disappeared down the stairway.

"Is Bree coming?" Danae asked, realizing she hadn't seen her sister-in-law yet.

Her mom looked up from the huge bowl she was loading with candy. "She went to pick up CeeCee. They should be here any minute."

The back door opened and Dallas stepped through wearing his wolf mask and hairy gloves with fierce looking rubber claws. Grace and Emma took one look at him and broke into howls.

"Dallas!" Danae put down the spoon and shook a finger at him. "You're scaring them."

Looking sheepish, he yanked off his mask and smiled big at the girls. But that just made it worse, since he had fangs.

"Take out your teeth," Danae hissed.

"Huh?"

"Your fangs! Take them out." She turned back to the babies and cooed, "It's OK, girlies. It's just Uncle Dallas."

He turned aside, removed the mouthpiece, and tucked it into his shirt pocket before approaching the high chairs, grinning and talking baby talk. "That's right. This ol' wolf wouldn't hurt you—"

The babies were having none of it. They screamed at the top of their little lungs until Landyn came running.

"What happened?"

Danae couldn't help but laugh. She rose and made a production of shooing Dallas outside. "Out, Mr. Wolf," she scolded him, for the girls' benefit. "Get! Get outside where you belong!"

When the wolf had been properly dispatched and the babies calmed down, Danae finished feeding them and offered to put them to bed upstairs.

"That would be awesome, sis," Landyn said.

"Let me get some pictures of you guys first."

She wiped their tiny hands and faces and cleaned off the high chair trays. Landyn and Chase each picked up one of the "dice" and the little family posed beside a display of pumpkins and squash that Mom had arranged in a corner of the large kitchen.

"You're sure you don't mind putting the girls down?" Landyn gave Danae that look of pity she was learning to loathe.

"No, of course not. Are their pajamas up in the room?"

"The room" was one of the inn's guest rooms that Dad had finally designated for family after first Landyn and Chase, and more recently, Corinne and Jesse's family had needed to move back home temporarily. As much as they'd all had trepidation about their childhood home being turned into a bed and breakfast, the Chicory Inn had been a haven when they'd needed it. For

Landyn, while she and Chase put their marriage back together. For Corinne's family, while the two couples had made the big house switch.

Danae wondered who might need the sanctuary of the old house next.

"Yes, pajamas and diapers too," Landyn said. "And you don't even have to rock them unless you just want to. They pretty much put each other to sleep these days. Just put them in the crib feet to feet and maybe sing a couple of songs, and you're golden."

"OK. Come on, girlies." She picked Emma up from the high chair and parked her on one hip, then waited while Landyn put Grace in her other arm. "Let's go night-night with Aunt Danae."

She headed upstairs, nervous about tripping or dropping a baby. She was always a little self-conscious with her nieces, feeling like everyone was evaluating what kind of a mother she would be. And usually feeling like she was failing the test. Not that they ever said anything, but she sensed their judgment.

She was good with kids. And it would be different when she had her own. She nudged the door to the bedroom open and knelt to put the girls on the floor. They both flopped into crawling mode and made a beeline for the open door. She retrieved Emma, and by the time she turned around, Grace was escaping.

"You silly girls," she said in her best baby-talk voice. "You're giving a whole new meaning to 'roll the dice.'" She giggled at her own joke and made a mental note to be sure to find an opportunity to try it out on Link, which made her laugh harder thinking about it. The twins seemed to think she was laughing at them, and they upped their antics.

"Come here, you little wiggle worm." She scooped up one twin—three dots on the Onesie . . . that would be Emma—and plopped her into the crib, then nabbed Grace before she escaped.

The two quickly pulled to standing and peered over the rail at her while she gathered diapers and wipes and pajamas. She didn't know how Landyn and Chase did it. *But I'd be willing to give it a go, Lord. Even twins.*

The sweetness of her youngest nieces brought tears to her eyes as she sang the same lullaby Mom used to sing to them when they were kids. *Sleep my child, and peace attend thee, all through the night.* They finally settled down and she took turns patting their little backs, lulling them to sleep.

Within a few minutes, their even breaths told her they were out, but she lingered upstairs, playing the game she so often did when she had a chance to care for babies—pretending just for a minute they were her own. Making believe her prayers had been answered and her dreams had come true. She should have come dressed in costume as a mommy because that was all she really wanted to be.

The sound of unfamiliar voices in the foyer below brought her out of her little charade, and she gave each pajamaed bottom a final pat, made sure the baby monitor was turned on, and closed the door behind her.

She looked over the stair rail to see Mom in the foyer handing out candy to some kids who looked too old to be out trick-or-treating. Her mother had changed into a terra-cotta sweat suit and a crazy hat covered with flowers. Maybe she was supposed to be a flower pot?

Danae tiptoed back and checked on the babies one last time, then took a deep breath, put the hood up on her Red Riding Hood cape, and went down to join the festivities.

"Did I really scare the twins that bad?" Dallas still felt awful about making Grace and Emma scream like that. His hairy "paws" lay on the console between them—along with the set of fake fangs.

Danae just laughed. "I think they'll survive. It was kind of funny actually, but for a minute there, I was afraid you were going to scar them for life."

"Me too. I didn't even think about how they might react when I came in the house. Corinne and Jesse's girls didn't seem to be fazed. I hope the twins don't have nightmares."

"Don't worry. I'm the one who put them to bed. They were out in ten minutes, smiling all the way, so don't flatter yourself."

"I still can't believe your Dad gave your brother the prize for best costume."

Danae giggled. "You've got to admit, it was pretty good."

He snorted. "For throwing something together last minute, maybe. Man, we could have used that twenty bucks!" Link had come upstairs stuffed into one of Audrey's maroon jogging suits with the hood up, folded into a puffy tan sleeping bag, and calling himself a hot dog. He'd looked amazingly like one too.

"At least you out-punned him by calling him a sausage 'link.' Good one, babe!"

He chuckled, basking in her pride. "That *was* pretty good, huh?"

Something caught his eye as they crossed Sprigg Street, and he slowed the car and pointed. She followed his gaze to a group of late-night trick-or-treaters heading up to a house. "They're out a little late, aren't they?"

The clock on the dashboard said nine twenty-seven. "I'm going to guess those are college kids."

He nodded. "I remember those days."

"Me too. And I can't say I miss them."

He laughed. "No . . . me either. Tonight was fun. You make a very cute Red, by the way. Good enough to eat." He took his hands off the wheel long enough to make wolf claws.

"It was a fun evening. It always is."

"But . . . ?" She hadn't acknowledged his teasing, and there was something in her voice that made him think something was on her mind.

She shook her head. "No. No 'but.' I'm doing better, Dallas. I really am. I think it's been good for me to have the distraction of the shelter. It just really feels good to be doing something that makes a difference, you know?"

He reached for her hand across the console. She'd talked about nothing else since coming home from her first night volunteering at the shelter. It was a refreshing change. "I'm proud of you. I really am. But . . ." He didn't want to rock the boat when she'd been so positive lately, but he had to ask. "You're sure you feel safe there?"

"Absolutely. They're very careful with security, and like I've told you before, most of the women's abusers live out of town and have no idea where their wife or girlfriend is."

"I was thinking . . ." He paused, not sure this was the right time to bring it up, but he'd started, so may as well finish. "I don't want to horn in on your thing, but I wondered about going with you sometime."

"Really? You want to do that?"

"If that's OK with you."

She didn't answer immediately. "Sure. I think there are some couples who volunteer. There's always maintenance that needs doing on the house, so they'd let a guy volunteer for stuff like that. I think I'd have to get permission for you to be there."

He couldn't tell if she was pleased or not about his desire to see what the safe house was all about. He'd expected her to be pleased and he wasn't sure what to do with her lukewarm reaction.

"I just thought it might be good if I see where you're working, meet some of the people you've talked about." He shrugged. "You know how I like to be able to picture things."

"I know." She squeezed his hand. "And I'd love to have you there. If you *want* to come. But don't do it only on my account. I'm getting along fine there, and I've never felt unsafe."

"I'm glad. And I'm proud of you for going through with this. I . . . I'm sorry I made a stink about it to start with."

"I know you were just taking care of me."

"I do what I can."

She loosened her seat belt and leaned over to kiss his cheek. "And you do it so well." She rubbed the stubble on his usually smooth cheek. "You big bad wolf, you. Did you really grow all this fuzz in three days?"

"Give or take."

"Wow. What a man."

He puffed out one cheek and leaned toward her, one hand on the wheel. "You like this? There's plenty more where that came from. Just give me a couple days—"

"Don't go too wild on me there, Wolfie."

He gave a low growl that made her giggle like a little girl.

Elation took him by surprise. How long had it been since they'd found this playful way with each other? He felt like he was eighteen again. Except he'd never gotten lucky with Danae Whitman at eighteen. For the thousandth time, he shot up a silent prayer of thanks that he hadn't had the privilege of meeting this woman until he'd become a man halfway worthy of her.

Just enjoy the moment, Brooks. Don't go all serious on her. He pulled her into a one-armed hug.

"Both hands on the wheel, buddy." She wriggled out of his grasp. "Ten and two. Ten and two."

"Actually, that's not right anymore."

"What do you mean that's not right?" She looked at him like he was crazy. "Try telling that to Mr. Bates, my drivers' ed teacher."

"Um, no offense, but that was a long time ago."

That earned him a playful slug.

"No, I'm serious," he said. "It's because of the airbags. Apparently ten and two is a dangerous spot for hands and arms if the airbag deploys."

"Really? Well, aren't you just a fount of information?"

"I've got some more information for you too."

"Oh yeah? What's that?" She was flat flirting with him now.

"I love you." And he did. *So much.*

"I love you too, babe." She turned serious. "Despite all this stuff we've been going through, I still feel like the luckiest woman in the world."

"So . . . does that mean I might get lucky tonight?"

She laughed. "You might . . . you just might."

Afraid of losing the almost giddy place they'd reached, and not wanting the subject to turn to "all this stuff they'd been going through," he turned on the radio to an oldies station and pulled her close again.

She didn't resist him this time, but leaned into his one-armed hug, then intertwined her fingers with his, and let out a sigh that boded well for the rest of the evening.

It was so good to have his wife back. So good.

11

Everybody, this is my husband, Dallas." Danae took his hand
and pulled him into the dayroom at Cape Haven where the cur-
rent five residents, including little Austin, sat watching TV. The
show was not one she was familiar with, but from what she could
see, it didn't look appropriate for Austin. She'd had to bite her
tongue more times than she could count over the things Misty
allowed that sweet boy to see and do.

"It's not our business," Berta had reminded her more than
once. Still . . .

"Hey, ladies." Dallas lifted a hand, then quickly dropped it to
his side. "Nice to meet you all."

He seemed uncharacteristically shy, and Danae scrambled to
think of a way to make him feel more comfortable. She was proud
to have him by her side. They'd gotten the director's permission
for Dallas to work with Danae tonight, since Berta wanted to take
a couple of hours off to attend a piano recital of one of her grandkids. She'd be back before the next shift of volunteers came on,
but Mary, the director, had been adamant that there must be two
volunteers on site at all times. Berta said they'd let Dallas slide
through since he'd attended two of the training sessions at the
church. And of course, Danae could vouch for him.

The women finally looked up from the television and gave
half-hearted waves before turning back to their show. Danae was

embarrassed for Dallas at their almost-rude reception. Of course, all but Misty and a young woman named Jeri were new since the last time Danae had worked.

Misty had been here for over three weeks now. In fact, after another client had moved in with a relative yesterday, Misty had become the senior resident. She acted like it, too, sometimes bossing the newbies around as if she ran the place. But judging by her aloof demeanor tonight, something was bugging her.

"Did you guys already have supper?" Danae put on her most chipper attitude.

And got nothing in return.

Misty mumbled something that might have been "yeah," while the rest of them ignored her.

Then it struck her: it must seem to these women like she was rubbing it in. Each of them was likely looking at divorce or at least separation. Each wore deep scars—both physical and emotional—inflicted on them by men who were supposed to love them. Men they likely still cared for on some level.

And here *she* stood, holding her husband's hand as if he were a trophy she was lording over them. She hadn't thought of that when she'd told Dallas she didn't mind if he came with her tonight.

"Does anyone want popcorn?" She asked, feeling reproved. "We're going to make some kettle corn."

Murmurs of *no thanks* went around the room. They all seemed to be avoiding meeting her eyes.

Even Austin hid his face in his mother's sweater.

But he peeked up at Danae, and she wrinkled her nose at him, a game they'd played last time she was here.

He wiggled his little nose, then tugged on his mother's sleeve. "Mama? Can I have some corn?"

But Misty shushed him, pulling him into her lap and physically turning his face back toward the TV.

Danae took the hint and motioned for Dallas to follow her out to the kitchen. "I want to talk to Berta before she has to leave."

The older woman was bent over the dishwasher, pulling out clean dishes and setting them on the counter. Danae had introduced her and Dallas briefly when they first came in.

"Berta? I can't believe you're doing their dishes," Danae teased. "You give me so much trouble about doing their jobs for them."

The woman straightened, her glasses fogged over with steam. Her cheeks beneath the wire rims colored. "I know, I know . . . but they wanted to watch that stupid show, and I was bored." She straightened, put her hands on her hips, and shot Dallas a look of aggravation. "Does she give you this much guff?"

Dallas feigned a stern look. "And then some. Why do you think I send her here as often as possible?" He seemed immediately comfortable with Berta, unlike with the younger women.

"I should have known." Berta laughed, but just as quickly sobered. "I understand you're not crazy about letting us have your wife here at the shelter, but I promise you we're taking good care of her."

"Thank you," he said, putting an arm around Danae and drawing her close. "I appreciate that. Despite all the guff she gives me, I do kind of like her."

"We do too," Berta said seriously.

Danae could have hugged her. "I'm going to show him the rest of the house, OK?"

"Of course." Berta winked. "I'll just be here slaving away in the kitchen."

Danae took her husband's arm again, knowing Berta Salmans had already won Dallas over.

As they turned to leave, Misty appeared in the doorway with Austin in tow. "Is it too late to change our minds about kettle corn?" She dipped her head and refused to look any of them in the eye—the way she'd done when she first came to the shelter. Danae had forgotten how intimidated Misty had seemed then. And she hated that Dallas's presence had undone in two minutes the confidence Misty had already regained. The cowering hunch wasn't a becoming look on her. But if even a good, respectful man like Dallas had this effect on Misty, then she had some work to do before she was ready to make it in the world.

She wondered if Misty's husband had any idea the pain and life-changing angst he'd inflicted on his wife. Or if he even cared. How could he not care about his own son? Austin was so sweet, and most of the time he seemed like a normal little boy, but Danae had also seen him turn somber and pouty for no reason, and cling unnaturally to his mother—evidence that he hadn't come out of this unscathed. And who would expect him to? She could scarcely imagine a man using hands that had been created to love a son, to instead, inflict wounds. Wounds that wouldn't heal easily.

"Of course it's not too late," Dallas said. His nudge made Danae realize she'd zoned out for a minute.

She flashed a falsely bright smile. "Not at all. We'll make plenty."

"So you're a big popcorn fan?" Dallas reached to tweak Austin's nose the way he often did with his little nieces. But Austin flinched, and Misty swooped in to grab him like the eagle Danae had once seen nab a rabbit on Chicory Lane.

"Sorry, buddy," Dallas said. "I didn't mean to scare you." He reached out and gently touched the boy's arm.

But Misty pulled her son out of Dallas's reach. "We'll be in the dayroom," she said over her shoulder as she carried Austin out.

"Well, that was stupid," Dallas said, shaking his head. "I didn't even think how that might be—"

"Don't think another thing of it," Berta said. "You didn't mean anything by it."

"I just wasn't thinking."

"It'll be OK." Danae rubbed his back, hating that the incident had happened. She wanted to go shake Misty for being so defensive and paranoid. And yet, her rational mind understood that Misty had good reason for being overprotective of her son.

"Maybe I should make myself scarce—after we make popcorn."

"Don't be silly," Berta said before Danae could answer. "It will do these women good to see what a decent man looks like. They may hold you at arm's length, but don't let them scare you."

He looked to Danae, asking in that unspoken language they shared, if she agreed with Berta.

She took his hand briefly. "Berta's right. And Austin will warm up to you. He's just a little gun-shy right now."

"Sure he is. I should have thought of that."

She went to the cupboard and found the popcorn. "Here, you start this, and I'll get some drinks ready."

Dallas liked Berta, the older woman Danae had talked so much about, and who often worked the same shift with her. Just meeting Berta, and seeing the house where the shelter was, made him feel better about Danae being here. Though he could have kicked himself for scaring that little kid.

He was seeing a different side of Danae tonight. And he liked what he saw. She obviously enjoyed showing off her new project, and he liked seeing her tease Berta and navigate the shelter's kitchen as if she owned it.

The three of them worked together to fix a cart with snacks and drinks, then Danae rolled the cart out into the dayroom. There was a commercial playing, and the woman were considerably friendlier under the spell of fragrant fresh-popped kettle corn that Dallas had suggested they bring. In fact, despite the fact they'd all said no when Danae first offered, suddenly every woman had a bowl in her lap, and if he were a betting man, he'd bet they'd be making another batch soon.

Once drinks were distributed, Berta excused herself. "I should be back by nine at the latest," she told Danae over her shoulder, wheeling the cart back toward the kitchen.

Danae pulled a couple of dining chairs up to the TV, and Dallas reluctantly sat down.

He picked up a kernel of popcorn and absently tossed it into the air, then caught it in his mouth. Repeating the action, he looked and noticed Austin watching him.

Holding the boy's gaze, he launched another kernel—higher this time—and caught it on his tongue.

Austin's eyes grew round.

Dallas grinned and popped another piece into the air, but missed it with his mouth, and had to fight to catch it in his hand before it hit the ground. He looked over at the little boy and grinned.

A second later, he saw something white fly through the air.

By now Austin's mother and the three other women were watching with silent smiles.

Dallas tossed up another piece.

The little copycat did the same. Only this time, Austin caught it like an old pro. The stunned look on Austin's face sent them all into convulsions of laughter.

Dallas felt bold enough to lean over with an outstretched palm. "Give me five, buddy! It took me a week to learn how to do that and you nailed it practically on your first try!"

The boy puffed out his chest and beamed.

"Misty," Danae said, feigning a glare at Dallas, "you have my permission to kick this guy out of here at any time. He's a bad influence." She swung her arm back to give Dallas a playful slug, but just as quickly reversed her motion. The sheepish look she gave him beneath hooded eyes said she could totally understand how he'd done the same thing earlier tonight.

Misty gave a wan smile and turned to shake her index finger at her son. "Just so you pick up anything you drop. You hear me, son?"

"I *won't* drop any of it, Mama. See? I can do two of 'em!" He scooped a small fistful of kernels from the bowl and threw them into the air like confetti. One kernel hit his nose and the others landed on the rug in front of the sofa.

Misty opened her mouth to scold, but before she got a word out, Austin slid from the cushion and scrambled to retrieve the errant popcorn.

"Good boy, Oz," his mother said.

Dallas cleared his throat and tried to look sheepish. "Sorry. I hope I didn't cause trouble with that trick."

Misty waved him off. "He knows the rules now."

"My brother and I didn't know any other way to eat popcorn. That's how our dad did it, so that's how Drew and I did it. Shoot, I thought that was *why* it was called popcorn. Because you popped it into the air." He demonstrated with the dregs of his bowl.

"That's the truth," Danae said, laughing. "Whenever we babysit my three nieces, they beg for popcorn so they can watch Uncle Dallas eat it his special way."

"Except their mom banned all popcorn eating from the house," Dallas added. "They have to go outside now."

"I can see why," Misty said, picking another of Austin's missed kernels out of the carpeting.

Dallas noticed she had warmed up considerably.

"So . . ." Misty tilted her head, curiosity in her eyes. "You guys don't have kids?"

"Not yet," Danae said.

He couldn't help but notice that there was no trace of the usual melancholy in his wife's voice. She said it matter-of-factly, as though any day now, they *would* have kids.

And in that moment, he wanted that for her more than he'd wanted anything in a very long time.

12

By nine o'clock the women started drifting back to their own rooms. Berta was still in the office catching up on paperwork, and Danae sent Dallas on home. She wished she could go with him. She was eager to learn his impressions of the shelter. But after the whole popcorn thing with Austin, she was pretty sure he would have only good things to say. She smiled, thinking about how cute Dallas had been with the little boy.

Not so many weeks ago, their exchange would have only made her sad—or even angry—for what she didn't have. But something had changed inside her in recent days. Some holy alchemy had transformed her, altered her very soul. And finally, she wanted God's will more than she wanted her own.

Misty had put Austin to bed around eight thirty and had come back through the dayroom with a basket of dirty clothes on her way down to the laundry room. She came back to the dayroom now with an armload of little boys' clothes. She plopped down on the sofa across from Danae and started folding.

"Want some help?" Without waiting for an answer, Danae went to sit on the other end of the sofa. She pulled a warm T-shirt out of the pile and folded it in half.

"I don't think I can come up with the money to pay for these." Misty held up one of the shirts they'd gotten for Austin.

"You're not expected to pay for them, Misty. That's part of the service we offer."

"Why?"

The question took her aback. "What do you mean?"

"Why do you all do this?"

"The shelter, you mean?" She shrugged, feeling like she was walking on eggshells. "I guess just because we care about women in your situation. We want to help you get back on your feet."

"I don't get that."

"Nothing to get. When you get . . . trapped in an abusive situation it's hard to get free. Even harder if you don't have a safe place to go." She was grasping at straws. They hadn't covered the answer to questions like these in the training sessions. "We just want to show God's love and be that safe place . . . until you can get back on your feet."

"Yeah, well, I don't see that happening anytime soon. I don't see I have a whole lot of choices."

"The counselors will help you." This wasn't the time to remind Misty that the shelter had a two-month limit. She doubted they'd be too strict with that, especially since it involved a child, but they would be urging Misty to find work and a place to live. As long as they didn't make her feel she had no choice but to go back to her husband. "You've talked with a social worker, right?"

"Yeah, I did. For all the good it did," she muttered under her breath.

An early-news channel droned on low volume in the background as they worked together in comfortable silence.

"You've got a nice hubby," Misty said, not meeting Danae's eye—and looking guilty for having said it. "I didn't mean nothin' by that or anything," she added quickly.

Danae waved a hand. "Oh, I know you didn't. And thanks. He's a good guy, Dallas."

"I see that. I think . . . that's what I hate most about what Hank did."

Danae had never heard her use her husband's given name. She hoped it didn't mean Misty was softening toward him. If she took Austin back into that . . . She shook off the thought. She couldn't let herself go there. "What? What do you hate most, I mean?"

"That Austin don't have nobody to, you know, look up to. Be a role model."

"Does he have grandparents around? Or do you have any brothers? Or uncles?"

She shook her head. "None I'd want for a role model." She gave Danae a half grin and rolled her eyes. "I haven't made the best choices. I know that. Not that I had a say in my family. But the ones I chose and the ones I didn't—they're all a bunch of lowlife perverts. I just . . . I don't want my kids—my boy—around any of them. I don't want him to be the one to pay the consequences for my mistakes."

"Well, you're making good choices now. You were right to get Austin away. Somewhere safe. I know that couldn't have been easy for you."

"No. It wasn't. That's for sure."

They finished folding the laundry and Misty took it back to her room and returned with her hairbrush. She started messing with her hair, trying to put it up in a braid. She had long dark, wavy hair. It had been dull and in need of washing when she first arrived, but now it was freshly shampooed and it shone even in the dim lights of the dayroom.

"Do you want me to braid your hair?" Danae was a little surprised when Misty held out the hairbrush to her. She grabbed a bar stool that served as a side table near the sofa. "Here. Sit here."

Misty settled on the stool and slipped a covered rubber band off her wrist and handed it over her shoulder to Danae. "You're lucky to have your smooth blonde hair."

"Hey, I'd trade you any day. My youngest sister has even curlier hair than yours—except hers is blonde like mine—but I always tell her I'd trade her too." She stroked the brush through Misty's hair and separated it into three hanks.

"I guess we all want something different than what we got. I guarantee if you had my hair, and I had yours, you'd still be trying to trade me."

Danae laughed. "You're probably right."

She finished Misty's braid, tucking in wayward strands of hair here and there. But she couldn't quit thinking about what Misty had said, and wondering if she'd intended it to mean more than just about hair.

She thought of her sweet sisters and how bitter and jealous she'd let herself become toward them. Jealous because they had the babies she so desperately wanted. But not counting the blessings she did have . . . ones that they could have been equally jealous of, but weren't. Her beautiful home, a husband who made enough money that she could stay home, enough money that she enjoyed many luxuries her sisters only dreamed of—entire days spent at the salon spa, a lovely wardrobe, beautiful furnishings for their home.

And still enough money that they could afford the fertility treatments.

How many women struggling with infertility would have given anything for this privilege she took for granted?

She suspected Misty would trade her lives in a heartbeat. Except for Austin, of course.

But oh, how much she had to be thankful for. And she was ashamed for how ungrateful she'd been. And how blind she'd been to her blessings.

She secured Misty's braid with the twist of a rubber band, and as she performed the simple, mundane task, she determined to begin, this very night, to live a life marked more by gratitude. And less by petitions.

Old habits were hard to break, but with God's help, she would break this one. She would break free.

The Friday lunch crowd had died down by the time Danae found a parking place near the restaurant. Port Cape Girardeau was a favorite of hers and Dallas's, and she was shocked to learn that neither of her sisters had ever eaten there. "My treat," she'd told them when she called to invite them.

She didn't realize until then how rarely she did anything like that. How deeply ingrained her ungrateful thinking was! But the greater surprise was that God seemed to be assigning her exercises in generosity in an effort to teach her an attitude of gratitude.

An attitude of gratitude. She smiled to herself, remembering mom singing the catchy Sunday school song. She could remember nearly all the words, but apparently she hadn't learned the lesson they contained because she was finding this little experiment more difficult than she imagined that night at the shelter when she'd marked the beginning of a journey toward freedom.

She locked the car and put her head down against the cold mid-November wind that blew off the Mississippi. An opening in the mural-covered floodwall across the street from the restaurant afforded a glimpse of the wide river that formed Cape Girardeau's eastern boundary. Low whitecaps pocked the gray-blue water, and gulls dived for lunch in the wake of a river barge.

The barge's low horn sounded as she crossed the street to the old restaurant with its distinctive painted Coca-Cola sign taking up half the northern face of the building. The luscious aroma of hickory barbecue assaulted her the moment she opened the door, and her stomach growled in response.

She hadn't seen her sisters' cars in the parking lot, but they were seated at a table just inside the door. There were only a few other tables taken in the dining room and jazz notes wafted out from the speakers somewhere above her. Corinne and Landyn were deep in conversation and didn't see her approach.

"Hey, sisters." She pulled out a chair beside Landyn.

"Danae!" they said in unison.

Corinne scooted back her chair and gave Danae a hug. The small mound of Corinne's belly surprised her. She held her older sister at arm's length and noticed she was wearing a loose-fitting shirt. Not a maternity top, but the closest thing to one.

"You're starting to show!" She put a hand lightly on Corinne's tummy, feeling genuinely happy for her sister. "I'm so glad you guys could both get away."

Landyn looked at her watch. "Yeah, well, don't let me stay past three. I promised Chase I'd relieve him before the girls woke from their naps."

"I should probably leave by then, too," Corinne said. "How are you?" The way she asked—almost with a grimace—made Danae regret how she must have made her sisters dread even being around her recently.

"I'm doing good," she said, smiling. She looked from her oldest to her youngest sister and saw in their eyes that they thought she was going to tell them she was pregnant. "And no, I'm not pregnant."

They both visibly deflated.

"Oh, I'm so sorry, sis." Corinne touched her arm.

"It's OK. It really is. We're taking a little break from trying. I mean . . . we'll take a baby any time God wants to give us one, but I'm going to stop the fertility treatments until, well, for a while. I'm not sure how long."

"You're OK with that?" Landyn looked doubtful.

"I really think I am. We need a break. I started my last round of the meds this morning. I'll be off them by Christmas. I guess . . . if I'm not pregnant by then, we'll have to decide what's next. How are you feeling, Corinne?"

"Good. Other than having to pee every five seconds. Speaking of which . . ." She scraped her chair back and excused herself. "I'll be right back."

Danae and Landyn laughed as they watched her head toward the back. And Danae was surprised to realize that she felt only a tiny twinge of envy.

"You look great," Landyn said when Corinne had disappeared around the corner. "I like the way you're wearing your hair."

"I'd still trade for your curls in a heartbeat. I told one of the girls at the shelter that just last night."

"You're still volunteering there?"

"I am. And I love it. It's been really good to have something like that to fill my time."

A few minutes later, Corinne appeared and slid back into her seat. "Have you guys ordered yet?"

"No. I haven't even looked at a menu." Landyn took a sip of water and opened the menu.

Danae slid her menu to the edge of the table. "I already know what I want."

Twenty minutes later they were feasting on the best barbecue in town and laughing in a way they hadn't in far too long. And Danae knew it was her fault.

Their server came and refilled their drinks and when he brought them back to the table, Danae took advantage of the lull. "I don't want to get all serious on you guys and spoil the fun, but"—she swallowed the huge lump in her throat—"I just want to say I'm really sorry for being such a pain to be around these last few months. Oh—who am I kidding?—the last few years."

"Well," Landyn deadpanned, "I didn't want to say anything . . ."

Danae smacked her arm. But she was grateful her sister hadn't let things get too maudlin.

Corinne was more serious. "Hey, we get it, Danae. This has been really hard for you. And we're all praying for you. I hope you know that."

"I do. And thank you. I promise I'm not going to be such a drama queen from now on."

"Don't make promises you can't keep." But Corinne was smiling now.

"And you know you can always talk to us. Just because you're not going to be a drama queen and be all mopey and act like a jerk and make the rest of us miserable with your constant whining doesn't mean you can't." Landyn's eyes held a playful spark.

Danae laughed, but partly to keep from crying. She had been all those things. But she wasn't about to ruin the lighthearted mood of the day. She was so grateful to her sisters for loving her anyway. She wasn't so sure she would have been so patient if she were in their shoes. *Grateful.* One more thing for her gratitude journal—sisters who stood by her no matter how big of a jerk she was.

She reached to grasp a sister's hand in each of hers. "Seriously, I love you guys. Thanks for putting up with me. Now, how about we change the subject before I start crying like a little girl?"

That made her sisters laugh.

"Let's get dessert," Landyn said. "My treat."

Corinne gasped dramatically. "Oh, my goodness! Mark this day down. Our baby sister is buying!"

"Excuse me?" Danae reared back in mock dismay. "Do I not get credit for buying the *meal*?"

They ignored her and pored over a dessert menu.

She grabbed the menu from Corinne's hand. "There's really only one choice, sisters." She summoned their server, who came running. "Blackberry cobblers all around, please."

Corinne and Landyn each nodded hearty approval.

The server smiled. "Three of those, coming right up."

Blackberry cobbler. One more thing to be grateful for.

13

Danae drove over the November-gray streets of Cape Girardeau, winding her way through the neighborhood to the women's shelter. The month was nearly over and the towering trees in the neighborhood had finally given up trying to hang on to their leaves.

Autumn was such a poignant time, with the leaves dying and flowers fading. And yet, she thought it was no accident that God had designed this season of dying to be one of the most beautiful of all. It had been a glorious fall. And the winter snow would be beautiful. But these weeks between the last leaf and the first snowstorm always made Danae a little sad.

She hoped Berta would be at Cape Haven today. She and the older woman had become unlikely friends, and she usually tried to arrange her schedule so that she volunteered the same days Berta did. But Berta had been working nights lately because they were short of help on that shift. For Dallas's sake, she tried to be home in the evenings when he was, but she always felt safer and more confident when Berta Salmans was at the shelter.

The shelter had been especially quiet over these weeks leading up to Thanksgiving. She hadn't heard how many of the women would be at the shelter Thursday, but Berta had said many of them would probably try to go home for the holiday.

Danae had been aghast. "Surely you don't mean home to their abuser?"

Berta had frowned. "Usually home to their parents or siblings—but even that puts them at risk of their abuser finding them. And sadly, sometimes that's exactly what they want. These women are hopeful their abuser will 'behave' over the holidays, so they can have a warm family Christmas together. Unfortunately, the stress of the holidays just makes things worse."

Danae slowed the car as she neared her turn. A flicker of light against the gray sky caught her eye. There it was again. It came from between two houses ahead of her. Surely people weren't putting up their Christmas lights yet. The only thing that drove her more nuts than people who still had their holiday decorations up in February were the ones who put them up too early. At least wait till Thanksgiving, people.

Straining to make out the flashes of light, she slowed the car and rounded the last curve before the shelter. She slammed on the brakes when she realized what the lights were, and where they were coming from.

Two police cars were parked in the driveway of the shelter, blue and red lights strobing against each other in a frenetic rhythm. The front yard was swarming with uniformed officers.

"Lord," she whispered, her breath coming in shallow gasps. "Whatever's happening, please be with everyone inside." Austin! *Oh, please let him be OK! And Berta.*

She started to pull into the driveway, then thought better of it. There was no ambulance, which should be a good sign, but she had a bad feeling about this.

She fished her cell phone out of her purse and dialed Berta's number.

The woman answered on the first ring. "Danae? Don't come in today. We've got stuff going on here. I'll explain later, but you stay home."

"I'm right outside, Berta. What's going on?"

"You're here? Where?"

"I'm on the street, across from the house and down a ways. I can see the police cars. What happened? Are you OK?"

"I think so. Misty's husband paid us a little visit."

"What? He's there now?" How had he found her?

"No. The police arrested him. He's gone. They're just trying to figure out how he found out about the place."

"Do you think she told him?"

"I don't know. I hope not." Berta sounded breathless.

Who could blame her for being shaken? Danae's hands were trembling. "You're sure everybody's OK?"

"He shoved Misty around pretty good, but she's OK."

"Did Austin see it happen?"

"No, thank goodness, he was down for his nap."

Thank you, Lord. "What should I do?"

"It's up to you. Since you're already here, if you want to go ahead and work, you can. But let me talk to one of the officers first."

"OK. I'll wait."

"Don't hang up. I'll be right back."

Berta appeared at the front door, and Danae drove the car forward a few feet and rolled her window down. She saw Berta speaking with the officer and pointing in her direction. The officer turned to look at her and then waved her forward.

She thought about calling Dallas, but he would have a fit and probably make her come home. She would tell him about what happened. Just not yet.

One of the officers motioned for her to park behind a police cruiser. She did so and got out of the car, locking it behind her—something they'd taught them in the training, but that had never seemed so important until today.

"You work here, miss?"

"Yes, sir. Well, volunteer, that is. What's going on?" She was curious to hear his side of the story.

"The director can explain it. Everything's under control now. It's safe to go inside, but we'd like to ask you a few questions first."

"I just got here. I . . . wasn't here when it happened."

"When what happened?" Suspicion—accusation?—was thick in his voice. "I thought you weren't here."

She held up her phone, feeling sheepish. "I talked on the phone to one of the other volunteers who's inside. Berta Salmans."

"OK." That seemed to satisfy him. "We just have some routine questions."

"OK." Maybe she should call Dallas in case this made the news before she got home.

The officer showed her a list of all the shelter's volunteers and asked her to verify her name and contact information. Then he asked questions about Misty and Austin and asked whether she'd ever met Misty's husband. Apparently they thought one of the volunteers must have tipped Hank off. She didn't know all the volunteers, but none she knew would have done such a thing.

It seemed more likely that Misty—or maybe even Austin— had slipped up and said something that clued him in.

"So, is her husband—Hank—in jail?"

He looked at his watch. "He's probably out by now."

"What?" Surely he was kidding.

"The wife didn't want to press charges. Probably because she knew if she did, the beating he'd give her when he got out would be twice as bad."

"What? Why would he be getting *out*?" She hadn't meant to sound as if it was the officer's fault. But why was Misty's jerk of a husband going free? It made no sense. He was obviously a danger to his wife and child—and everyone else in the shelter. This event had no doubt traumatized the other women, who thought they were safe from that kind of assault here. That was the whole point of the safe house, after all.

She was just grateful Austin hadn't had to witness it. Or get hurt again. "Is Misty OK? She didn't have to go to the hospital or anything?"

"She'll have a pretty nice shiner but no broken bones. She refused treatment. From what the director said, this was minor compared to what he's doled out before."

"Yes. It probably is." She hiked her bag up on one shoulder. "Can I go inside now?"

"Sure. Be aware we may call you with further questions if we need to."

"That's fine. You have my cell number"—she pointed to the shelter's contact list he held—"and I usually have my phone with me whether I'm here or at home."

"OK. Thank you, ma'am. We're just about finished here. Y'all take care tonight."

"Am I OK to stay parked here?"

The officer eyed her car, then nodded. "You might want to come and move it once we clear out, but it should be fine there. I won't give you a parking ticket or anything."

She smiled uncertainly, not sure if he'd meant it as a joke.

His expression gave no hint either. When he turned and strode toward another policeman, Danae walked across the street to the shelter. She took the steps up to the front door two at a time, nervous about what she might find inside. She punched in the security code and waited for the lock to release. How had Hank gotten in? Unfortunately, she knew the answer. He'd probably simply knocked.

They'd gotten lax. The first night she was there for training, Renee had made it sound as if they'd be under lock and key twenty-four seven. But in reality, no one seemed to worry much about security beyond the alarms to alert them when someone came or went from the house, and those got ignored too much of the time, with each of them assuming any alarm was another volunteer coming on shift, or a resident going out for a cigarette or a stroll. They weren't running a prison, after all.

It was quiet inside, but Berta met her in the front hall. "You missed it, girlie." She threw her arms up and waggled her hands, obviously still pretty wound up.

"Were you here when it started?"

Berta dipped her head. "I'm the one who let him in. I feel like a fool."

"Oh, Berta . . . But I probably would have done the same thing. Any of us would. I never saw a picture of him, did you?"

She shook her head. "But I shouldn't have believed the jerk."

"What did he say?"

"That he was here to spray for termites. He had me convinced. He even had a logo on his shirt. Next thing I knew, he was dragging Misty out of the dayroom, and she was screaming bloody murder. It's a wonder Austin didn't wake up."

"I'm *so* glad he didn't."

Berta nodded. "I called 911—and Mary. She and the police got here about the same time."

Mary was the director of the shelter. She ran several safe houses in the Greater St. Louis area and spent more time there than she did in Cape. Danae had only met her a couple of times, but she liked the woman.

"How do you think Hank knew where to find Misty?"

Berta shook her head. "I'm half afraid she told him."

"Misty? Why would she do that?"

"Honey, a woman gets lonely and forgets all but the good parts of her man. One part in particular."

"Berta!" She wasn't sure the woman meant it how it sounded.

"I'm just sayin'"

Apparently that was exactly what she meant. That didn't sound like Misty to her, though. But who knew? "Where is she now? Is she doing OK?"

Berta pointed over her shoulder. "She's resting. It's a plum miracle that Austin slept through the whole thing."

"Thank the Lord," Danae whispered.

"You got that right. But Mary won't let them stay here now that he knows where they are."

"Where will they go?" A wave of sadness rolled over her, thinking about never seeing Austin again. Misty too. They'd become a surprisingly big part of her life over the past few weeks.

Berta shrugged. "I don't know. But it's not fair for the rest of the women to be put in danger because she's here. The police said they'd keep a watch on the place for a few days, but this is *not* going to make the neighbors very happy."

She hadn't thought about that. "I don't blame them. I wouldn't be very happy if my neighborhood was swarming with cops."

"Or men like Hank either."

An involuntary shudder went down her spine. It had more to do with telling Dallas what had happened than it did any danger she might be in. It was a conversation she was *not* looking forward to.

Feeling nervous and uncertain, Danae went into the dayroom where Misty was curled in the corner of the sofa, looking small and alone. "Are you OK?"

Misty didn't look up. "Do I have a choice?"

"I'm sorry. That was a stupid question. Of course you're not OK." She sat on the edge of the sofa. "I'm so sorry for what happened."

Misty shrugged. "It wasn't your fault."

She didn't have a reply for that. "Berta said you'd have to find another place. If . . . if there's anything I can do to help. Maybe help you call some of the other shelters . . . ?" She felt so helpless. She couldn't fathom how terrified Misty must be. And yet she seemed surprisingly calm, sitting here. Calmer than Danae felt herself.

"There is something you could do."

"Sure," Danae said, leaning forward.

"I need to go home—to my sister's—for Thanksgiving. My brother is going to be there, and they don't exactly get along. Big surprise." She shook her head, looking embarrassed. "Could you watch Austin for me until Sunday?"

"But it's Thanksgiving. Won't your family want to see him?"

Misty shook her head vehemently. "It don't matter. I can't risk it now. Not with Hank the way he is. I can't risk him coming after Austin."

"No. Of course not. But . . ." This wasn't what she'd expected when she offered to help. She didn't know what to say.

Misty seemed to sense she needed convincing. "I could come back Saturday if that would help. But my brother will be there until Sunday afternoon, and he was gonna give me a ride back, so . . . there's that." She eyed Danae.

"I'll have to ask Dallas," she said finally. "And make sure it's OK by the shelter's rules. But . . . I don't know why it wouldn't be. We always go to my parents' house for Thanksgiving. It's just outside of Cape near Langhorne. Is it OK if Austin goes with us?"

She shrugged again. "He won't care. As long as Mr. Dallas is there, he'll be happy. And you too," she added quickly. "He thinks you're—"

"Don't worry," Danae said, laughing. "I know Mr. Dallas is *way* higher on Austin's list than I am."

Misty looked up at her with a hint of a smile "Maybe if you changed your name to Bug Tussel?"

Danae laughed out loud. It was so uncharacteristic of the somber young woman, and it touched her that Misty remembered their conversation from that first night when they'd talked about Dallas and Austin both being named after Texas towns. "I don't think I'll be changing my name any time soon. I guess I'll just have to live with being second fiddle to Mr. Dallas."

Misty uncurled from the corner of the sofa and stretched her legs out on the ottoman in front of her, looking much relieved. "I can't thank you enough for this."

Danae held up a hand. "It's not for sure yet, Misty. I really do need to check with Mary and Berta—and, of course, Dallas—first."

She wasn't worried about Mary or Berta, either one. But if Dallas refused, she'd rather assign the blame to the shelter than to her husband. Misty had enough prejudices against men without making Dallas a bad guy too.

14

Well, that pretty much cinches it for me. I don't want you going back there, Danae."

"Dallas." She turned off the water at the kitchen sink and dried her hands. "I knew you'd freak out and be irrational about this, but—"

"Irrational?" *Was she serious?* "Since when is it irrational for a man to do everything in his power to protect his wife? And for him to prefer that she not willingly go places where crazy men are breaking in and beating the—"

"Dallas!" She threw the dish towel on the counter in a heap. "Can we please just talk about this?"

"I'm willing to talk about it. But it's going to take some pretty heavy-duty convincing." He picked up the towel and twisted it into a knot. What had she been thinking to stay there and work her entire shift after that man had weaseled his way into the shelter and beat up his wife? Did she not have a brain in her head? Dallas shuddered to think what might have happened if Danae had been there when it happened. Knowing her, she would have tried to intervene and it might have been her with the black eye—or worse.

"OK. Before we talk about the whole volunteer thing, there's something else I want you to please consider."

He pulled out a stool at the bar and straddled it. "I'm listening."

"They're letting Misty stay for another week. She's going home—to her sister's in St. Louis—for Thanksgiving and to try to figure out where to go next."

He didn't know where she was going with this, but he hoped it wasn't where he thought it was.

"Hear me out, babe."

"I'm listening, I'm listening."

"Misty asked if I'd be willing to take Austin over Thanksgiving weekend."

"What? She doesn't want to spend Thanksgiving with her son?"

"It's a long story, but she doesn't want to take Austin with her because she's afraid Hank might show up at her sister's house. Austin could come with us to my parents', and I'd stay home— not volunteer at the shelter, I mean—during those days. Most of the women are leaving for the weekend anyway, and—"

"I like that part. You not volunteering." He tossed her a crooked grin.

"Dallas . . ."

"Sorry. Go on."

"We'd have Austin for about four days. I'd go pick him up from the shelter on Wednesday night, and Misty promised she'd have something worked out by Sunday, and I can take Austin back to the shelter then. She won't have transportation, so she can't pick him up," she explained.

"The shelter is OK with all this?"

"Berta talked to Mary. She said it's a little unconventional, but they don't have any problem with it as long as Misty makes arrangements with us personally and doesn't involve the shelter."

He wasn't sure why, but he didn't like the sound of this one bit. Except, on second thought, he did know why. Danae had grown attached to the kid. And she was going to get her heart broken. Misty couldn't stay at the shelter, which meant Austin couldn't stay there either.

"This is for four days?"

"Yes." She sat up straighter and her eyes sparked. "Wednesday night through Sunday night. He can sleep in the blue room on the daybed."

The woman knew she was wearing him down. After all, what kind of jerk would say no to such a request, especially when they had the extra room in their house? Two of them, in fact.

"What if Misty doesn't find a new place to stay by then? That doesn't give her much time, Danae. And I know you—you'd have them both moved into our house before I knew what hit me."

"I wouldn't do that." She studied a fingernail as if she'd never seen one before. "Not without asking you."

"Danae. That is not even an option."

"I never said it was."

"I see that gleam in your eye." He shook his head and groaned.

She smiled. "I promise. I'm only asking if we can babysit Austin for four days."

He knew when he'd been had. "Do you promise you won't cry when you have to say good-bye to him on Sunday night?"

Her blue eyes filled with tears and she went back to inspecting that fingernail.

He slid off the stool and went to her, pulling her into his arms. "This is exactly why I'm nervous about doing this. You're going to fall in love with the little guy, and then you're going to be heartbroken when Misty takes him back to St. Louis."

"Dallas, I fell in love with him the first night he showed up at the shelter. But I know I can't save the whole world. I know that. And don't tell me you aren't a little bit in love with him too."

He nuzzled her neck. "He's a cute kid. But I'm not going to cry my eyes out when he moves because I'm not going to get attached to him." He pulled away and waited until she looked him in the eye. "You need to promise me you'll guard your heart too."

"I can't make a promise like that."

"Then I'm not sure we should babysit."

"Dallas, it's just four days. If I want to cry about it when he moves, what do you care?" She clenched her fists and sucked in her cheeks the way she did when she was fuming.

"Babe, I just don't want you to get hurt."

"I'll be fine. I told you . . . Please, can we do this for Misty?"

"Isn't there anyone else at the shelter who could take him?"

"She asked me, Dallas. Us. She's never met any of the other volunteers' husbands, and as you can surely imagine, she doesn't trust just anyone. She liked you. And Austin likes you too. That's one of the reasons she asked us."

He grabbed up the dish towel again. "OK, now you're not playing fair."

She giggled. "Well, it's true."

He sighed. What was keeping him from agreeing? It was only for a few days. And Danae was right. It wasn't his business whether she let herself get too attached. Her passion was the reason she'd been drawn to volunteer at the shelter in the first place—and why she was so good at the job. He blew out a resigned sigh. "All right. We can do it. But it won't be my shoulder you cry on Sunday night, you understand?" But he knew better. He would always be there for her. Always.

Danae nodded, beaming, all but jumping up and down.

"And we're not keeping him any longer than that. Sunday night he goes back to Misty."

"I know."

He'd been had again. This woman . . . "Come here." He held his arms out and she filled them.

"I love you, Dallas Brooks."

"I know you do. And that's where all my problems begin."

She smacked him one for that. But her kisses said she knew exactly how he meant it.

15

Still trying to warm up since plowing the driveway on the open tractor, Grant rubbed his hands together and watched out the front windows as white flakes drifted down from a gray sky. It had been snowing since seven a.m. and already the boughs of the fir trees were flocked with an inch of the stuff. "We may not have a white Christmas," he told Audrey, "but we're going to get a white Thanksgiving."

She came to stand beside him, clucking her tongue at the sight beyond the window. "I just hope everybody gets here before the snow closes the roads."

He frowned. "I just hope everybody gets *home* before the snow closes the roads."

She chuckled. "Good point."

"What else do you need me to do? You have everything looking real pretty."

She turned away from the window and surveyed the inn as if trying to see it through his eyes. It sparkled with candles on white tablecloths and glittered greenery festooning the mantel and the tall windows on either side of the fireplace. "It does, doesn't it? Oh—you know what you can do? Take some pictures before the kids get here and destroy it. White tablecloths probably weren't the best idea."

"I wondered about that. But I wasn't going to say anything."

"Smart man. I wish we'd waited to shoot that video. I really like the way this looks better than what we shot."

Landyn was working on some Christmas promotion spots for the inn on some of her friends' blogs, and she'd arranged for a friend's husband to come and shoot some footage last week.

"Yeah, yeah, and if you'd shot it today, next week you'd be wishing you could shoot it again."

"I know. You're right."

"Come here, you." He pulled her into an embrace, which she only tolerated for a few seconds before she broke free and crossed the room to fiddle with some flowers she'd already rearranged twice.

He rolled his eyes and returned to his window watch. Not two minutes later, the first car pulled into the driveway, plowing a new path through the snow that had already accumulated since he'd come inside. "Bree's here with my mother," he called to Audrey. "I'm going to go help them in."

"I'll come too." Audrey frowned. "It might take three of us to get Cecelia up the stairs. She was so frail when she was here last Tuesday."

Grant had noticed too. He didn't want to think about what it might mean. *Lord, let us catch our breath with everything else before we have to deal with another crisis.*

He opened the front door as Huckleberry made a beeline for him, barking as if there was a rabbit at the door. "Audrey, I'm letting Huck out."

"Don't you dare!" she screeched. "Huck! Quiet. Grant, do not let him out." She raced to the door and hauled the Lab by the collar toward the laundry room. "You can let him out once everyone gets here, but this weather has him too wound up. Besides, I don't want him bowling your poor mother over."

"That's thoughtful of you," Grant said. He didn't wait to hear Audrey's comeback—if she'd even heard him—but stepped onto the front porch, wishing he'd thought to at least put on a jacket. Just when he was getting warmed up too.

"Happy Thanksgiving!" Bree shouted over the top of the car, her breath forming a cloud in the frigid air.

"You too, sweetheart! Thanks so much for picking up CeeCee."

"I'm happy to." Bree left the car running and came around to help CeeCee from the car. "How's she doing today?" he whispered over his mother's head.

CeeCee straightened and looked up at him with an expression he knew well from boyhood. "I'm doing just fine, thank you. I'm not dead yet."

He tightened his grip on her thin arm. "I can see that, Mother. You're very much alive."

She scowled. "What does that have to do with anything?"

"You said you're not dead yet, and I'm just saying—"

"Deaf," she barked. "I said I'm not *deaf* yet. But apparently you are. Now get me inside. It's cold out here in case anyone hadn't noticed."

Bree's shoulders shook with suppressed laughter, which made Grant laugh.

"Bree Whitman, did you not hear my mother say, 'I'm not dead yet?'"

She threw him a stern look and held up a hand. "I am staying completely out of this one."

"Good decision if you value your inheritance, young lady."

But over CeeCee's bent head, Bree gave him an exaggerated nod and mouthed, "She did say *dead.*"

"Don't think I didn't see that, young lady."

Bree cringed in a way that made Grant roar.

"You two go ahead and have your fun at my expense." But CeeCee wore a smile that said she was in full entertainment mode.

He and Audrey had noticed in recent months that his mother was a little mixed up from time to time. Of course, at eighty-four, almost eighty-five, who wouldn't be slipping a little? But today, his mother appeared to be in fine form. It would be a good Thanksgiving.

Dallas and Danae's car turned into the driveway and the Penningtons' right behind it. He turned his mother over to Audrey and Bree, grabbed a jacket from the hall closet, and went to carry in granddaughters. Along with the pumpkin pies.

Dallas pulled to a stop, and Grant opened Danae's door. "Happy Thanksgiving, you two."

"Make that three today, Dad." Danae unhooked her seat belt and swiveled to the back seat. "This is Austin."

Puzzled, Grant gave a little wave, then opened the SUV's back passenger door. He chucked the boy under the chin. "Hey there."

"We're babysitting Austin for a couple of days."

"Well, hi, buddy. Nice to meet you." Grant held out a hand and the boy shook it solemnly. "How old are you?"

"Free," he said, then stuck a thumb in his mouth.

"He turned three in August," Danae said, climbing out of the passenger seat to stand beside Grant.

The boy popped out his thumb long enough to hold up three fingers. "Do you gots any kids?"

He pulled Danae into a sideways hug. "This girl right here is my kid. But, yes"—he pointed to where Corinne and Jesse were unbuckling their crew—"do you see that car right over there? Full load of kids in there. I hate to tell you, though, sport, but they're all girls."

The boy scrunched up his nose. Grant laughed and tousled the dark mop of hair. He was a cute kid. His olive skin and dark eyes and hair said he might be of Mediterranean descent. Greek? Maybe Latino. Audrey hadn't said anything about Danae bringing a guest. Who sent their kid to a babysitter on Thanksgiving Day? His curiosity was getting the best of him, but the boy was old enough—and obviously bright enough—that he didn't want to ask questions in front of him. He guessed it had something to do with the women's shelter.

He still wasn't crazy about the idea of Danae spending time there. But Dallas seemed convinced it was safe, and Grant had pledged to God—and Audrey—when he handed off his daughters at the front of the church on each of their wedding days, that he would try to stay out of their business.

He'd blown that promise with Landyn and Chase, sticking his nose where it really didn't belong when they were struggling in their marriage a year ago. Of course, when they decided to move in with him, it sort of became his business. But he didn't have that excuse with Dallas and Danae—at least not yet—so he was going to do his best to "mind his own beeswax," as his mother liked to say. Not that his mother ever minded *her* own beeswax. But that was another story.

"Come on, Austin." Danae held out her hand. "I'll introduce you to the girls. And Huck."

"Now there's a boy you can play with," Grant said. He whistled for the lab.

"Who's Huck?" The boy looked skeptical.

"You'll see. You're going to have fun, buddy."

He didn't look too sure about that, but he took the hand Danae offered and tromped through the snow to the front porch.

"Wipe your feet!" Grant called. Audrey had been mopping floors all morning, which he'd told her was stupid. Understandably, that hadn't gone over very well. Forty years of marriage and he still hadn't learned to keep his mouth shut when appropriate.

He followed the crowd inside and helped Audrey get casseroles in the oven and salads in the fridge, then went to help hang up coats in the hall closet. The kids went downstairs to play, and Grant ended up in the hall with Danae.

"What's the story on your little guy? I can't imagine anyone not wanting to have him at their Thanksgiving dinner."

"His mom is from the women's shelter. It's a safety issue. She's going home but she was afraid Austin's father might show up. He . . . beat Austin, and that's what finally convinced her to come to the shelter. Apparently she could handle him smacking her around, but it was another thing when he went after her son."

"I would hope so," Grant said, shaking his head. He felt sick to his stomach to think a man could do that to his child. To his wife. The world was a sick place—and getting sicker by the minute.

16

The little boy sure gets along well with Corinne's girls," CeeCee said from her perch in the recliner by the living room window overlooking the backyard. "What did you say his name was?"

"It's Austin. And yes, they've played really well together," Danae agreed. She came to kneel by CeeCee's chair and followed her grandmother's line of vision out to the yard where Jesse, Chase, and Dallas had some sort of game going with the kids in the snow. Huckleberry was in hog heaven darting from one kid to the next, tail wagging. Even the twins were getting in on the action, bundled in snowsuits with only their pudgy faces sticking out, cheeks rosy from the cold. Chase carried one and Dallas had the other hiked up on one hip as if he carried babies all the time. Danae's heart twisted at the sight.

She watched, feeling herself drift into that fantasyland she'd tried so hard to stop living in. But she couldn't help it. She could so easily imagine that they had a baby girl. Dallas would be such a good daddy.

Austin seemed to be having the time of his life, running in circles, flopping in the snow, and laughing with the little girls as if they'd known each other forever.

"It must have warmed up out there," Mom called from the kitchen. "Nobody seems to be in a hurry to come in."

"Yes, and let's keep it that way," Landyn said through a yawn. She playfully scooted Danae out of the way and eased into the chair beside CeeCee's, closing her eyes. "I feel a nap coming on."

"Mom, do you need help in the kitchen?" Danae called.

Landyn opened one eye. "Oh, sure. Pour on the guilt just as I'm getting my first nap all month."

"Don't worry, sister, I wasn't offering *your* services."

"Nor mine, I hope," Corinne chimed in.

Mom stepped through the archway that divided the living room and the great room and kitchen. "You can all quit fighting because I don't need any help. Not until it's time to get leftovers out for supper."

"I can't believe the Sillies are giving up football for a romp in the snow," Corinne said.

They laughed. Dad had started calling the three sons-in-law "the Sillies" after Corinne had sent him a text message with the acronym SIL, meaning sons-in-law. Dad didn't get it and had replied with something stupid that no one could even remember now. But the guys had earned a new nickname out of the deal— one that would probably stick for life.

"Actually, I think it's halftime," Danae said. "The Sillies might be silly, but they're not dumb."

"Ah, that explains it." CeeCee rolled her eyes. "I knew there had to be some explanation. And I still don't understand why Grant calls them silly."

Without opening her eyes, Landyn reached over and patted their grandmother's knee. "It's technology, CeeCee. Don't worry about it."

"So Austin spent last night with you?" Mom joined them in the living room, untying her apron as she slumped onto the opposite end of the sofa from Corinne. "How did that go?"

"It went well. I was a little worried he'd have trouble sleeping in a strange house, but he was asleep by nine and never made a peep until we woke him up at seven this morning."

"What's his story? Or can you talk about it?" Corinne curled up in the corner of the sofa. Her pregnancy was evident now.

"We're really not supposed to say too much. But obviously, you can figure it out, given that they're living at the women's shelter. His dad got abusive toward Austin too. That was the last straw, I guess."

In getting a medical release for Austin and contact information for Misty before they took Austin home, they'd actually found out more than Danae had known through the shelter's records. Since they used a first-name-only policy with volunteers, she hadn't even known that their last name was Arato. Misty had laughed and said, "Hank's mom always told people it was Italian, but his old man swore his ancestors were from Japan. Mama only *wished* they were Italian." She shrugged. "I don't know the truth. His folks are dead now. My side is mostly mutts, so it probably cancels out any pedigrees on Hank's side anyway."

Danae had simply felt grateful that her family wasn't like either side of Austin's family. And then she felt arrogant and judgmental for having such thoughts.

"Well, he's an awfully cute little guy," Mom said. "It's amazing how resilient kids are. Does he ever talk about his dad?"

"Not a lot." She knew they were all curious, but she was growing uncomfortable with the information being revealed. Trying to steer the subject away from things she wasn't supposed to talk about, she asked, "Is Bree coming back for supper?" Her sister-in-law had left shortly after lunch to be with her own family.

"She wasn't sure," Mom said. "Her family was going to her aunt's in Sikeston today, so she said not to wait supper on her."

"As if we ever have a schedule for supper," Landyn said.

Danae tossed a sofa pillow at her. "I thought you were sleeping."

"I talk in my sleep sometimes," she quipped, launching the pillow back at Danae without opening her eyes.

They laughed and then Corinne pointed at CeeCee—who was sawing logs while sitting straight up in the recliner—and they laughed some more. Again, Danae was guiltily grateful for her family.

"I thought Dallas's brother was coming too." Mom jumped up and wiped an invisible smudge off the wood floor with a wrinkled tissue. The woman didn't know how to relax.

"We invited him," Danae said. "I'm not sure if he's coming or not." Now that Dallas and Drew's parents were gone, they often included Drew in the Whitman family holidays. Most years, he had a girlfriend and declined their invitation. But he'd broken up with someone recently—a girl she and Dallas had never met. Knowing Drew, it wouldn't be long before he had another one lined up. Dallas got frustrated because his brother wouldn't settle down and marry one of them. But she wanted her brother-in-law to marry because he was truly, madly, deeply in love. Not because his big brother thought it was time he settled down. "I hope he doesn't come too late. We're probably going to take off a little early because of Austin."

"Oh? You have to take him back tonight?" Corinne moved a sofa pillow and motioned for Mom to sit beside her.

"No. We have him until Sunday," Danae said. "But he's used to—"

"Wow, till Sunday? I'm surprised his mom would want to leave him over Thanksgiving."

"She didn't really have much choice. And . . . I really shouldn't say any more about the shelter."

"Oh. Sorry." Corinne affected a wince. "I really wasn't fishing. I know you have to keep everything confidential."

"Anyway, what I was saying is he's used to going to bed pretty early, and I don't want to get him off his schedule while we have him."

"His mom will appreciate that," Corinne said.

Despite what Corinne claimed, they *were* fishing. All of them. She didn't blame them. Her family had always been open with each other. And maybe she could have told them a bit more than she had. But given the fact that Hank had somehow found out where Misty was, it seemed wise to keep the details to herself. There was no reason her family needed to know this stuff anyway.

Mom jumped up again. "Well, maybe we should start getting supper on the table then?"

Corinne gave Danae a look, and they rose in unison, each taking one of their mother's arms and escorted her, laughing, to the sofa.

"Sit down, Mom!" Corinne used her stern voice—the one usually reserved for when her daughters were misbehaving.

"Yes, please! You're making the rest of us look like slackers."

Landyn popped awake and sat straight up. "Who are you calling a slacker?"

Their laughter woke CeeCee, which prompted more laughter.

Bree arrived a few minutes later, and by the time the guys and kids straggled in from outside, the subject of Austin's situation had been dropped. Until after supper when she and Dallas were loading the car getting ready to go home.

While Dallas bundled Austin up for the trip home, Dad followed her out to the car, offering to help her carry out the dishes she'd brought.

"You don't need to, Dad. I can get them in one trip now that they're empty."

"I don't mind."

She didn't argue, even though it felt silly, the two of them trudging through the snow, each carrying one little casserole dish.

"He's a cute little guy," Dad said without prelude.

"He is. He sure took to the girls."

Dad smiled. "That he did. They made him feel real welcome too. I was proud of them."

The yard lights on either side of the driveway cast a pool of sparkle on the snow, and the night air had that wonderful hushed quality about it. When they reached the car, Dad handed her the dish and waited while she secured it between the front seats. "So, how long did you say you had him for?"

"Just until Sunday. His mom will be back at the shelter then, until they can find another place to go. Dallas told you what happened? At the shelter?"

He nodded, his gaze too piercing for comfort. "Just . . . You be careful," he said, putting a hand on her arm.

"I'm not worried, Dad. The police are watching the place and Misty will be mov—"

"That's not what I mean." Frowning, he looked at the ground and carved an arc in the snow with the toe of his shoe. "I mean be careful with your heart, honey."

Her breath caught. Was she that transparent? She pasted on her bravest smile. "Don't worry, Daddy. He—Austin already has a mommy. I know that."

"When do we get ta play with those girls again?" Austin tossed off the quilt Dallas had just tucked him in with.

"You mean Sari and Sadie and Simone?"

"Uh-huh. And those babies."

Dallas put the quilt back on, taking care to secure the edges of the bedcovers, buying time. How could he answer that question when the answer was *never*? "The babies . . . Emma and Grace, you mean."

"Yeah, them. And that dog. Hunk-a-betty."

Dallas curbed a grin. "Yep, Huckleberry." Austin had been taken with Grant and Audrey's chocolate lab, and the feeling was mutual, judging by how the dog had shadowed him all day. "So you had a good time today, huh?"

"Yeah. Those people gots a *biiig* house." He steepled his hands over his head. "You gots a big house too."

"Yep, we do. We both have pretty big houses, don't we?"

"Uh-huh, and they gots lots of food and lots of toys and lots of stuff and—" Austin closed his eyes, obviously trying to think of something to keep the conversation going.

Dallas laughed and made a rake of his fingers, ruffling the little boy's hair. "Now I think you're just stalling."

One eye popped open. "What's stally?"

"*Stalling.* It's when you're supposed to be going to sleep and you keep talking."

Austin looked appropriately guilty.

"I'm going to cover you up one more time, OK, buddy? If you throw the covers off this time, you're on your own."

He made a production of shaking out the quilt and spreading it over Austin, then tucking him in on the sides, the way his father used to do with him. He hadn't thought of that in years, and it put a lump in his throat for his dad. He wondered if Drew remembered those tuck-ins.

He was curious where Drew had spent Thanksgiving. He'd invited his brother to the Whitmans', but Drew had begged off. Dallas would give him a call tomorrow if they weren't too busy with Austin.

He had to admit he was taken aback by how much work a kid was. Maybe it was different when it was your own kid. But there were car seats and meals and baths and teeth-brushings and nose-wipings and vitamins and night-time Pull-Ups and constant safety checks . . .

And he'd sort of loved it all. Well, except for the nose-wipings and Pull-Ups.

He and Danae had babysat for Jesse and Corinne's girls before, but never overnight, and there was just something different when it was nieces and you knew the parents. With this kid, it felt like a bigger responsibility. Bigger stakes.

Part of him wanted to tell Drew about their time with Austin. But he knew exactly where his brother would steer that conversation: adoption. The elephant in the room . . . in the *world*. His world anyway.

He'd lectured Danae about getting attached to Austin. He couldn't tell her that after barely twenty-four hours, he was as smitten with the kid as she ever was. And with the idea of having a kid. The feelings had taken him by surprise. He'd always wanted a family, of course. It just seemed like the natural progression of things.

But until now, it had been mostly for Danae's sake that he wanted kids. Because she seemed to feel that life wasn't worth living if you didn't have kids.

He wouldn't go that far, but having this kid in their house had definitely made the prospect of a family something he could now envision. And look forward to.

"You guys doing OK?" Danae's shadow fell across the daybed, and he turned to see her standing in the doorway.

He knew she was checking up on him more than Austin. And he didn't blame her. He had almost zero experience with kids. But he was turning out to be kind of a natural, if he did say so himself. He gave her a thumbs up over his shoulder.

Austin threw off the covers again and peered up at Danae. "Can I stay up a little longer?"

"No." He and Danae answered in unison.

Austin sighed and flopped back on the pillow. "G'night."

"Sweet dreams, Austin," she said, a smile in her voice.

"Good night, buddy. See you in the morning."

Dallas gave one last tuck and rose, turning toward the doorway.

Danae still stood there, leaning against the doorjamb. The expression on her face was one he would have paid any sum of money to see again and again.

17

Come on, Austin. You need to get your coat on. I bet your mama can't wait to see you." Danae could scarcely choke out the words. But she needed to be matter-of-fact about this. Not just for Austin's sake, but for her own.

She couldn't believe how quickly the weekend had flown by. They'd built a snowman in the backyard on Friday, built tents with quilts and sheets in the living room on Saturday, and played hooky from church this morning—which seemed easier than trying to explain Austin's situation to their friends—and made a feast of pancakes, bacon, and eggs.

"Is my mama gonna get beat up?"

Her hands stilled on the buttons of his jacket. She looked into his dark, serious eyes. "No, sweetie. Why do you think that?"

"'Cause my dad beats her up." He hung his head. "And sometime he beats me up."

She grabbed the lapels of his jacket and pulled him into a hug, hiding her tears behind his shoulder. After a minute she held him at arms' length and looked into his dark eyes. Eyes that held far too much sadness for a three-year-old. "No, Austin. You're both safe now. Your mama just went to visit her sister and brother, remember?"

"But I don't have no sister and brother."

"No. *Her* sister and brother. You're right. You don't have any sisters or brothers yet. But someday you might. Would you like that?"

"Like Sari and them other girls at that big house?"

"Yes, Sari and Sophie and Simone."

"And them two babies."

"Emma and Grace. The twins."

"Yep. An' Hunk-a-betty too."

She laughed through tears. She'd never be able to think of Huckleberry by any other name.

"You would be a very good big brother, Austin."

"'Cept if I had a big brother I—"

"No, silly, you would *be* the big brother."

"I know. And if I had a big brother he could sleep in my bed with me 'cause we don't got no baby bed." Austin had been intrigued by the crib that was set up in the nursery where he'd slept on the daybed.

"Well, if you ever got a baby brother or sister, I bet you'd get a baby bed too, so—"

"I'm too big for a baby bed!" He snorted. "I'm a big boy."

"No . . . I meant you'd get a bed for the baby, so you wouldn't have to share your bed." She released him and finished zipping his jacket. This conversation was getting complicated—especially since Misty and Hank weren't even together any more. "We'd better get a move on, sport."

"How's come Mr. Dallas isn't comin' with us?"

"He had to go in to work for a little while."

"My dad don't go to work."

"He doesn't?"

"No. He just sits on his butt all day."

"Austin . . ." She couldn't contain a snicker. "That's not a very nice way to talk."

He looked at her as if he didn't know what she meant, and she felt bad for correcting him, knowing he was only echoing what Misty must have said about Hank.

"Come on. Let's get in the car. Your mama is going to wonder where you are."

"No, she won't." he said, as if she was the biggest dunce alive. "I'm right here."

"You crack me up."

He grinned as if it were the biggest compliment he'd ever received.

They'd only heard from Misty once, on Friday evening. She'd left her sister's phone number as the emergency contact, but when Danae had called that number an hour ago, it went straight to voice mail. She assumed that meant Misty was on the road home.

She opened the door and helped Austin down the two steps into the garage. In just four days, they already had a routine. She tossed his little suitcase full of freshly laundered clothes behind the driver's seat, then went around to help him climb up into the car seat they'd borrowed from Corinne and Jesse. She buckled him in—for the last time.

And her heart literally ached.

She'd actually been glad when Dallas got called in to manage an issue at work. She'd been determined not to let him see her cry as he'd predicted she would. But who was she fooling? She was on the verge of blubbering like a baby. And she probably would do just that right after she dropped Austin off. Not before, she hoped. And she prayed Dallas wouldn't be back from the office by then. She just might have to go for a little drive afterward—to compose herself.

She backed out of the garage and turned the car toward the shelter, feeling as if she was going to the gallows.

⸺⸺

When they pulled into the driveway of the women's shelter a few minutes later, Austin pointed out the window. "That's where me and Mama live, right?"

"It sure is. I bet your mama is watching out the window for you."

"And you live here too. Right, Miss Danae?"

"No. You know where I live, silly. Where you stayed in the room with the green curtains?" Austin had been taken with the green-and-white chevron curtains in the blue-painted nursery. He'd said they looked like dinosaur teeth. She smiled, remembering.

He tilted his head and studied her reflection in the rearview mirror. "Miss Danae, what's so funny?"

She shot him a smile. "You are, buddy. Now let's go see your mom."

She parked the car along the edge of the drive. Someone had plowed the driveway and shoveled the sidewalks and stairs. She took a deep breath, steeling herself, feeling a strange mixture of sadness and relief.

She went around to unbuckle Austin from the car seat.

She took his hand and reminded him to look both ways before crossing the driveway. Once across, he scrambled up the steps to the porch.

"Be careful on the steps. They might be slippery."

"I get to push the button. Me!"

"Yes. Good for you for remembering." She was surprised he knew about the security alarm.

She pressed in the code and lifted him up to push the entry key. Once the lock released, she opened the door and waited for him to climb over the threshold.

"Mama?" He tore down the hall to the family room where he and Misty had been staying, but his mother didn't answer. Not knowing where Misty was, Danae called him back.

He turned and gave her an inquisitive look.

"Hang on, bud. I'm not sure if your mom is in your room or out in the dayroom. Let's go check."

She scooped him up and carried him down to the office to check in and see who was working today.

Mary, the director, looked up from the desk. "Hi there."

"Hi. Did you have a good Thanksgiving?"

"I did. Too short though. How about you?"

"It was good, thanks."

"And how about you, young man?" Mary rose and reached across the desk to squeeze the toe of Austin's boot.

He buried his face in Danae's shoulder and her heart squeezed tighter. "Is Misty back?"

Mary shook her head. "Not yet."

Danae looked at the clock over the desk. "She hasn't called?" It was five o'clock, and after not being able to reach Misty, she'd purposely waited till a little later in the afternoon, so Austin wouldn't be disappointed.

"Not yet. Berta's doing the night shift tonight, and I called Renee to come in, but we're shorthanded till she gets here. Would you mind staying until Misty gets back?"

"No, that's fine. I'll wait with him. I have her sister's number, where she was staying. I'll see if I can reach someone there and find out when they left. I think her brother was bringing her back."

Two hours later, Danae was still waiting. And no one was answering the sister's phone.

"I'm not sure what to do here," Mary said. "We don't have any other contact numbers for her. Would you be willing—since you already have the medical forms and Misty's permission—to take him home again tonight? Or, if you'd rather, stay here with him? We don't have the staff to watch him in case she doesn't show up until late."

Danae looked at the clock again. "Let me try to call one more time." She wasn't sure she could go through the agony of doing the one-last-time routine again tomorrow. And what would Dallas say? She needed to call him.

She dialed the sister's number, but didn't bother leaving a message when it went to voice mail this time.

Austin sat at a small table in the corner of the office, coloring with some markers Mary had hunted up for him. He seemed unconcerned that his mother hadn't showed up yet. It made Danae sad that he would be so cavalier about her tardiness.

She went into the entry to call Dallas without being overheard. She'd called him around six to let him know she was waiting on Misty, but hadn't talked to him since.

He answered on the first ring. "Hey, babe. How are you doing?"

"Are you still at work?"

"No, I'm home now. Are you on your way?"

"Yes, but . . . there's a complication."

"What do you mean?"

"Misty still isn't back."

"Oh? And let me guess—you want to wait till she gets there?"

"Actually, we've been trying to get hold of her sister for hours. No one's answering and Misty hasn't called the shelter." She explained about them being shorthanded. "They're suggesting I bring Austin home with me and let him stay the night. I can bring him back tomorrow."

"Danae . . ."

"I know. It was hard enough saying good-bye today. But, I wouldn't feel right leaving him here. Mary's nervous about having him here with such a slim staff. It's just her and Renee, until Berta gets here later. Would you rather I stay here with him?"

He sighed heavily into the phone. "It's up to you. I don't care if you want to keep him another night. As long as that's OK with Misty."

"We can't reach her. That's the whole problem."

"Oh. Sorry. I wasn't thinking." Another sigh, then, "Yeah, bring him back here. That's fine."

"Thanks. I'll have to pack him up again, but we should be home in half an hour or so."

"OK. Do you need supper?"

"I'll stop and pick up fast food on the way home. Or a pizza. Have you eaten?"

"Not really. Pizza sounds good."

"OK. Pizza party it is."

"Be careful. It's supposed to sprinkle and the roads could be slick."

"I will."

She started to hang up, but Dallas spoke her name.

"What?"

"You don't think she's . . . trying to dump Austin, do you?"

She hadn't let herself think about that possibility yet, but the longer they waited on Misty with no word . . . It did happen sometimes. Even with mothers who loved their children. Sometimes things simply grew too overwhelming.

But she said, "I really don't think so. She loves him, Dallas. I can tell she does."

18

"Good night, buddy. You sure you don't have to go pee again?" Dallas held the blanket a few inches from Austin's chin, waiting for a final tuck.

"I already did. 'Sides, I gots a push-up on."

He hid a smile. "I know, buddy, but the goal is to wake up with a *dry* Pull-Up, OK?"

Austin nodded, looking like he was in trouble, and Dallas wished he hadn't said anything. He'd been a little alarmed that a three-year-old—almost three and a half now—still had to wear diapers to bed, but Danae assured him it wasn't unusual. A lot of kids—boys especially—still peed the bed long past toddlerhood. Thank goodness for the miracle called Pull-Ups. Even if they did cost a small fortune.

"Night-night, Mr. Dallas."

"See you in the morning." They'd fallen easily back into the routine of the past four nights. Dallas turned to leave and reached to pull the door almost closed.

"Wait!"

"What is it, Austin?"

"What if my mama gets back there and she doesn't know where I am?"

He went to sit on the edge of the bed again. "She'll know where you are. Miss Danae told everyone who works there, and she left a message with your uncle and aunt." About a dozen of them, in fact. And still, they hadn't heard a word from Misty. Something was fishy, and he didn't like it.

"OK." Austin's thumb went to his mouth, but he stayed in bed, under the covers.

Dallas could tell the boy sensed something was going on. How could he not?

Danae had done bath and Pull-Up duty and was downstairs trying to contact Misty again. Dallas found her on hold on her cell phone in the kitchen. She shook her head with a frown. "Nobody's answering anywhere," she mouthed.

He went to the fridge to get a glass of iced tea and poured one for Danae too.

He set it in front of her, and she hung up and gave a little growl of frustration. "Where could she be?"

He shook his head. "I don't know, but she'd better have a good excuse for bailing on us like this."

"You'd think she'd at least call to check on Austin. She has to know he's wondering where she is."

"Maybe she thought we'd cover for her."

"I'm not going to lie to him."

"Do you think she does though? Lies?" He hadn't been around Misty as much as Danae had, but somehow the woman hadn't struck him as a bastion of truth and integrity. But then, maybe she'd learned to lie to protect herself and Austin from her monster of a husband.

"I don't know," Danae said, taking a sip of her tea. "Did he ask about her again when you were putting him to bed?"

"Yes, but he seemed pretty sleepy. Hopefully he'll fall asleep, and by morning we'll have an answer if he asks again."

Danae shook her head. "It's just so inconsiderate of her."

"You've got that right," he said. "As if it wasn't enough that she asked us to keep him for almost four days—and over a holiday." He winced. "I'll feel bad if we find out she was in an accident or something. But it's pretty presumptuous of her to just expect that we'd take him another night."

"Without even calling." Danae put her empty glass in the dishwasher.

He drained his glass and handed it to her across the island counter. "Well, there's nothing we can do about it. Might as well get a good night's sleep. We can deal with it in the morning."

Danae seemed not to have heard him and grumbled out loud. "I would have rather she just asked us to keep him tonight in the first place. At least then we could have enjoyed having one more night with him."

He agreed. This being in limbo was no fun for anyone. He went around the island to where she stood at the sink. He wrapped his arms around her from behind and kissed the back of her neck. "Let's go to bed."

She leaned back against him and he felt her body relax. "Mmmm . . . That's a good idea."

Together, they went through the house turning off lights and checking the door locks. She followed him up the stairs to their master suite across the hall from the nursery where Austin was.

He stopped at the door and pushed it open enough to peek in. Austin lay on his back, his arms over his head, his little mouth slack in sleep. He sensed Danae behind him and turned to her with a smile. "He's a cute little snot."

"He is. And not a care in the world."

Dallas stepped into the room and pulled the quilt up around Austin. He sensed Danae at his side and pulled her to him. They stood there, arm in arm, watching Austin sleep. And again, he felt himself moving closer to Danae's dream of filling this house with children. *Let it happen, Lord. Please. For my sweet wife's sake.*

She lay her head on his shoulder and sighed. "I sure hope she shows up in the morning."

"She will." She'd better.

But . . . He wasn't sure why, but he was starting to get a bad feeling about this whole thing.

Danae tossed and turned half the night. Finally, after Dallas's alarm went off and the drone of his shower lulled her back to sleep, she got in another good hour. She was just stirring again when he appeared in the doorway of their room.

"You awake? I'm heading to work. Austin's still zonked, so you might as well sleep in as long as you can."

"Thanks. I'll see you tonight."

"Give me a call after you hear from Misty, would you?"

"Sure." She stretched and hunkered down beneath the blankets again. "I'll call the shelter a little later. She probably just got in late last night and they didn't want to call and bother us."

"I hope that's all it is." But Dallas sounded skeptical.

She listened to the distant hum of the garage door going up, then back down. She was wide awake now, and started to push back the covers, but just then, Austin burst through the doorway, giggling.

She patted the bed, and he crawled up in it with her as he'd done the last two mornings. He burrowed under the covers until only the mop top of his head stuck out. She tickled him and he escaped to the end of the bed, taunting her to tickle him again.

She reveled in this "bonus" morning with the little boy. But the thought of Misty—and the realization that it was almost eight thirty and still no one had called from the shelter—sobered her. "We'd better get you dressed and get some breakfast in you."

"How's come?"

"So we can get you back to your—" Her cell phone rang on the nightstand beside the bed. "See there," she crowed. "I bet that's her now."

Austin's eyebrows went up in a comical slant, and he watched her as she answered the call.

The caller ID said Cape Haven. "Hello?"

"Danae?" It was Berta. Something was wrong.

She turned slightly away from Austin. "Hi, Berta. Is . . . everything OK?"

"You'd better come in. And don't bring Austin. Can Dallas stay with him?"

"He already left for work. What's going on?"

"Can you call him?"

"Berta, what's happened?"

"We have a . . . *situation* with Misty. She's in jail."

"Oh, no. For what?"

She heard a commotion over the lines, and Berta's muffled voice. Finally she came back on. "Just get here as soon as you can. If you have to bring Austin, I guess we can work something out."

"Berta?"

The phone went dead. *What on earth?*

She hung up and called Dallas. It went straight to voice mail and she left a cryptic message, eyeing Austin as she did. He was still watching her, his dark head cocked to one side, as if he knew this concerned him.

Her phone rang again as soon as she hung up. *Dallas. Thank God.*

"Hey, babe. Sorry I missed your call."

"Stay here for a minute, sport," she told Austin. "Hang on, Dallas." She crawled out of bed and slipped into the hallway, speaking just above a whisper into the phone. "I don't know what's going on, but Misty is in jail."

"For what?"

"I don't know. Berta wants me to come in to the shelter but not to bring Austin."

"That doesn't sound good." His tone expressed the dread she was feeling.

"I know. Is . . . is there any way you can come home?"

"Oh, man. I'm swamped after the holidays and I was supposed to meet with—" He stopped abruptly, then let out a long sigh. "I'll be there. Give me about fifteen minutes."

"Thank you."

She turned to see Austin standing in the doorway. He looked so forlorn it tore her up.

"Is my mommy dead?"

She gasped. "Oh, honey, no! Of course not. Why would you think that?" She bent to wrap him in a hug. What kind of world had this poor kid grown up in that he would even ponder such an awful thing?

She wished Berta had told her more so she could prepare Austin. But what possible reason for being in jail could you talk to a three-year-old about?

It seemed like an eternity before Dallas finally arrived home. Danae had distracted Austin with breakfast and had laid out his clothes for Dallas to help him with. "I'll call you as soon as I know anything," she said quietly as they kissed good-bye at the garage door.

Driving to the shelter, her mind swirled with a thousand different possibilities. None of them good.

Nerves on edge, she punched in the security code and went inside. Before she could get halfway down the hall, Berta came from the office and headed toward her. "Thank goodness, you're here."

"What is going on, Berta?"

The older woman closed her eyes briefly as if steeling herself to deliver bad news. "You're going to want to sit down for this."

19

Hey, Kurt. Sorry I had to back out on our meeting. We have a . . . family situation I needed to deal with."

Dallas was handling work issues from home as well as he could, and he knew his boss understood that he wouldn't have left the office like this unless it was truly necessary. Still, he felt like he was letting everyone down at work. And yet, looking over at Austin snuggled into the corner of the sofa, watching some kids' show that Dallas hoped and prayed wouldn't scar the kid for life, he knew he was right where he needed to be.

He wrapped up the phone call with Kurt Troyfield as quickly as he could and checked to be sure his phone's battery had enough charge left.

He looked at the clock for the twentieth time in as many minutes. Danae should be at the shelter by now. He wished she'd hurry up and let him know what was going on.

A screech came from the corner of the sofa and Dallas's heart went into overdrive. He jumped up and leapt over the ottoman. "What's wrong, Austin?"

"I hafta go! I hafta go!"

"Go where?"

"Go pee!" He rose to his knees on the sofa, held himself, and did a frantic dance on the sofa cushion.

"Well, don't just sit there! Let's *go!*" He picked Austin up by the armpits and made an awkward race to the hall bathroom with him. They made it with no time to spare.

He helped Austin get washed up and dressed. As much as he'd enjoyed helping Danae with the boy during the days they'd babysat him, it made him nervous to be here alone with him. He wasn't sure how Danae seemed to instinctively know what a three-year-old needed, while he didn't have the first *clue*.

But Austin could almost dress himself, and when they were finished, including shoes and socks, Austin looked like he was supposed to. Zippers in front, shoes on the right feet, and everything right side out. Unless there was something he didn't know, he was doing good so far.

He was starting to second-guess himself about letting Danae go to the shelter. Maybe he should have let her stay here with Austin while he went to receive whatever news was waiting about Misty. And yet, even though Misty had warmed to him—enough to feel comfortable with Austin staying with them over Thanksgiving—she wouldn't likely feel comfortable talking to him about whatever it was that was going on. He couldn't even guess. Except that it likely involved her abusive husband.

And that scared him to death. What if Hank was trying to get to Austin through Danae? The thought paralyzed him.

"Huh, Mr. Dallas? Is it?"

He pushed through the fog of foolish conjecture and focused to see Austin tugging on his pant leg.

"Sorry, buddy. Is it what?"

"Is it time to go see my mama?"

"Pretty soon. We're waiting for Miss Danae to call."

Why *wasn't* she calling? He had a bad feeling about this. Really bad.

Danae followed Berta down the hall to the office, where Mary was already seated. The two women exchanged a look Danae couldn't interpret. Berta waited until Danae was seated before taking the chair across from them.

"We have a major situation on our hands," Mary said, looking hard at her. "As you already know, Misty is in jail."

Danae leaned forward. "What happened?"

"She shot her husband last night."

"Oh, no. Is he going to be OK?"

"He's dead." Berta spoke the words in a monotone.

Her breath left her. She scrambled to think what to say, what she could even do. "Did he beat her again? Was it self-defense?" Where would she have gotten a gun?

"According to the officer who came to talk to us, she shot him in the back. In cold blood."

He must have attacked her again. "She seemed like she was doing so well. Why would she do that when she'd finally gotten away?" And yet, she hadn't really been safe here. Hank had found her here. Probably because Misty had told him where she was. No one seemed to know for sure how he'd found her.

And Austin. "What . . . what will happen to Austin?" Her voice broke. Surely they wouldn't make him go back to the family Misty had described as "a bunch of lowlife perverts."

Mary cleared her throat. "That's why we needed to see you, Danae. Misty left a written request that you and your husband take Austin."

"What? Take him? What do you mean? When did she leave it?"

"Apparently, she told the officers they'd find it in her room. Here at the shelter. They searched the room and found the note." She slid a folder from the stack on her desk and placed it in front of her.

"But that means . . . Misty *planned* to shoot him."

As if Mary had read her mind, she said, "It's a tangled mess. Misty turned herself in. She said it was self-defense. There was no witness, but they—the police—are saying there's no doubt he was shot in the back. And the fact that she left a letter concerning Austin points to premeditation."

Danae stared past Mary, trying to make sense of it all, trying to piece together what this might mean for Austin. "Would they let us have him? Even if the letter proves she killed him in cold blood?"

"We're trying to figure out what to do. Misty has a court-appointed attorney. I suppose it will be up to him. And the state, of course."

"Please don't let them take Austin. Don't let him get sucked into the system. Please. We'll do anything. Whatever it takes." She'd heard horror stories of children being placed in foster care, and then their families—loving families who had the child's best interest at heart—unable to get them out of the system. Sometimes for months. Or longer.

"So, you'd be willing? You and Dallas would be willing to take him in until—"

"Of course. Yes. We'll take him."

"You need to think this over, Danae." Mary sounded alarmed. "This could get very complicated. I don't know who Misty has for family. Or who Hank's survivors are. But there's surely someone in the family who will want him."

"No." Danae shook her head so hard it hurt. "Misty was clear that there was no one in the family who she would want for role models for Austin. In fact, she called them perverts. She didn't even want Austin around them. Surely they have to honor her letter?"

"We're trying to find out about that."

"Do you have the letter?"

"We have a copy. The police took the original." Mary rummaged through the folder in front of her and came up with a single sheet of copy paper. She handed it across the desk to Danae.

It was hard to tell from the copy, but it looked as if it had been written in pencil on a piece of notebook paper torn out of a spiral binder. A memory flashed into her mind . . . Her dad had just taken her down to the Home State Bank in Langhorne to open her first checking account. Dad had made her practice writing a check correctly. He'd warned that she should never sign a check in pencil because it would not be legal—or maybe it was that the details, amount or signature, could be altered. She couldn't remember for sure, and now she wondered, was that true of a note like this—what was, in essence, Misty's will?

She read the brief note, trying to process what it would mean for her. For Austin. For Dallas.

To whom it may concern:

My name is Misty Shavonne Morrison Arato. This is about my son Austin Franklin Morrison (we called him Austin Arato but that is not his real name). It is my wish that my son Austin is put in custody of Dallas and Denay Brooks. I do not want my son to be with any of my family or the family of Hank Arato (also goes by the name of Henry Arato). Hank is not Austin's real father. His birth father has never had nothing to do with Austin. My son should go only to Dallas and Denay to take care of him if I can't.

Misty Shavonne Morrison Arato

How could Misty do this? *Why* would she? Had she killed him just for revenge? It had always been clear that she loved Austin. Why would she have risked losing him just for revenge? How could a mother give up her son for *any* reason?

The thought startled her. Dallas's mother had done that too. But . . . that was different. She'd given him up at birth. Dallas never liked to talk about it, and he didn't know all the circumstances, but from what little he had told her, his mother was still in her teens, unmarried. And it was a blessing . . . *he* considered it a blessing that he'd been spared that kind of existence and had instead grown up with his adoptive parents. And with Drew.

Dallas. He didn't know what was going on. Didn't know any of this. And he was probably wondering why she hadn't called.

But what on earth would she tell him? She couldn't think straight. She didn't even know what any of this would mean. The only thing she did know was that she would not let Austin go with any of his relatives in St. Louis. She would break the law first, if she had to.

Berta put a hand on her arm. "This isn't a decision you need to make now, Danae. It may be out of your hands. It will depend on whether they find Misty guilty."

Maybe it was all a horrible mistake, and they'd figure out what happened, and Austin could come back to the shelter with his mama in a few days. And yet, why else would she have written such a letter, unless she knew she would not be coming back?

"Where did you find Misty's letter?"

"It was in the top drawer of the dresser in her room," Mary said. "Apparently, she told the police where to look for it. And we found it there, just like she said."

Berta shook her head. "She must not have thought about the fact that the letter would incriminate her."

Danae scooted her chair back. "I need to call Dallas. He's swamped at work, and he came home to watch Austin." A wave of nausea came over her. "What do we tell Austin?"

"He's three, is that right?" Mary hadn't spent as much time with him or Misty as Danae and Berta had.

"Almost three and a half." *Oh, dear Lord, help us. Help Austin. How will we make him understand?*

Berta inhaled deeply, and they both turned to face her. "I'm going to go out on a limb here and suggest that you might want to take Austin to a hotel or to another family member's house. Some of our volunteers may be questioned. It might be in everyone's best interest if you guys—and Austin—are unavailable for comment."

Mary winced, but then she nodded. "I'm inclined to agree. And if you quote me, I'll deny it. But I'll say one thing: I agree with Danae that we do not want that little guy going with either of their families in St. Louis."

Danae picked up the note and scanned it again. "If it's true that Hank isn't Austin's father, then his family wouldn't have any right to him, would they?"

"It depends," Mary said. "On whether he legally adopted Austin. Whether he was a legal guardian—although I wouldn't think that would give his *family* any rights." She shrugged.

Danae tapped the sheet of notebook paper. "Misty says here that Arato wasn't Austin's real last name. Wouldn't that indicate that Hank never officially adopted him?"

"It might," Mary said. "There are a lot of unknowns right now. But the first order of business is making sure Austin has a safe place to be. I think, in light of Misty's letter, and the fact that she put Austin in your care this weekend, that it would be best if he stays with you. You and Dallas currently have guardianship of him at his mother's request. You have the medical release forms to prove it. Like Berta said, it might be best if you and Austin are just"—she chalked quote marks in the air—"'conveniently' not at home, on the chance that someone from DFS comes looking."

Danae's pulse raced. The Division of Family Services and foster care were a godsend when a child actually needed protection, but over her dead body would they take Austin away and put him into the system. They'd all heard too many stories of children who got sucked into the foster care system. It practically took an act of Congress to get them out again. "So . . . what do we do next?"

Mary shook her head. "I'm not sure. We have the shelter's attorney looking into it. She's the one who helped with the legal aspects of getting the shelter up and running. She's served as a guardian ad litem—a child's advocate—in some other child protective situations, so I think she'll be able to give us some direction. Until then, if you and Dallas are willing, I think the prudent thing to do is leave things the way Austin's mother chose for him. She cared enough to put it in writing. And if that's wrong, I plead ignorance."

Berta nodded.

Danae tried not to think about the fact that there might be people who wanted to take Austin. Whether it was family members of Misty or Hank, or child protective services, or whoever. "Would we be doing anything illegal if we disappeared for a while?"

"I'm not an attorney," Mary said. "But I can't imagine it would be wrong to protect Austin from any of those possibilities."

"No. No, I can't either." Danae inhaled, steeling herself for what was to come. "I have to call my husband. I can't leave him hanging any longer."

"Of course." Mary waved her away. "Go."

Danae left the office and walked blindly through the house. There were two women she didn't recognize in the dayroom. She didn't want anyone to overhear her conversation, so she punched the security code and went out to her car. Her legs could barely hold her up.

She closed the car door, took a deep breath, and dialed her husband.

Dallas answered on the first ring. "Is everything OK?"

"No. Oh, babe . . . I don't even know where to start. What's Austin doing right now?"

"Hang on." She heard him talking in that precious voice he used when he spoke to children. She could hear him moving to somewhere he could talk more freely. "He's watching TV. I know you don't like kids watching too much TV, but I've had to field some work stuff, so yes, I'm using the TV as a babysitter."

"Stop—I don't even care about that. Dallas, Misty killed her husband."

"Killed him? What do you mean?"

"I mean she shot him dead. She's in custody right now, and from everything they know, it sounds like she shot him in the back and that it was premeditated."

"How could they know that?"

Strangled, inappropriate laughter came from her throat. "That's where we come in."

"Danae? Are you OK? What's the deal?"

20

I think we need to take him." Dallas wasn't sure where the conviction in his voice had come from, but even hearing himself speak the words aloud, he knew—as crazy as it sounded—he believed them.

His in-laws had come and picked up Austin and taken him out to the inn. Ever since, he and Danae had paced the house like zombies trying to absorb the news.

Now, half standing, half sitting on a barstool, she twisted the wedding ring on her finger, unable to sit still, but seeming to need the support of a chair at the same time. "I don't want him to get put in the system. I know that. But, Dallas, we don't even know what we're getting into. How long would we have him? A few weeks? A few *years*? I . . . , I don't know if I could do that." Her voice rose on the word and tears sprang to her eyes.

"If we don't take him, who will?"

"I know. I know. But—"

"Misty asked us—*trusted* us to take care of him."

"She *used* us, Dallas. She knew what she was going to do when she left for St. Louis on Wednesday. When she wrote this note." She jabbed at the copy of the note Misty had left. A copy of a copy, actually, since Mary had felt the shelter needed to keep a copy on hand too.

He picked it up and read it again. "She spelled your name wrong."

Danae gave a humorless laugh. "She spelled a lot of things wrong and—" A little gasp escaped her. "You don't think that would keep this from being valid, do you? A valid document?"

"What? Because your name is spelled wrong? I wouldn't think so. They could see from the rest of the note that she's not the sharpest crayon in the box."

"Dallas!" She glared at him. "That sounds awful."

"You know what I mean."

She ignored him and jumped up from her chair for the dozenth time. "I feel like we're the ones who did something wrong!"

"Well, maybe we are. I'm not sure I like the idea of hiding out at your parents. It feels a little too close to kidnapping."

She shuddered at the word, and he knew she was remembering a few months ago when an unstable woman Jesse had worked with lured Sadie and Simone into her car. This world sure had its share of nutjobs to go around.

Danae stood at the window for a few minutes, and then she turned, staring past him. "What if someone comes and tries to take Austin? He's not going to understand what's happening."

"He doesn't know what happened yet," Dallas reminded her.

"I know. And how do you even tell a three-year-old that Mommy killed Daddy?"

"Well, the man he called Dad, anyway. I wouldn't dignify him with the label."

Danae nodded, but her face was a mask of anguish and confusion.

Dallas went to her. "We'll get through this, babe."

She buried her face in her hands. "What are we going to tell him?" she said again.

He rose and went to her, wrapped her in his arms. "Shhh . . . shhh . . ." He opened his mouth, then promptly closed it, not knowing what else to say. But he did recognize the silent, persistent nudge inside him. Still, he hesitated.

He kissed the crown of Danae's head, unaccustomed to praying aloud. Yet the insistent nudge finally won out. "God, we need your help," he whispered. "Give us wisdom and show us what's right in this situation. Help us tell Austin in a way he can understand, and in a way that won't break his spirit." Words left him then.

But Danae nodded against his chest, and wrapped her arms around his waist. He didn't know how long they stood that way but he realized that it had grown dark outside. "We probably should let your parents know what's up."

"What is up? I don't have a clue what we should do."

"We just . . . we need to do the next thing. One foot in front of the other. We need to explain to Austin as best we can. And we need to be sure he's safe and with people he knows and loves. I think that's the most important thing right now."

"Yes. You're right." She straightened and took a deep breath. "I sent his suitcase with Mom and Dad. Is there anything else we need?"

"No. Except our own clothes and stuff. I think we should stay at your parents', like Mary and Berta said. It's better if we just aren't here. And . . . I wouldn't answer your phone unless you can see who it is."

So many questions they didn't know the answer to. Supposedly, Misty was in the city jail in St. Louis, the town where the murder had occurred. But whether she would soon be out on bail or . . . He didn't know. And it didn't matter. She wasn't their responsibility.

But Austin was.

Gently, he let Danae go. "Let's finish packing and getting the house closed up."

"OK." She seemed grateful to have "marching orders," and after calling her parents to see if they could stay at the inn, she followed him throughout the house, gathering things they would need, turning off lights, and locking doors.

The drive to the inn was the longest twenty minutes he could remember. "I think we should tell him together, don't you?"

"Yes, but I want to talk to Mom and Dad first. Just about how we should tell him. How *much* we should say. I don't even know how much a three-year-old can understand."

"Probably at this point, until we know what's going to happen to Misty, the less we say the better."

Danae nodded. "Misty already pretty much told him that he wouldn't be seeing Hank again because of the beating. And I don't think Austin is going to be torn up over that. But what if they won't let him see Misty?"

"They probably won't. She killed a man, Danae."

"I know. But surely they'll at least let her have visitation, don't you think?"

"I don't know."

The yard lights from the inn appeared in the distance through a low mist that veiled the woods. The lights were on inside the inn and two cars with out-of-state license plates were parked in the driveway. "Are you sure your parents have room for us?"

"I didn't even ask if they had guests. I . . . I don't know. Surely Mom would have said something."

They went quietly into the house, and Austin came running before they even got past the foyer. Audrey was right behind him.

"Shhh, buddy, people might be sleeping." Dallas lifted Austin into his arms, overwhelmed with sadness.

"Come on in," Audrey said. "Our guests are all at the game in Cape, so you don't have to worry about being quiet just yet."

"I'm sorry, Mom," Danae said. "I didn't even think about you having guests this weekend."

"It's OK. Your room is open and the guests are in the two far rooms, so it shouldn't be a problem. They won't get in till late tonight, and they asked for an early breakfast, so they won't even know you're here."

"Thanks, Mom."

Dallas could see that Danae was near tears. "Is Grant around? We wanted to talk to you two before we talk to this one—" He angled his head toward Austin pointedly.

"Of course. Let me get him. You guys come on in the kitchen. I just took some cookies out of the oven. Your favorite, Dallas."

He wasn't hungry, but he never turned down one of Audrey's famous chocolate chip cookies.

"Can I have one, Mr. Dallas?" Austin wiggled to get down, and Dallas released him.

"Has he already had a cookie?" Danae asked.

"No, I made him wait for you to get here."

Dallas gave Austin a thumbs up. "Yep, you can have one. But you have to sit at the table with it. Let Gram show you where to sit."

He'd called Audrey by her grandmother name without even thinking. Dallas wondered if anyone else had noticed.

But they seemed not to, intent instead on getting cookies and milk set up at the small table in the kitchen. He watched Austin devour a cookie, and it struck him that the scene was like something straight out of a Norman Rockwell print.

If only they didn't have to deal with the grim reality that was about to unfold.

21

Austin? Hey, buddy, look at me." Danae sent up a prayer that she would be able to tell him as much as he could understand.

Her parents had added so much wisdom to the discussion, and she felt relieved that Mom and Dad didn't feel they needed to give too many details to the little boy—at least until they knew what would happen to Misty, and whether Austin would be able to see her. Her parents had felt—and Dallas agreed—that Danae should be the one to tell him. As much as the boy clung to and looked up to Dallas, Danae was the one Austin had the longest and closest relationship to.

He looked up at her now, his big brown eyes bright, as if she was about to reveal a wonderful surprise. "We need to tell you something really important, OK?"

He nodded, and tugged at the string on his hoodie, unable to sit still.

"Your mama is going to stay in St. Louis for a while, and she asked me and Dallas if you could stay at our house until she gets back. Is that OK with you, sport?"

"I play bassetball with Mr. Dallas. And I make a basset!" He shot an invisible three-pointer.

Danae could almost hear the nothing-but-net *swoosh*.

"You sure did, buddy. High five." Dallas put up a hand and Austin stretched to match palms with him.

The infernal lump came back to Danae's throat and she tried unsuccessfully to swallow it. At her dad's suggestion, they'd decided it was best not to even mention Hank or the fact that Misty was in trouble. Her mom agreed. "If he was even a year older," Mom had said, "my advice would probably be different, but I think all he needs to know at this point is that his mom will be away for a while, but that she's made provisions for him, and that he'll be safe and taken care of."

Something about hearing her mom voice it that way—that Misty had made provisions for Austin, and she and Dallas *were* the provisions—helped Danae feel a bit more comfortable about taking Austin into their home and into their care.

Dallas seemed so sure of the decision. And that, frankly, surprised her. She was afraid his certainty was because this might all be very temporary. Ironic when most of her own anxiety was wrapped in the possibility that they would have Austin just long enough to fall in love with him. If that were to happen, she didn't know how she could ever face losing him.

She snuggled closer and put an arm around Austin. "Buddy, you know your mama loves you, right?"

"Uh-huh." His thumb went to his mouth.

"It might be a while before you get to see her, but your mama is making sure everything is OK for you, do you understand?"

"And my mama will come an' pick me up in a little bit, right, Miss Danae?"

She threw Dallas a desperate glance.

"Well, not today. It might be a while. But you can stay with Miss Danae and me as long as—"

"Dallas . . ." She cleared her throat.

"As long as you need a place to stay," he finished weakly.

She sighed, supposing Dallas's words didn't exactly constitute a commitment on their part, but desperate not to make Austin promises they couldn't keep.

They would know more after they met with Misty and her attorney. She didn't know when that would be or how she would face Austin's mother when the time came. And she had no clue what the outcome might be. But she would be glad when that meeting was over and they knew what the next hurdle was.

———

"Mom? You there?"

"Up here, honey . . . laundry room." Audrey pulled another load of warm towels from the dryer and started folding.

Danae appeared at the top of the stairs. "I thought I heard the dryer. Can I help?"

"Always. We have two couples coming in this evening and I'm behind on getting the rooms made up." Audrey sorted hand towels and washcloths from the bath towels and piled them in front of her daughter. "Where's Austin?"

"He finally fell asleep. I just hope he doesn't sleep until supper like he did yesterday."

"It's not the sleeping till supper part that's bad. It's the waking up at five a.m. rarin' to go."

"Ha. You've got that right."

"Maybe you should wake him up if he's not up by four or so."

"Yes. I think I will. Actually, Mom, we're thinking about going back home to sleep tonight. It's been three days and nobody's tried to call us or the shelter. It's almost like they've forgotten Austin existed."

Audrey shook her head, frowning. "That's kind of sad."

"It really is. But it's a relief too."

"I'm sure it is. Just knowing he's safe. But you know you're welcome to stay here as long as you need to. I've appreciated your help with the laundry and cooking."

"I knew there was an ulterior motive in wanting us to stay on." Danae's grin faded. "Only one problem."

"Oh? What's that?"

"Mary—the director of the shelter—called, and we're supposed to meet with Misty and her lawyer in St. Louis tomorrow.

Would you guys be willing to keep Austin for the day? We need to leave by eight. I'm guessing we'll be home before supper. Would that work?"

"I'll check with your dad, but I don't know why it wouldn't."

They folded the fragrant linens in silence for a few minutes, but Audrey's mind roiled with worries. She finally worked up the courage to broach a subject she couldn't quit thinking about. "How do you think he's handling everything?"

Danae shrugged. "It's hard to tell. To me, he seems like he's taking it in stride. He's had a few meltdowns, but to be honest, I saw him have a couple of those in the shelter. It's hard to know whether he's reacting to his mom being gone—or everything he went through with his dad before. I suppose at some point it might be wise to look into some counseling." She creased a towel into thirds and added it to the stack. "Does that sound crazy to you? Putting a three-year-old in counseling?"

"I'm not sure what I think. And it's not my decision to make."

Danae cocked her head and eyed her. "It sounds like you're saying it's not really *my* decision either."

"I—" She released a slow breath and put down the stack of towels she'd been folding. "I suppose that is what I was saying. And I'm sorry. It wasn't my place to say it. I . . . I don't want to see you and Dallas get hurt over this."

"You don't think we should be taking care of Austin?"

She shook her head. "I'm not saying that. That has to be between you and God. I just . . . I can see how attached you already are. What if he ends up having to go into foster care?"

"Mom, Misty has asked us—in writing—to take him. Surely that counts for something and if—"

"But for how long, Danae? Even if she ends up in prison, would you guys be required to take him to visit her?"

"We'd *want* to, Mom."

"What if they send her to Lansing or—"

"We'll cross those bridges when we come to them. Dallas and I have been talking about this a lot. We're not going to jump into anything until we know what we're getting into. But even if it meant making long trips every few weeks to visit Misty, I think . . . I think it'd be worthwhile."

"I just don't want to see you get hurt. I'm not meaning to be discouraging. I know you well enough to know that you love so deeply and so fully. If you go into this whole hog and then things go south, that would kill you, Danae." She did not want to fall apart in front of Danae, but she was glad she'd had a chance to speak her mind.

"Mom, I may as well tell you right now. We're already in it 'whole hog,' as you say. And if anything happens that keeps us from being a part of Austin's life, it will devastate us. But I'm kind of starting to think—" She stopped abruptly as if collecting her thoughts. Or deciding whether she should finish her thought.

"Go ahead." Audrey patted Danae's arm. "I won't hold you to anything you say. I'd love to know what you guys are thinking. Maybe it will calm my fears so I can get some sleep."

"Mom. You don't need to lose any sleep over this."

"Oh, well thanks. *Now* you tell me."

Danae laughed, then quickly sobered. "I'm kind of bracing myself to have my heart broken. But I think Dallas and I are supposed to take care of Austin for however long he needs it."

Her face must have shown her trepidation because Danae gave her a quick hug.

"I know you worry about us, but Mom, I've been such a wreck. For three years I've been in turmoil over what I *can't* have. A baby. This whole thing with Austin has given me a sense of purpose I haven't felt in forever. It's not how I hoped or dreamed it would be. He's not a baby. He's not mine. But I feel like, for however long God lets us, we're simply supposed to love him as if he *was* ours."

"Oh, honey. I admire your attitude so much. I really do. I only hope—"

"I know it won't be easy. But honestly, I'd rather feel this kind of pain—pain because I loved somebody and then lost him—than be the way I've been up until Austin. I've been so self-absorbed, so turned inward that I made everybody else miserable. And myself too! I ruined Corinne's enjoyment of this baby that's coming—and it was already hard for her. I was such a jerk. And poor Dallas. He's put up with so much."

"I'm guessing he thinks you're worth it."

Danae cringed. "I'm afraid it was a toss-up for a while there."

"Oh, stop. I know better than that."

"Maybe. But that's the thing, Mom. It's better now. Dallas and I are in this together and if our hearts get broken, well, we'll be in that together too. And it'll be OK. Somehow, I just know it will. Even if it's hard."

Audrey couldn't speak for the ache wedged in her throat. She was so proud of this beautiful girl. This precious daughter.

Please, God, don't let her heart be broken.

22

The uniformed officer entered the room ahead of them and held the door open. The low-ceilinged space had a musty odor, like a cellar that hadn't been opened in months.

Dallas took Danae's hand, noting it was as clammy as his own. He steered her to the metal table where Misty sat, and beside her, her court-appointed attorney, a young man who looked like he should still be in high school.

Misty sat with her back straight, her hands cuffed in front of her. Dallas almost didn't recognize her. She wore no makeup and there were dark, puffy circles under her eyes. Her wavy hair hung loose and limp in front of her face.

As soon as they were seated, he reached for Danae's hand again.

"Hello, Misty." Danae's voice came out in a squeaky whisper and she squeezed Dallas's hand so hard it hurt.

"How is he?" Misty leaned forward. "How's Oz?"

"He's good," Dallas told her. "Austin is doing really well. He's no trouble at all."

"No. He's a good boy." Misty spoke in a monotone, almost as if she were high on something. But given that she'd been locked up for days now here at the jail housed in the Justice Center, it was more likely she'd closed off her emotions to the reality of what was happening to her.

Dallas looked to the attorney, hoping he would steer the conversation. Dallas didn't have a clue how this was supposed to go, but he assumed the purpose of the meeting was to iron out the details of Austin's custody.

Misty looked over at the attorney. "Can I talk to them, or do you have to?"

"You can talk to them. Just remember what we discussed."

"Yeah . . . I know." She looked down at her hands, clasped in front of her, the handcuffs looking tight and uncomfortable. When she peered up, it was Danae's eyes she met. "You got my note? About taking Oz . . . Austin?"

"We did. But we're not sure exactly what that means, Misty."

"I want you to take him. Please."

"You mean until you're out of jail?"

Misty looked to the attorney again. Leaning forward, the young man cleared his throat. "Mrs. Arato has pled guilty to murder in the first degree. She knowingly and after deliberation, in front of witnesses, shot her husband in the back. In the state of Missouri, murder in the first degree is a class A felony, and the punishment is either death or life without probation or parole. Because multiple witnesses corroborated Mrs. Arato's confession and because there is evidence that the murder was premeditated, we had no choice but to enter a guilty plea for Mrs. Arato."

"You're not even going to fight it?" Dallas asked. "What about the fact that her husband beat her and her son?"

"Physical abuse is not grounds for premeditated, cold-blooded murder." The attorney gave a smug smile, as if he were answering a question correctly on a test.

"Misty?" Danae reached across the table and placed a hand over the younger woman's. "Why did you do it?"

"Ma'am," the attorney said. "I'm sorry, but you're not allowed to touch my client."

Danae withdrew her hand.

Misty didn't answer her question, but looked at Danae with pleading eyes. "I need you to promise me you'll take Austin. You've got to take my boy."

"It . . . it's not that easy, Misty." Dallas said what Danae had been saying to him all the way to St. Louis. "We need to find out exactly what would be involved. We don't know where you might be . . . what it would involve for us to bring him to visit you?"

"No. No, that's exactly what I don't want." She lifted her hands, as if to fling them wide, but the shackles brought them back to the table with a thud.

"Misty?" Danae sounded confused. "You don't mean that. You can't just—"

"I don't want my son to see me in prison. I don't want that baggage on him. I know what that was like, and it's not what I want for my son."

"Is there anything that can be done?" Dallas turned to the attorney. "An appeal? *Something*?"

"Her husband beat her!" Danae said. "And Austin. He followed them to the shelter they'd escaped to, which is where we met Misty. Surely the courts have to take that into account!"

The attorney's demeanor softened. "I wish that were true, but when a man is shot in the back in front of witnesses, it makes it pretty difficult to build a case for leniency."

Dallas sighed. This was really happening. And Austin was going to need a home. "So what happens next?" he said. "Has the arraignment already taken place?"

"Yes, sentencing has been set for February"—he flipped open the folder on the table in front of him—"February 24."

"Will she be released until the trial?" Danae asked.

"No ma'am. And . . . I'm not sure you understand, but there won't be a jury trial. Mrs. Arato has pled guilty to murder in the first degree and has waived the right to a trial."

"Misty? Is that true?" Danae asked.

"What choice did I have? I don't want to die."

What was she talking about? Dallas gave the attorney a questioning look.

The man returned it with a one-shouldered shrug. "This judge won't set bail for murder one at any rate. But frankly, as I've told Mrs. Arato, unless she wants to take this to trial and risk the judge handing down a death sentence, she's chosen the wisest option. The law in the State of Missouri is clear about the penalty for murder one, and I'd say a guilty plea in exchange for life without parole is the best deal she could ask for."

"Surely she has other options?" It felt rude to talk about Misty as if she weren't sitting right there, but Dallas didn't know if they'd get a chance to speak with the attorney after they left this room.

He felt Danae tense beside him. Neither of them had imagined there wouldn't be at least the possibility of parole, but it was sounding as though Misty was doomed to life in prison. If not a death sentence. But he couldn't bear to bring this up with the attorney. Not with Misty in the room.

But if she'd shot her husband in the back as they said—as *she* admitted to—it wouldn't be right for her to get off without penalty either. He and Danae had only ever known Misty as Austin's mommy. And he assumed that, in her own mind, Misty saw her actions as a way of protecting her child. Dallas raked a hand through his hair. Who knew whether *he* might have done the same in similar circumstances?

But where did this leave Austin?

Danae straightened and slid a hand across the table, stopping just a breath away from Misty's hand. "Misty, I promise you we will make sure Austin is taken care of. I don't know if it can be us. We have a lot to talk about before we can decide that. But we won't let him be hurt. We'll see to it that he's—"

"No! It's got to be you. It's got to be you and Dallas. Your family. I never would have done it if I thought you'd say no. If I thought you'd let me down."

"What are you talking about?" Dallas wanted to reassure her, but he didn't like the implication of her words. He glanced at the lawyer, hoping to make it clear that he truly *didn't* know what Misty was talking about. "Misty, we never gave you any reason to think we'd be willing to take Austin under . . . under *any* circumstances."

"You love him. I can tell you do. And he's happy with you. I can't offer him nothing."

"Misty . . ." Danae put her hand over Misty's and glared at the attorney, daring him to stop her.

He let it ride.

"Austin loves you with all his heart." Danae's voice was barely a whisper. "Why did you do this when you knew it would keep you from him?"

"Like I already told everybody, I don't have anything to give. The shelter kicked us out, and I've got no money. If Hank got Austin back, God help us. And things was heading just that way because I couldn't take care of my baby anymore. I want my kids—" Her voice broke. "I want Austin to have a future. I don't want him growing up like I did. Kids making fun. Being marked like that. I don't want him ending up like I did."

"Oh, Misty—" Danae's words came out on a sob. "Why didn't you talk to us before? Why didn't you—"

"What good would it've done?" Misty's voice held a hard edge.

"We could have helped you find someplace. We could have—" She stopped short, swallowing a sob.

Dallas wanted to pick up the plea for her, but he couldn't honestly say what they would have, or could have, done to stop what happened. And it didn't matter now. It was too late. The damage was done.

And Austin was so much more than collateral damage.

―◌◌◌―

The sun rode low in the sky, framed by the towering Gateway Arch as they drove east on Walnut Street, trying to get back to the Interstate. She'd lived in Missouri, not three hours from St. Louis, all her life, and she'd never been up in the arch. She wondered if the view from the top might somehow give her a perspective she certainly didn't have now.

And needed desperately.

Dallas drove in silence, the hum of the tires on the highway affording an invisible wall of privacy between them. But when the city landscape gave way to rolling hills and wooded fields, he reached across the console and took her hand. "What are you thinking?"

"I wish we could see the future."

He nodded, knowing exactly what she meant. "If we knew for sure Austin would spend all his childhood and teenage years with us, it would be a no-brainer. We love him. He needs a home. We have one to offer."

"But if by some miracle Misty gets paroled five or ten years from now, could you give him back, babe? I don't know if I could!"

He heaved a long sigh and squeezed her hand. "It's *already* gut-wrenching to think about sending him back now."

Tears sprang to her eyes, and she let them run down her cheeks unchecked. "Everything in me wants to give him back now before we set ourselves up for the most painful thing we've ever experienced. But . . . I really think God is saying that Austin needs a family, and we are the very ones God has prepared to *be* his family."

Dallas started nodding hard. "Yes. That's what I think too. But we have to go into it knowing that we might be asked to give him up. We have to treat him as if he belongs to God."

"The way Hannah gave up Samuel in the Bible."

"That couldn't have been easy."

"No. But Dallas, sometimes God asks birth parents to give *their* babies up too. Remember when my cousin lost her baby?" Grant's brother's daughter had given birth to a stillborn baby. A perfect little boy, full-term. It had devastated them. But now their Christmas cards showed three precious little stair-step towheads about the age of Corinne's girls.

"So . . . you're willing to take Austin and raise him as long as God allows? Even if it means we might not be able to actually adopt him?"

She nodded, her throat full. "We have a little boy, Dallas. He might not belong to us in the way we'd hoped. But we have a little boy to love and to raise."

"For however long," Dallas reminded. "We don't know how this all works. There are still too many unanswered questions."

She nodded, not wanting to let him put a damper on the overflowing of awe and joy and grief and confusion that bubbled up in her. "We need to start making lists!" She rummaged in her purse.

"Danae . . . We've got to talk to an attorney and see what this involves. To be sure we can get him medical care when he needs it and permission for whatever vaccinations and that kind of stuff he'll need."

"We need to talk to Misty about so many things. Surely they'll let us have a couple of hours with her to iron things out—"

"I wish we could convince her to let us bring Austin to see her. At least once in a while. And tell her that she'll always be his mother, but that we'll do our best in her absence."

Danae wanted to change the subject. She couldn't bring herself to admit it to Dallas, but she'd been relieved when Misty said she didn't want Austin to visit her.

"I just don't want her to think we're giddy about this," Dallas said.

Danae cringed. "Oh, Dallas. I *am* a little bit giddy. I know that sounds terrible. My heart is crushed for Misty, but I love Austin so much. As much as if he *were* my son. And we get the *privilege* of raising him. It seems so amazing!"

"Just guard your heart a little bit, babe, OK? Until we've talked to an attorney. Until we know for sure this is really happening. I don't want you to get—"

She held up a hand. "I know what you're saying, I do. But Dallas, I'm starting to wonder if this is what all our waiting has been for—preparing us for Austin. I think I'd rather pour my heart out—*our* hearts—and if we get hurt in the end, at least we know we gave it our all."

He looked at her with love in his eyes. "You are an amazing woman, do you know that?"

"Yeah, well, I have a lot of lost time to make up for. I've spent too much time whining. I'm so sorry you've had to put up with me. But now it's time to suck it up and man up and all that good stuff."

He laughed. "I love you."

"I know you do. And I'll be forever grateful for that."

He turned back to the road and she swallowed hard, trying not to fall apart. When she finally could speak again, she put a hand on his knee. "And in case you were wondering, I love you too. Now, could you drive a little faster? I'm missing our boy."

23

Grant turned away from the chaos that was currently reigning in his living room and adjusted the damper, then closed the fireplace doors, and took a step back to check his handiwork. The fire burned hot and the logs crackled—just the way he liked it. He turned to warm his back at the fire.

Christmas wrapping was strewn from one end of the house to the other, a veritable Toys"R"Us had popped up in his living room, and kids and adults in various stages of sugar-stupor were flopped on the furniture and floor. The guys were sprawled on the sofa, and NBA basketball droned in the background. Perfect Christmas music, all of it.

He loved every inch of the mess, every minute of the day. Christmas was his time. And this had been an extra good one. He caught Audrey's eye across the room and knew she was reciting the same litany of gratitude he was. Bree had taken CeeCee home and gone on to be with her family, but the rest of them had stretched out and made themselves comfortable in the lull between lunch and leftovers.

Corinne's girls chattered in the corner of the great room, playing a game of Candy Land with Austin at the kid-sized card table. Austin and the girls had hit it off from the moment they'd met at Thanksgiving. Seeing Danae so happy, so nurturing with little Austin, did his heart good. He'd fit into the family almost seamlessly, though with things still unsettled with the boy's mother, Grant still hadn't let himself think of Austin as a grandson. Although, he didn't know who he was kidding. He already loved the kid like crazy.

The sentencing for Misty Arato wasn't until well after the first of the year, and he was terrified Danae and Dallas might be setting themselves up for heartbreak. Missouri had notoriously tough murder penalties, and Misty's attorney had said there was no chance she'd escape with less than life without parole. Still, Grant had heard too many cases of criminals getting off easy for one reason or another.

It wasn't like he was rooting for Austin's mother to spend the rest of her life in prison, but she had killed her husband in cold blood, after all. And he couldn't even imagine what it would do to Danae if she and Dallas had to let Austin go back to his mother, or worse, back to the woman's family in St. Louis. Or God forbid, into the system. It had been a rough few weeks for all of them, waiting on the attorneys, agonizing over the decision whether to agree to Misty's request that they take Austin in.

He and Audrey had hashed out every possible scenario until they were sick of the subject. But ultimately he couldn't have been more proud of Danae's attitude. She and Dallas both had decided to be all in. To do what was best for the boy, even if it meant getting their hearts broken.

And given Austin's history of abuse, there were a lot of ways he could ultimately break their hearts—even if they got to raise him to adulthood. Abuse like that had to mess with a kid's mind pretty badly. He only hoped they—

A blood-curdling scream came from the great room, and Sadie shot from the room grasping something in her hand, waving it over her head. "It's mine! You can't have it. I chose the blue one!"

Austin chased behind her with fire in his eyes. He was wailing like a banshee and saying something over and over, but Grant couldn't for the life of him figure out what it was.

Sadie made a beeline for Audrey and buried her face in her grandmother's apron. "Don't let him get it, Gram! Don't let him! I had it first!"

"Did not! DID NOT!" Austin barreled into Sadie and Audrey, nearly toppling them both over, despite the fact that he was half as tall as Sadie.

Dallas and Jesse both jumped up from the sofa and headed to their respective kids.

"What is going on?" Jesse barked over the din.

Link grabbed the remote and turned the game down to a low murmur.

"Austin?" Dallas dropped to his knees and took the boy by the shoulders. "Tell me what's wrong. What are you guys fighting about?"

Sadie glared at Austin. "He stole my gingerbread man."

"Sadie." Jesse put a firm hand on her shoulder. "Uncle Dallas was not talking to you. Now be quiet."

"I did not stole anything!" Austin burst into tears and stood in the middle of the floor, mouth wide, wailing at the top of his lungs. Jesse and Dallas exchanged your-guess-is-as-good-as-mine shrugs and took the fighters to opposite corners of the room.

Sadie calmed down, but Austin would not be consoled.

Grant heard Dallas trying to pry the story from him, but the boy couldn't stop crying long enough to answer. Finally Dallas took him downstairs. They could still hear him crying.

"What happened?" Danae appeared on the staircase, casting about the room. "Was that Austin?"

Audrey pointed toward the front door. "Dallas took him to the basement to calm down."

"What happened?" Danae asked again, looking from Grant to Audrey to Corinne and Jesse.

"They got into a tiff playing Candy Land," Grant said. "I'm not sure exactly what the deal is."

"He took my gingerbread man!" Sadie sniffed. "I was almost about to win and—"

Jesse shushed her, then looked at Danae. "Is Corinne upstairs?"

She nodded. "She's helping Landyn get the twins down for naps. Do you want me to get her?"

He waved her off. "No, it's OK." He turned to Sadie. "Listen, Sadie, I'm sure Austin didn't do it on purpose. You've got to remember he's only three. He might not understand all the rules."

Danae looked near tears and Grant saw her slink off to the basement.

Sari hollered from the great room. "Come on, Sadie. Aren't you gonna play anymore?"

"No, stupid! Austin stole my gingerbread man!"

"Sadie, stop it right now. I don't want to hear another word about the game." Jesse turned to Sari. "You guys put the game away and find something else to play, you hear me?"

"But Da-ad!"

Jesse snapped his fingers and strode toward the great room.

Sadie ran to obey. She pouted, but both girls clamped their mouths shut, and Grant could hear them picking the game up.

Feeling uncomfortable at the tension, and not wanting to interfere, Grant went to the kitchen and rinsed the few dishes that had accumulated since the men loaded the dishwasher. Jesse had taken the girls back to the living room, and the TV filled the silence again, but Danae and Dallas were still downstairs with Austin. At least he'd quit crying.

Audrey came in and opened the refrigerator.

"Everything OK out there?" He kept his voice low.

"I think they'll get it worked out. Do you know what set him off?"

"No. They were playing together fine, and next thing I knew those two were going at it."

She scooted him over to fill a pitcher with water. "I think things are catching up with Austin."

"Well, the poor little guy has been through a lot."

"I just hope—"

The volume on the TV went down again and they heard Dallas's voice. Audrey moved to the doorway, just out of sight, and Grant followed her.

"Sadie, Austin has something he'd like to tell you," Dallas said.

You could have heard a pin drop. Grant moved to the other side of Audrey so he could watch the little drama play out.

Austin's voice was barely a whisper, but it sounded like, "Sorry I yelled at you."

"I forgive you, Austin." Sadie buried him in a hug.

It was the way he and Audrey had always made their kids make up after a fight. It was good to see. Except Austin tolerated it for about five seconds before he spread his arms and busted loose, running for the front door. Danae chased after him and caught him up in her arms. "Hey, buddy. Where are you going?"

"I want my mama!" He started in wailing again.

Danae crumpled into a heap on the steps with Austin in her arms. Her shoulders shook with silent sobs, and Grant went to her and sat on the step beside her. While she tried to comfort Austin, he tried to comfort her. But his heart broke for both of them, and he shot up a silent prayer for peace for all of them, but especially for this hurting little boy.

They sat that way for several minutes and Austin finally quit crying. He kept his head buried under Danae's chin, sucking his thumb for all he was worth.

After a few minutes, Grant sensed someone standing in front of them and raised his head to see Dallas. He started to get up and relinquish his spot to his son-in-law. But Dallas motioned for him to stay put.

"Danae, I'm going to go start the car," he said quietly. "I got that box of presents you'd gathered up, but what else do we need to take?"

"Just the dishes I brought. But I need to leave the salads for everyone else's supper." Her voice quavered with remnant tears.

"Are you *ready* to leave?" Dallas put a hand lightly on her arm. "I didn't mean to rush you, but . . . I just thought it might be best."

She nodded, then looked up at Grant with an apologetic frown. "I think we need to get Austin home to bed."

Grant put an arm around her and patted Austin's back with the other hand. "That's probably a good idea. This was a pretty big day for him. Do you guys want to take some leftovers with you—for later?"

"Maybe some turkey," she said. "We don't need anything else."

"I'll go get your coats and hats."

"Thanks, Dad."

Oh, Danae. The sadness in her voice just about killed him. He knew things would look brighter tomorrow, but right now, he wished he could turn the clock back about fifteen years when all his kids—all five of them—had belonged under this roof. No one was running off to another house, no one had suffered any worse heartbreak than a severe case of unrequited puppy love.

Of course, going back meant that half the people in this house would not be part of his family. The sons-in-law he loved like his own. Precious Bree. The granddaughters who had claimed a sizable hunk of his heart.

No. He didn't really want to go back. He wanted to make it so there were no more wars that tore sons and husbands from their families. He wanted to make it so every daddy loved his wife and son. He wanted to make it so mamas who wanted babies could have as many as they desired. He just wanted to fix everything so no one he loved would ever hurt again.

But that just wasn't possible on this side of heaven.

24

A brilliant sun streamed in through the window of the master bathroom. It was almost too bright for Danae to apply eyeliner and shadow. Nevertheless, she went through the motions, stroking on layers of mascara and brushing her eyebrows into submission. She took the same care with her makeup today that she had on her wedding day. And she wasn't sure why.

The new year had spawned a string of bright, sunny days, but she couldn't seem to shake the cloud that hung over her. She and Dallas had spent the entire week before on paperwork, securing the documents they needed to become Austin's guardians for however long he needed them to be. Filling out form after form, researching every possible contingency, wanting to be sure that they left no loopholes.

She had no regrets about their decision—despite Austin's blow-ups, which had happened with frightening frequency since the incident at Christmas at her parents' two weeks ago. But though that concerned her, it wasn't the source of her melancholy.

Today they would go visit Misty. Danae and Dallas had decided to ask Austin's mother to sign papers granting custody to them as legal guardians. Even though they were merely doing what Misty had asked—no, *begged* them to do—Danae felt as if they had somehow betrayed her.

Misty's attorney had all but guaranteed them that she would escape the death penalty by pleading guilty. Danae hoped he knew what he was talking about.

She'd rehearsed a thousand different speeches, trying to imagine what she would want to hear if she were in Misty's shoes, what would offer her the most comfort if she were losing her only son the way Misty was. Today would make it final for both of them. And the agony Misty was experiencing tempered the joy that wanted to bubble up inside Danae, because now she had a child to love.

Not a son of her flesh, not even a boy she could call "my son." And yet she didn't think she could have loved Austin more if he were her child. They had asked Misty's attorney if they could bring Austin to the meeting for Misty to see. And so Austin could see her. A sort of closure for both of them.

But the attorney consulted Misty and come back with her reply: absolutely not. She did not want her son to have a memory of his mother in shackles and a prison jumpsuit.

Danae understood, in a way. And was grateful. She was afraid seeing Misty might reverse the progress they'd made with Austin since Christmas.

And yet she wondered how a mother—one who hadn't seen her son for almost eight weeks now—could cheat herself of that opportunity. It was either fierce pride, or selfless love. Or perhaps it was simply God's grace poured over the whole thing. And certainly there had been enough people praying for exactly that, that she shouldn't doubt.

She smoothed lip gloss over carefully applied lipstick and checked her reflection in the mirror. She was a different person from the woman who'd looked back at her even six months ago when they'd first moved into this house. Different, and better, she hoped.

Today would test what she was really made of.

This time, instead of an attorney, it was a social worker—she introduced herself as Carol Blye—who met Danae and Dallas in the waiting area. The woman had graying hair and a rather dour disposition. She led them through the halls of the Justice Center to a room similar to the one where they'd met with Misty before.

As before, Misty was in handcuffs, although it seemed to Danae that she sat straighter this time, as if she'd grown accustomed to the restraints. Danae wasn't sure what she'd expected—that Austin's mother would be thinner and wan, maybe? But if anything, she'd put on weight.

"Hello, Misty." She forced a smile.

Misty nodded. "How is he?"

"He's good. Really good. He misses you, but he's doing well." Danae produced the envelope, the only thing the social worker had allowed them to carry in, besides the documents for Misty to sign. "I brought pictures. Would you like to see?"

Tears filled Misty's eyes, but she nodded. Danae pulled the packet of photos out and slid it across the table.

She'd brought only a few close-ups of Austin taken at Christmas. The pictures showed him happy and smiling, but she'd been careful to crop out anything that would show too much of their home, or her parents' house, or other family members. It seemed cruel to show how much more they could offer Austin than Misty had ever been able to. Such a strange dichotomy when that was exactly what they'd needed to prove to the social worker who was conducting their home study. That in itself had been a harrowing process. And they weren't finished yet. They'd apparently passed the home visits with flying colors, but there were still other hoops to jump through. If Dallas didn't already love Austin so much, Danae wasn't sure he would still be onboard.

She mentally flipped through the photos of Austin again, and wondered if she should have removed one that showed him with his head thrown back, laughing at some silly game Dallas had been playing with him. How would she have felt if the tables were turned and she saw photos of her own child looking so happy—without her?

And yet, wouldn't Misty want to see him happy? As wrong as Misty's actions had been, she was in this place, in part, because she'd loved Austin enough to sacrifice her freedom to keep him safe. To be sure he was happy.

Misty struggled over the handcuffs to open the packet that held the photos. The social worker sitting beside her didn't attempt to help her, so Danae didn't either.

When she finally got the small stack of photos out of the envelope and looked at the one on top, she broke down.

Which caused Danae to do the same.

Dallas put his hand on Danae's back, and after a few minutes, he spoke to Misty in a tender voice that made Danae love him all the more.

"Austin's getting along really well," he said. "He's such a bright boy and always wants to learn new things. Danae and I have fallen in love with him, Misty. We're honored to be his guardians. For as long as he needs us."

Misty only nodded, but Danae noticed that the hard set of her jaw, so often present while she was in the women's shelter, had softened.

Carol Blye seemed eager to keep the meeting moving along and pushed a folder full of papers across the desk to them.

"It's unfortunate," she said, "that we're going to have to do everything again—all the same papers—for the baby." She shot Misty a look of frustration. "I wish we could just do addendums—and maybe we can for a couple of these—but I'd feel more confident if the documents specifically named each child."

Dallas and Danae exchanged questioning looks.

"I'm not sure I understand," he said.

"They don't know," Misty told the woman, ducking her head.

Carol Blye turned to her, looking incredulous. "What?"

"I . . . didn't get a chance to tell them. They don't know," she repeated.

The woman slapped the folder on the table, her jaw tense. "Are you kidding me?"

"What's this about?" Dallas said.

The woman sighed. "It seems Mrs. Arato is pregnant. She just revealed this fact to me this morning. But she led me to believe that you had agreed to guardianship of her infant as well. Is that not correct?"

Danae couldn't hold back a gasp.

"No," Dallas said. "No. We . . . had no idea."

Danae noticed he couldn't meet Misty's eyes when he spoke.

Misty turned a silent stare on the social worker before addressing Danae. "I didn't say anything because these papers will be different. I've been doing research and I don't understand exactly what all has to happen, but I know it's not the same as what you done with Austin."

"What do you mean, Misty?" Danae had a feeling she knew, but she didn't dare let herself go there.

"I want you to adopt this baby." Misty looked self-consciously at her belly, and Danae realized that what she'd thought was weight gain, was her pregnancy starting to show.

"Misty—"

"Austin . . ." A faraway look came to Misty's eyes. "Austin's been mine for so long I can't see clear to let him go. How would that make him feel? But this one"—again, she looked at her belly—"this one won't ever know me. It's best he gets a clean break."

"He?" Danae blurted. "Do you know it's a boy?"

"No. I just call it 'he' because it don't seem right to call it 'it.' I had sonograms with Austin, but they won't let me do that here. But I probably wouldn't want to find out what it is anyway."

"When are you due?"

"April sometime. I think the doctor said April 11 was the official due date."

"Then"—the social worker sighed—"I guess we need to know first of all: are you willing to proceed with the adoption of this child?"

It was all Danae could do not to shout, "Yes!" But she looked to Dallas to make sure he was on the same page.

His complexion was pale, his eyes glazed. "We'll need to talk things over. Give us a few days to think things through. You . . . you've taken us by surprise."

"Dallas?" Her voice quavered against her will. But, what was he *thinking*? If they lost the chance to take this baby because they weren't ready to commit . . . Healthy American babies didn't come along every day. And this was Austin's brother or sister!

Without acknowledging Danae, he told the social worker, "This is not something we can decide on the spot."

Danae looked from him to the social worker. "May I have a few minutes to speak with my husband in the hall?"

Carol's lips were pressed into a hard line, but she pushed her chair back. "I'll see if I can get another consultation room. It's understandable you're feeling a little blindsided."

"Dallas, please . . ." Misty pleaded.

Danae didn't remember ever hearing her call him by name.

"You wouldn't separate my babies, would you?" Misty's expression was distraught. "This is the last thing I can give Austin. It's the only way I can go on—if I know they'll have each other. Be raised together. Please. Danae? I don't have anybody else. You know that."

"Dallas?" Danae gripped his knee under the table. Hard. "Let's talk about this, please." *Why* was he hesitating? He'd been the one to convince her that they should take Austin. How was this any different? It wasn't. It was better. It was an answer to prayer. An ending to their quest for children. An ending that made everything they'd been through make sense! She would have Austin, but she would have a precious baby to love as well. How could he even hesitate?

The social worker excused herself and went into the hall.

"Why are you changing your mind?" Misty asked, looking hard at Dallas.

"How can you say 'changing your mind' when this was something we knew *nothing* about? Why didn't you tell us?"

She looked at the table where her handcuffed wrists rested. "I wasn't absolutely sure I was pregnant until I saw the doctor. Here in the jail."

Something was off. Danae didn't think she was being completely honest. "You said you're due in April? Misty, that means you're . . . six months along. How could you not have known? Did Hank know?" Maybe she shouldn't have asked, but she needed to know.

But Misty didn't reply. They waited in awkward silence, each of them avoiding the eyes of the other two in the room.

Finally Carol returned. She stood holding the door open and motioned to Dallas and Danae. "Come this way and I'll show you to a room where you can talk."

They followed her blindly out into the hallway.

"I'm sorry to spring this on you." The social worker shook her head, looking almost as stricken as Danae felt. "Like I said, I just found out this morning myself. I've landed in some crazy situations in this job, but in all my years, I've never had anything like this."

"I don't see how they couldn't have known."

"You've got me," Carol said. She riffled the edges of the sheaf of papers she carried. "With the baby due in April, we're really going to be pushing the clock to get everything in order in time. The home study and background checks you've had for Austin's guardianship should be valid for the infant's adoption as well. But I'll have to do some checking to be sure. I'd like to get any additional paperwork started as soon as possible."

25

A guard led them down the hall to a room almost identical to the one where they'd left Misty.

"Ring this buzzer when you're finished. We'll escort you back to the other room." He closed the door behind him, and a metallic click sounded.

Danae looked at Dallas. "Did they just lock us in?"

He shrugged. "Probably."

She took a chair at the table in the center of the small office, but Dallas paced the length of the room, head down.

"What are you thinking? Why are you so hesitant?" He'd suddenly become a stranger to her.

"Do you remember when we talked to Misty the first time we came here, right after her arrest?"

"Yes."

"She said something then. She said, 'I want my kids to have a future. I don't want them growing up like I did.'" He looked up, met her eyes. "Danae, she knew then. She said 'kids,' plural. She knew she was pregnant. She's had this up her sleeve all along."

"You mean, getting us to take her kids."

He nodded. "Maybe it was her contingency plan—if she didn't get away with Hank's murder. But she's smarter than she lets on."

"But what does that have to do with us taking the baby?" She rose, feeling antsy, almost frantic. If they didn't decide in the next few minutes they might lose the chance to take this baby.

Dallas crossed to the window and looked out to the street below. Without turning, he spoke. So softly she had to strain to hear.

"Austin, we know," Dallas said. "But, we don't know anything about this baby. If I'm figuring out the timing of everything right, Hank beat her while she was pregnant. What if something happened to the baby? What if that damaged it?"

"Dallas, I seriously doubt any—"

"And you think Hank is the father of this baby? What if his anger issues, his abusive personality—what if that's genetic? Nobody really knows, do they? We sure don't. We haven't had time to check any of this out."

"But Dallas, how can we take Austin and *not* take this baby? Would he ever forgive us, once he knows he has a sibling? He's lost so much already. Would you really take this away from him too?" She felt like she was manipulating him, but these were legitimate questions.

"We don't even know for sure if Hank is the father, but if he is, he may have family that have rights to the baby first." He still wouldn't turn to face her.

"No, he doesn't." She took a step closer to him, testing. "Misty said, back at the shelter, that Hank's parents were both gone. No other relatives would have rights over what Misty wants. And she's made it clear she wants us to take her baby."

"OK, but just be realistic for a minute. What if something *is* wrong with the baby? If we agree to this, and then the baby is born with . . . defects, or something that required long-term care, would we still be obligated?"

She had to admit, in the brief time they'd known there was a baby at stake, she'd only imagined a perfect, beautiful child. A cross between Misty and Austin. Still, it didn't make any difference to her if the baby was perfect. "If I were pregnant, Dallas, we'd face that same possibility. You wouldn't reject *our* baby if it turned out to have something wrong with it. I know you wouldn't."

"Of course not, but that's different. Totally different."

"I'm not sure it is." She didn't like the way he was thinking. And she didn't understand it. He'd embraced the idea of raising Austin so wholly—even before she had. Why did he have such cold feet when it came to a baby? *A baby!* The very thing they'd been trying for all along! It didn't make sense.

Finally he turned to face her, bracing his hands on the window ledge behind him. "Have you thought about this? If we take these kids in, we're as good as adopting Misty too."

"You're the one who told Misty we'd bring Austin to visit her. Is that what you mean?"

"Yes. That, and . . . we'd have a tie to her—because of the kids—that would be forever. How would you feel about that?"

She hadn't considered it. Hadn't had time to consider anything. How had he come up with all these questions—all these roadblocks—in the short space of time since they'd learned about Misty's baby?

"I guess . . ." She sorted through her thoughts, wanting to speak truth, not just to say what would get him to agree to taking that baby. "To be honest, I wish we could break all ties with her. I wish we could adopt Austin, and this baby, as our own. That's what would be easiest. For us. Her attorney doesn't think she'll ever get out. But what if she does? What if she gets off on some technicality? That scares me. I admit."

He nodded. "Me too. But—and this sounds awful to say, but honestly, chances are very good—" He stopped. "*Good* isn't the right word. But the probability is high, if not certain, that even if she somehow got paroled, it wouldn't be for years. After Austin is grown. At that point, it will be his decision whether he has a relationship with Misty."

"I know you're probably right." She bit her lip until it hurt. This was too hard. Like driving blind. "But what if she got out early? What if five years from now when we've raised that baby as our own—grown to love Austin even more than we do now—what if she gets out somehow, and she wants to take them back?"

He shrugged. "I suppose we have to go into this knowing that could happen. And how could we blame her? She loves Austin as much as we do. This baby too. And Danae, you might not like this, but I don't think I'd be willing to do this unless Misty would promise to keep up a relationship with the kids."

She stared at him. "What?"

His Adam's apple moved up and down in his throat. He reached for her hand. "I need to tell you some things. Things you don't know about me."

She'd only seen Dallas cry two times in their entire marriage, but he looked near tears.

"What is it?" She could barely push the words out. Fear gripped her beyond anything she'd yet felt over this whole situation with Austin. "What don't I know about you? I thought I knew everything there was to know about you." Her attempt at laughter came out thin and hollow. She did not need any more surprises to deal with right now.

"It's nothing bad. Not like you're probably thinking anyway. Except I should have told you. Long before now. I'm sorry."

"Dallas? What is it? You're scaring me."

He went to the table and pulled out a chair, then motioned for her to sit down.

She did, gladly, since she didn't trust her legs to hold her right now.

He sat down across from her. "I've always skirted around the subject of adoption. There's more reason for that than what I've told you. Or anybody. Drew doesn't even know. Only my parents. I guess . . . I kind of hoped this had died with them."

"I don't understand."

She must have looked terrified, because he reached for her other hand and squeezed it. It helped. A little.

"It's just that"—He swallowed hard and raked his fingers through his hair—"I was fine with my own adoption. You know that. Mom and Dad always made it matter-of-fact. I never knew anything but their love. And Drew's. But when I was eighteen, I got it in my head that I wanted to meet my birth mother. So I started searching."

"Dallas? Did you find her?"

"I found her all right. And then I found out that she didn't want to be found."

"Oh no." She squeezed his hand harder, her heart breaking for how that must have hurt him. "So . . . what happened?"

"I called her. Like an idiot I blurted out who I was and that I wanted to meet her. She hung up, but I'd played detective—not that it was that difficult to find her. I found out where she lived and I went to see her."

"Oh, Dallas." She could scarcely breathe, and she could imagine how he must have felt. How high his expectations must have been to meet the woman who'd given birth to him. He'd told her not long after they met, that he'd "thought about finding my birthmother," but that he'd given up the search and hadn't ever wanted to try again. She'd never heard this part of the story, and she was afraid it didn't have a happy ending.

"The woman answered the door, and the minute she heard my voice and put two and two together from the phone call, she yelled that she never wanted to see me again. She even threatened to call the police."

"Oh, babe. I'm so sorry."

"Oh, it gets better."

Danae closed her eyes, as if somehow that would make it easier for him to talk about this humiliating experience. But she clung tightly to his hand.

"About that time some guy in the house—I assume it was her husband—comes up behind her and asks if everything is OK." His voice grew distant. "Maybe it was my father . . . I don't suppose I'll ever know. And honestly, I don't care now. But anyway, my birth mother hisses that if I say one word she'll make sure my life is ruined—and some other things I wouldn't repeat. She pretty much disowned me and told me to get off her porch."

"Dallas . . . I'm so sorry. What did you do?"

"I'm not proud of it. Remember I was only eighteen. But, I called her a not very nice name and hightailed it out of there. I got back in my car and drove to the end of the street. I got out of my car just in time to throw up." He gave her a sheepish sidewise glance. "And then I cried all the way home. I mean, cried so hard I could barely see the road."

She put her arm around him and lay her head on his shoulder. "I'm sorry, Dallas. She doesn't know what an amazing man she missed the privilege of getting to know that day."

He straightened. "Well, I wasn't all that amazing at eighteen. That came later. After I met you."

She laughed softly.

He pulled her closer. "I still don't understand how a stranger could hurt me that much. But I won't lie. It stung. In the end, she didn't even seem like someone worth knowing, and yet, I can't— *couldn't*—seem to quit missing her."

Danae didn't miss his use of the present tense. Did her husband still feel the pain of that rejection all these years later? But she remained silent.

"It's weird to long for someone you don't even know," he said. "Someone who makes it clear they don't care about you or want you in their life. And then to feel guilty because, after all, I *had* a mom. And she was great. She and Dad were great. The best. But there's always something there, you know?"

She forced down the lump in her throat. "I *don't* know, Dallas. I think maybe only someone who's lived through it can truly understand. But what if that's the whole reason we're getting Austin? Because if he goes through that same kind of pain, you'll be there for him. You'll understand."

He kissed the top of her head, then gave a short huff that ruffled her hair. "I guess I never thought about it that way. For a long time I thought I'd outgrow it—that horrible tender spot—and I have learned to ignore it most of the time. But I think no matter how old you get, you can't help but always wonder how your mother could just . . . give you up. Like you were a worn out pair of shoes or—"

"Babe, it's not fair to assume it was easy for your birth mother."

He shrugged. "I know the whole identity thing is a huge issue for a lot of adopted kids. Especially when they reach a certain age."

She knew she was treading on shaky ground, but this was the most open he'd ever been about the subject, so she risked the question. "Is that why you've been so against it? Adopting?"

"That's part of it. I didn't ever want to put a kid through what I went through. But I think maybe I didn't want to have to ever revisit that time in my own life either. It was selfish, I know."

She reached to stroke his cheek. "You don't have a selfish bone in your body."

"You just go on thinking that. I know better. But . . . something about telling you all this now helps. I'd give anything if I could keep Austin from ever having to go through that. He's been through so much already. But if he does struggle with this same kind of pain, if he goes through an identity crisis—"

"He'll go through it whether he's with us or with someone else," she said softly. "If even your amazing parents couldn't heal that pain in you . . ."

"You're right." He pushed her gently away from him, tucked a wayward strand of hair behind her ear. "If he has to go through it, it might as well be with us."

26

A knock on the conference room door made them both jump. The lock clicked and the same guard poked his head in the door. "You folks about ready? Ms. Blye is waiting for you."

Dallas held up a hand. "Give us just a few more minutes."

The guard nodded. "I'll be right out here." He pulled the door closed again.

Dallas took her face in his hands. "You want to take this baby?"

"I do," she breathed. *He was going to say yes.* Her heart swelled. "I do too."

Aware of the guard waiting outside, still she didn't feel rushed or pressured. It just suddenly seemed so very right. "I think . . . these may be the kids God has had for us all along."

He nodded. "I think you're right. If we ask ourselves what's best for Austin, what's best for the baby Misty is carrying, we know the answer."

"Yes. And if we walk away, Dallas, that baby will go into foster care. Yes, *maybe* it would get a warm, loving family. Or maybe it would be tossed from one family to another for twenty years."

"But could Austin ever forgive us if we kept him from his only sibling? Could we ever forgive ourselves?"

"We have to take them, Dallas. Both of them. God's got this. Whatever happens, He'll get us through."

He sucked in a deep breath and blew it out as if gearing up to shoulder the weight of the world. "Yes. You're right. I don't think we have a choice."

She couldn't stop the smile that bloomed. "Let's go tell Misty."

Misty's shoulders shook and she couldn't seem to catch her breath. Dallas looked from Danae to the social worker, wondering if they would be able to continue.

Finally, Misty choked out two words. "Thank you."

Dallas watched Danae start to reach across the table, then quickly draw her hand back. He knew it was killing her not to be able to touch Misty, to somehow convey, physically, how much they were mourning for her.

And though it hadn't quite soaked in yet, he knew another emotion would come soon. Gratitude. This was the mother of the children they would raise. And he was grateful. For Danae's sake, if not for his own yet.

It would take some time to get used to everything. To let the idea of having an infant soak in.

Carol Blye, the social worker, waited until Misty had composed herself a little, then turned all business again. "We can work out some of these details in the months to come, but it is Misty's desire that you legally adopt this baby."

Dallas reached for Danae's hand beneath the table, knowing it was all she could do to contain her joy at this news. Even though it was a strange joy—one profoundly tempered by what this gift would cost Misty.

"I can't—" Misty put a hand over her mouth, still struggling. When she finally spoke again, her voice quavered. "But I can't do the same to Austin. If he remembers me, I don't ever want him to think I was willin' to give him away."

Her words healed Dallas more than she would ever know. He committed them to memory for the day Austin would need to hear them. "He *will* remember you, Misty. We want him to see you as often as we're able to bring him and we—"

"No. I don't want that." Her voice came strong and clear now. "I don't want that on him. I want him to be a normal kid. Not a kid with a mom in jail. Not an outcast the way I was. Not—"

"We'll work everything out. I promise you, Misty." Dallas stretched his palm over the table, as close to hers as he dared.

"I just wanted my babies to have a good life." She started crying again.

It was like a knife in his gut, knowing that their answer to prayer came at such a high cost.

"I did wrong by them. I know I did. I don't know why I couldn't stay away from Hank—from men like him." She bowed her head.

And in the hunch of her shoulders, Dallas saw so many regrets, so many wasted moments.

As if she knew what he was thinking, she began to spill her heart to them, raw and honest. "I told you already Hank isn't Austin's father. I didn't meet him till after Austin was born. Hank . . . he seemed like he was gonna be a good man. He didn't want a kid, but he was good to Austin—at first anyway. But he turned. He changed. Before I knew it, he had me in a corner and he knew it."

She sniffed, and pushed a strand of hair off her forehead. "He might've ruined my life, but I couldn't let him ruin Austin's too. Except"—she held up her shackled wrists—"I guess he did that anyway."

Dallas opened his mouth to speak, but words wouldn't come.

Misty shifted in her chair. "I had no choice, I hope you see that. I hope you can make Austin understand that. I blew it big-time when I told Hank where I was. But it didn't matter anyways. My days were numbered there. And once he found out about this baby . . . we were all dead anyway. Like I said, he never wanted a kid. He only took Austin because I didn't give him no choice. Isn't it strange that, in the end, I was the one who didn't have no choice?"

The social worker cleared her throat and shot Dallas and Danae an apologetic frown. "Misty, this isn't information that Mr. and Mrs. Brooks really need."

Misty's jaw clenched, and she turned an angry stare on Carol Blye. "These good people are going to raise my son . . . my babies. And yes, ma'am, this *is* information they should have."

"We *would* like to have Austin's medical information," Danae said softly. "And any family history that might be important for future medical treatment."

Misty's eyes narrowed. "Well, now see, that's where we have a problem." She lowered her head again. "I don't know who Austin's father is. That was a . . . rough patch in my life. I needed the money—if you get what I'm saying."

Dallas looked over to see Danae close her eyes, and he knew she felt awful for opening another wound.

"I want you to know I stopped that—livin' that way. Even before I came to the shelter. No booze, no drugs, no men. Not for a long time." Misty looked Danae in the eye, but avoided Dallas's gaze.

Danae held up a hand. "Misty, you don't owe—"

"No, but . . . I did. I swear, as soon as I decided to leave him—Hank—I started livin' clean."

He wondered if she understood how that sounded, coming from the mouth of a woman who'd shot her husband in the back.

But she went on as if it all made perfect sense. "I never wanted my babies growing up the way I did. And I'd rather die than have them in the system . . . or have them visiting their mama in jail. I know what the shame of that is like, and I don't want that for my kids."

Dallas wanted to tell her that as bad as that shame might be, what Austin would imagine if he was told nothing, would be even worse than the truth. Instead, he said, "Your children will know that you loved them. And that you wanted the best for them, that everything you did, you did out of love for them." He hesitated, not wanting to sound like he condoned what she'd done. "I promise, Misty, your kids will know that, no matter what, you loved them. That's all they really *need* to know."

"Thank you." Misty stared past him, unfocused. And no doubt emotionally exhausted.

"But . . . I don't want Danae and I to have secrets to keep either. Secrets are never good."

He understood that now. For himself. Even so, he wondered how it might have affected him if he'd learned that his own birth mother was a murderer. How could they ever tell Austin that? And yet, it could not be kept a secret. Not for too many years anyway.

He couldn't curb the sigh that came at the thought. When he'd been searching for his own mother, he'd had to navigate a maze of legal documents, public records, and newspaper archives. Austin would be able to find Misty's sordid past with the click of a few keys on a laptop. They would have to tell him someday. But not today. *One day at a time . . .*

He put a hand palm-down on the table beside Misty's. "We have time to talk things over," he said quietly. "We all have a lot to think through. But I know we can make this work in a way that's best for Austin and your baby, and for you, Misty."

And for him and Danae. But that went without saying.

Carol Blye released a sigh that sounded like relief. She opened the folder in front of her. "Shall we sign some papers?"

27

Do you hear me, Austin?" Danae hollered from the kitchen at the inn, quickly retrieving the last shard of glass from the broken vase. "You stay on that sofa until I tell you it's OK."

She wrapped the broken pieces in newspaper and started for the dumpster in the garage.

"Here, I'll take that." Corinne took the bundle from her.

"Thanks, 'sis." She turned to her mother. "I'm so sorry about your flowers."

The roses from the Valentine's bouquet Dad had sent Mom were flopped in the sink and didn't really look worth saving.

Her mother waved off the apology. "Don't think another thing of it. I got to enjoy them for a few days."

Sighing, and embarrassed, Danae tossed the flowers into the trash can under the sink before quickly taking a damp paper towel to the wood floors to catch any slivers of glass she might have missed.

"I didn't mean to!" Austin shouted from the sofa in the living room.

"I know you didn't, buddy." She hurriedly washed her hands and went to sit beside him. Huckleberry sat on the floor next to the sofa, his canine head propped beside Austin, silky ears drooping, as if he was in time-out too.

She patted Austin's leg. "I know you didn't do it on purpose, but that's why I told you not to jump on Gram's sofa. Because I knew this would happen. Do you understand what I'm saying?"

He gave a begrudging nod and went back to pouting.

"If you had obeyed me, this wouldn't have happened. Now Gram doesn't have her pretty flowers that Poppa gave her, and you have to sit in time-out on the sofa. We could have saved all that trouble if you just would have listened and obeyed what I said in the first place."

More pouting.

"Austin, do you understand what I'm telling you?"

"Yes. Are you gonna still keep talkin' and talkin' at me?"

She heard her mother and Corinne chuckling in the kitchen, and despite her embarrassment over Austin's behavior, she had to bite back her own laughter. "No. Not if you've learned your lesson."

He bounced on his bottom causing the sofa cushions to come halfway off the seat. The kid was a veritable Tigger. "Now can I go play with Sari-n-Sadie-n-S'mone?" He jumbled the girls' names together as if they were all one word.

Sari was out of school for Presidents' Day so Corinne and Danae had brought the kids to the inn for the day. The Pennington girls were fast becoming his favorite playmates, so it was pure torture for him to have to sit in time-out.

Danae glanced up at the clock. "You need to sit here for three more minutes." She'd already shortened his time by several minutes, but ten minutes was starting to seem like an eternity—even to her.

She waited until it wouldn't seem like she was caving in, then released him. "OK, you can go play. But don't forget what we talked about." She picked up a stray puzzle piece from the carpet. "Give this to Sari. I think that goes to her puzzle."

"No, Sari don't gots any puzzles."

"She doesn't have any puzzles," she corrected. They'd been working on Austin's grammar. He'd improved too. But every time

Danae was around Misty, she realized why Austin spoke the way he did. Part of her felt guilty—for Misty's sake—trying to change his speech. And yet, he would be handicapped in so many ways if he didn't learn to speak correctly. Misty was proof of that. She put her hands on his face and made him look at her. "Did you hear what I said? Can you say that? She *doesn't have* any puzzles."

He stomped his foot. "That's what I *awready* told you! Didn't you hear me?"

She hid a smile and gave him a gentle swat on the behind. "Go play, silly. And settle down, OK? You play nice with the girls."

But he was halfway down to the basement playroom, Huckleberry in tow, before she finished her sentence.

She rejoined her mom and sister at the kitchen table, slumping dramatically into the chair. "How do you do it, Corinne? And Mom! *Five* of us? Seriously, how did you survive?"

"This too shall pass," Mom said.

"And pass, and pass, and pass, and pass," Corinne deadpanned.

"It seems like we just get over one hurdle and then he's doing something else we have to discipline him for. He probably thinks he lives in time-out, but I don't want to let him get away with stuff."

Mom patted her arm. "You're doing just fine, Danae. He's a sweet kid. But he's had a huge upheaval in his life, and even if he can't understand exactly what's happened, he knows something's up. It's going to take some time."

"Not to mention, he's a boy!" Corinne said. "When I get together with Liz, my friend with the four little monsters . . . er, I mean *boys*, it's a whole different dynamic."

"And vive la différence," Mom said.

"I guess." Danae blew out a weary breath. "At least he always seems to settle down when Dallas is around."

"That's because he's needed a daddy all his life, and now he finally has one worth the title," Mom said. "You'll get through it."

"I'm a little nervous about how things are going to be when we add a baby to the mix."

"I know the feeling," Corinne said, patting the swell of her June baby beneath her maternity shirt. "Everything going good with your baby?"

Danae laughed and patted her own flat belly.

Corinne laughed. "That's not very nice. I am seriously jealous of your figure, sister."

"Well, that makes us even. Though I must admit I'm not quite as jealous as I used to be. I think I might go nuts if I found out I was pregnant right now."

"I'm here to tell you," Corinne said, "it would all work out just fine if you were pregnant too."

"You can't know that yet." Danae looked pointedly at her sister's belly. "Come back in two months and we'll talk."

It was so good to laugh together. She was still getting used to her sisters commiserating with her about baby things. It was what she'd always dreamed about. And she loved the feeling of fitting in and not feeling on the outside of those conversations. Although in truth, the "privilege" was a little anticlimactic now that it had been granted.

"You never answered my question though, Danae." Corinne turned serious. "What is the news on the baby?"

"Really nothing new. Misty's healthy, the baby's growing as it should. The time is going a lot faster than I thought it would." She rolled her eyes. "Austin sees to that. I was feeling kind of bad that Dallas is working such long hours and handling nearly all of the legal stuff with custody and guardianship for the kids. But I'm telling you, I'm working overtime, too, just keeping up with that one." She pointed toward the basement.

As if her words had summoned them, the clomping of little feet on the stairway made them all look that direction.

"Can we have a 'nack?" Simone asked.

"Yeah, can we have a 'nack?" Austin echoed.

"Ask Gram," Corinne said.

"Gram?" Austin looked up at her with his big puppy dog eyes. "Can we?"

Mom jumped up with a wink at Danae. "How could I say no to *that*?"

"If you can, you're a stronger woman than I."

Mom laughed, and her little shadows followed her to the pantry to rummage for "'nacks." Danae's heart swelled with pride in her boy. *Her boy*. It had been hard not to think of Austin as her *son*. But she'd begun to refer to him as "my boy," and that felt like the next best thing.

"What do you think about that, buddy? A new brother or sister? Won't that be awesome?"

Judging by the roll of Danae's eyes, Dallas guessed he might be overhyping the announcement just a bit. But he was dying with his audience.

Austin shrugged. "Can I play a bideo game?"

Dallas shot Danae a questioning look. Was this a normal reaction from a little boy on hearing he was going to be a big brother? He and Danae had decided to treat the coming baby as if it was a casual, everyday event. They intended, when the baby came—about a month from now—to present it to Austin as a gift that Misty had given him, and all of them. They wanted the whole event to be a warm remembrance of his birth mother, something for Austin to look back on fondly.

And frankly, something to ease the sting of telling him that Misty wasn't coming home. Ever. They'd agreed that, at his age, it wouldn't be something they'd sit down and make an announcement about. Instead, they would answer his questions as they came up, and hope that he "absorbed" the truth slowly. Still, it was something he'd have to know eventually.

"Can I?" Austin eyed the basket that held the video game controls.

They certainly hadn't expected this nonreaction to the news about the baby.

Danae shrugged, apparently taken aback by it too. "You can play your video game, sport," she said. "But not until after supper. And then just for a few minutes."

"*If* you eat all your vegetables," Dallas reminded.

"Awww, Dad, do I hafta?"

Dallas's heart nearly stopped beating. Austin looked up at him with an expression he couldn't quite decipher—a cross between ornery and . . . testing? "Did you just call me Dad?" He tweaked Austin's nose, trying to keep it light.

Austin squirmed, looking embarrassed. "Is that OK?" he squeaked.

Dallas exchanged looks with Danae, who shrugged, looking as shell-shocked as he felt. "What do you think, Mo—" He'd almost called Danae, "Mom." But they hadn't had time to think—or talk—this through, and he wasn't sure how to handle it.

"What made you ask that, buddy?" Danae scooted closer to Austin on the sofa and put her arm around him.

"'Cause that's what Sari-n-Sadie-n-S'mone call their people."

He and Danae laughed out loud, which made Austin bury his head in his lap, squirming harder.

Dallas patted his back. "Hey, we're not laughing at you, sport. We're laughing because that makes us happy."

"Look up here, Austin," Danae urged. "Look at me."

He peeked out beneath his elbow, and she prayed for the right words. Words that would heal and not do more damage. "Do you remember your mama, Austin?"

He sat up straighter. "She gots me a bwack-and-white ball."

"A soccer ball. That's right, she did." Danae looked up at Dallas. "He had it at the shelter."

"I wonder what happened to it," Dallas said over Austin's head.

"Probably got put away after he broke something with it."

"Huh-uh, I never braked anything" Austin wagged his head.

"I know, buddy. I'm just teasing. Hey"—she put a finger under his chin and tilted Austin's head until they were eye to eye—"your mama loves you very much. You know that? And she misses you."

He cast down his dark gaze.

"Austin?" Danae's voice went gentle. "Do you remember . . . your daddy?"

The way she said it, through gritted teeth, Dallas knew she hated to use the name she called her own father to refer to Hank Arato. But it was what Austin had called Hank.

Austin shook his head hard. "Mama said he hurts me."

"Yeah, buddy. He did. I'm so sorry that happened, Austin," he said. "But that man is . . . He's not ever going to hurt you again, OK?"

Dallas scooted closer until Austin was squished between Danae and him. What his own parents had called a "fam sandwich" when he and Drew would squeeze in between them on the couch. He hadn't thought of the memory in years, and it warmed him.

Austin looked up at him with big, round puppy dog eyes. Dallas understood now how Danae could never say no to those eyes.

"I think—" He willed his voice to hold up against the huge boulder in his throat. "If you want to call us Mom and Dad—like Sari-n-Sadie-n-S'mone call their people—I think that would be just fine. Don't you . . . Mom?" He threw a wink at Danae.

The tears that had brimmed in her eyes spilled over now, but she was beaming like a floodlight too. "I think that would be just fine," she said, half laughing, half crying.

Austin studied her and wrinkled his forehead. "Are you cryin' . . . Mom?"

She lost it then. The full-on ugly cry. And Dallas had to fight not to follow suit. "You know what, buddy. Sometimes people cry because they're happy."

"That's silly!" He giggled, and then he feigned a pathetic wail.

Dallas tickled him. "You goof! You must be happy too, huh?"

"I'm not a goof!"

"Oh, I think you are a goof. I think you're the biggest goof I know."

"Tickle me some more, Dad."

Dallas gave him a perfunctory tickling before putting a finger under Danae's chin and forcing her to look at him.

He was gratified to see that she was a weepy mess—happier than he'd ever seen her.

28

Danae turned the page on the calendar and pinned it back on the bulletin board in the kitchen. *April.* The month their baby was due. In some ways, it seemed like they'd just celebrated Christmas. But in other ways, it seemed like that had been eons ago.

This waiting wasn't easy, even when you weren't the one heavy with child.

She heard the garage door grinding open. Finally. Dallas had worked late every night last week, and he'd promised her he'd be home in time to go with them to her parents' for supper.

Austin had come to live for Tuesday nights at Poppa and Gram's. But with Dallas working longer hours, Danae knew he would rather have had a night at home. She didn't blame him, but it was tradition. A tradition of only a couple of years, but she wouldn't have missed those nights for anything. Not to mention, she didn't have to cook on Tuesdays. At least not the whole meal. Tonight, she was on dessert duty. They were celebrating Emma and Grace's first birthdays so, besides a cake for the adults, she'd volunteered to bake two little round cakes the girls could dig into.

Dallas came in and plopped his briefcase and a stack of mail on the counter. He gave her a perfunctory kiss and sifted through the mail. "Where's my buddy?"

"He's up in the playroom. Are you going up? Tell him to bring his shoes when he comes down."

"I'll put them on. I'm going to change clothes first. You think we'll be outside tonight?"

"Knowing Mom, yes. Better get a jacket for Austin too."

"What did you make?" He lifted the top from the cake-taker that held her perfect six-layer carrot cake. "Hey, I think somebody had better test this before we try to serve it to company."

"Get out of there! Dallas Brooks, there had better not be one fingerful of frosting missing from that cake!" She swiped the lid from him and swatted him away, loving their life. Loving the simple, wonderful routines of being a family.

And it was about to get better. The cradle was set up in their bedroom and stacks of diapers and outfits in pink, blue, and neutral yellow, waited on a shelf above the changing table. They'd probably move the baby into the second nursery in a few months—unless it was a boy, and then they'd have to paint over pink walls first. But for now, she loved going to sleep with a view of their makeshift nursery at the end of the bed. And she felt just a little bit vindicated for all the grief Dallas had given her over having *two* "nurseries" in their house. The thought brought a smug smile.

Dallas took the steps two at a time, and her smile changed to one of delight when she heard Austin's cries of, "Dad! You're home!" She picked up the little birthday cake boxes to carry them out to the car, but her cell phone trilled from the living room where Austin had been playing "bideo" games on it.

She set the cakes down and ran for the phone. The Caller ID said St. Louis County. It was still at least two weeks away from Misty's due date, but she knew babies sometimes decided to come early. She really didn't want an April Fool's baby, but she wasn't going to be picky. She pressed Talk, her senses heightened.

"Danae? It's Misty."

"Misty? You're not in labor are you?" She couldn't keep the smile out of her voice.

"No. Sorry. Not yet. But that's why I'm calling. They're not gonna let you in the labor room."

"What?" She slumped into a chair, feeling like a deflated balloon. She'd known it wasn't a sure thing, but Misty had requested that Danae be with her for the labor and delivery, and Danae had been so excited about the possibility she could hardly stand it. "What happened? Do you think if I called someone it would make a difference? Or if Dallas did?"

"No. They said no exceptions. It's policy for someone of my . . . status." She spit the word out.

Danae took a deep breath. She didn't want to cry, not when Misty sounded bummed about it already. But she was crushed. "So . . . who will be with you?"

"Only medical staff is allowed, they said."

"Oh, Misty. I'm so sorry."

"I . . . I want to ask you something though."

"OK . . . sure." Misty's tone made her nervous.

"I was thinking. I don't want Austin to see me in jail. But in the hospital, that wouldn't be such a bad memory, would it?"

"No." She wasn't prepared for the ripples of—was it jealousy?—that went through her. "No. That would be a good memory, I think. You . . . you could even see him meet the baby."

The magnitude of what Misty was giving up—handing over to them—rolled over her with the force of an ocean wave.

"I'd like that, I think. I might chicken out. I have to think about it some more. I know he'll understand more when he gets older. But until then, I don't ever want him thinkin' I just walked away and never looked back, you know?"

"Oh . . . he wouldn't think that, Misty. We'd never let him think that. We were telling him just the other night how much you love him and miss him. He was remembering that soccer ball you bought him."

An overlong pause. "He remembered?"

"He did. We don't have it anymore. It didn't come with his stuff from the shelter, but he still remembered that you got it for him."

"Maybe I can get him another one somehow."

"Hey, would you like us to pick one up and bring it, so you can give it to him?"

"Would you?"

"Of course. We'd be happy to."

"I'm sorry you can't come in. For the baby, I mean."

She swallowed hard. "It's OK, Misty. It's not your fault."

"Well, yeah, it is."

"You know what I mean."

"Yeah . . . I know."

Dallas bounded down the stairs with Austin on his shoulders.

She shushed him and turned away with the phone. "Thanks for calling. We're praying for you, Misty. And we're sitting on pins and needles."

"Yeah. Tell me about it."

That made her laugh. It was a good way to end a disappointing call.

"Who was that?"

"Misty," she mouthed, not wanting to get into this conversation in front of Austin.

"I don't get to go into the delivery room." Her voice cracked.

"Oh. I'm sorry, babe." He slid Austin from his shoulders, set him on the floor, and came around to embrace her. "I know you were really counting on that."

She melted into him, trying to gather herself. "It's not the end of the world."

But if she were honest with herself, at the moment it sort of felt like it.

"I'll get the cake," Dallas said, lifting it from the table under the pergola.

"Oh, sure. The big hero saving the carrot cake." Jesse laughed and slugged Dallas in the arm. "Watch him, boys," he told Chase and Link. "Somebody be sure that cake makes it into the house."

"Well, doesn't that just take the cake," Link quipped.

Danae laughed, loving the guys' banter. But she marched over and took the cake-taker from her husband. "*I'll* take the cake, thank you very much. You go get something that requires muscles. Like Austin, for example."

They'd tried to eat outside tonight, but before they even had the table spread, a chill breeze came up, making it miserable for everyone. Now they'd formed a brigade to get all the food back in the house.

Spirits were high as they gathered around the table and laughed at the birthday girls' antics with their cakes. Danae was so grateful the hard news about not getting to be with Misty for their baby's birth had come on a day she was scheduled to be with people she loved. It was hard to feel down around this crazy family.

Link was cracking jokes and making his brothers-in-law laugh so hard they'd soon be shooting milk out their noses. She put the disappointing news out of her mind and focused on simply enjoying the moment.

When dishes were done, all the guys took the kids to the basement playroom to show them a new game Jesse had "invented" for one of his college courses.

Mom and Corinne and Landyn headed upstairs to get the twins bathed and put down for the night. Danae found Bree and CeeCee in the living room, deep in conversation. Her grandmother and Bree had always had a special bond, and she started to leave, thinking she'd interrupted. But they both beckoned her into the circle, and she curled into a sofa in the corner opposite Bree.

She listened while they finished their conversation. Something about Bree's job. Danae realized she hadn't asked her sister-in-law about her work as an event planner for quite some time. She'd make a point to be more interested next time.

Bree turned to her, smiling big. "So when's your baby due, Danae?"

CeeCee gasped and clapped her hands. "You're not!"

Danae laughed. "No, CeeCee. I'm not pregnant. Bree just means the baby we're adopting. You remember? It's Austin's brother or sister. His birth mother is due in two weeks." Mom and Dad had mentioned they were concerned that CeeCee had been slipping a little, but tonight was the first Danae had seen it for herself.

Danae had always admired her grandmother deeply. Cecelia Whitman still lived alone, and up till now had been as independent as they came. Danae could scarcely imagine their family without CeeCee someday.

"So, tell me about this baby," CeeCee said. "Boy or girl?"

"We won't know until it's born. But Austin seems to think he's getting a little sister."

"Really?" Bree said. "Are you hoping for a girl too?"

"I don't know. It would be neat to have one of each, but I'd like Austin to have a brother too. I'm just thrilled to have babies."

"Who would have thought, this time last year, right?"

Danae remembered that night in September when Corinne had announced her pregnancy. Danae had thought then that it would never happen for her. Bree had been so sweet to her that night. And just look where God had taken them since then. It still amazed her when she thought about their whole story.

"You said you wanted to be there for the delivery?"

Danae frowned. "No. I mean, I wanted to. But I just found out today that they won't let me in."

"Oh, I'm so sorry. You must be so disappointed, Danae."

"I am. It's not the end of the world, of course. I feel worse for Misty because she really seemed to want me there. And instead she'll be with strangers. They won't let anyone but medical personnel in."

"How sad."

"It is. And for me, I know I have no reason to complain. I'm truly grateful for everything God has seen fit to give us. It's just that I was so looking forward to being there. It seemed like getting to be there for the labor and delivery, watching a child come into the world, was God's way of letting me get a sense of that experience—as close as possible anyway. I know it sounds petty, but I just wanted that so badly."

CeeCee clucked in sympathy and put a hand on Danae's knee. "You won't remember this because you were just barely a spark in your daddy's eye then, but when your grandpa and I took our trip up to Canada in 1962, or was it '63? It seems like Grant was still in—"

Danae patted her grandmother's thin arm. "You've told us about that trip, CeeCee. I remember."

"Not the part I'm about to tell you."

Danae laughed, knowing there was a "Don't patronize me, young lady" attached to the gruff response.

Danae exchanged a look with Bree. They had all heard CeeCee talk about that trip. Danae had always assumed the trek to Canada had made such an impression because Grandpa and CeeCee rarely traveled.

A faraway look came to CeeCee's eyes. "You see," her grand-mother said, "some of the people on that tour had flown in to Silver Islet. Flying wasn't like it is now, and back then it was quite an experience to be able to say you'd flown. Well, Grandpa and I couldn't afford to fly. Gas was cheap back then, and we made the entire trip—more than a thousand miles—in our old '52 Ford. Took us three days to get there. Oh, there were some beautiful sights along the way, but nothing like those people on the air-plane got to see from a mile up in the air. Flying was more of a rarity back then. But you know what, Miss Danae?"

Danae smiled, knowing there was a moral to the story coming.

CeeCee took her hand and squeezed. "Once we all got to Canada, nobody gave a hoot how they got there. We were all too busy oohing and aahing at the vastness of Lake Superior and at our glimpse of the Aurora Borealis and all the other incredible sights there were to see. Sure, if someone happened to men-tion how they got to fly to Ontario, I felt a little jealous for a few minutes. But then I'd just smile and nod and wait until the con-versation turned back to whatever amazing thing we were experiencing at that moment. And you know, there were a few people who thought it was pretty amazing that we'd *driven* all that way. Sure it was a long, hard trip, but we had some stories to tell too."

Tears sprang to Danae's eyes. She got the message, loud and clear.

And she wasn't so sure CeeCee was "slipping" in the least.

29

W̲ell, I got them in the mail . . . nick of time."

"I wish I could be excited about that," Danae called from the kitchen.

Dallas hung the car keys on the hook in the mudroom. He'd finished their taxes after they got home from family night at the inn, and at eleven forty, he made his annual late-night race to the post office. Every year he *swore* he wouldn't wait until the last minute the next year. And every year he decided he should give up "swearing."

But this year he'd had a legitimate excuse. And he thought he might just be able to hang out his shingle as an attorney now, given the reams of documents and forms he'd filled out in the quest of getting Austin and the coming baby into their custody.

He found Danae at the sink and nuzzled her neck. She smelled like fresh laundry and something sugary. It was a good combination on her. "I can think of some ways we could celebrate," he murmured into her hair.

She laughed. "I'm *sure* you can. But FYI, I do not consider Tax Day a reason for celebration. Besides, I'm too excited to think about anything else." She wriggled around in the cage of his arms to face him. "*Why* haven't they called!"

"Maybe because there's nothing to report yet?" He kissed her forehead and went to rummage in the fridge for a midnight snack.

When he straightened he found her, hands on hips, study-ing him.

"Aren't you even a little bit excited?" she said.

He had to think about his answer. "I'm looking forward to a month from now, when we've settled into our new routine, and all this . . . transition stuff is behind us."

"Yes." She sighed. "I'm dreading the good-byes. Dreading them so much." Her frown quickly flipped to a smile. "But Dallas! We're getting a baby. Any day now. It's really happening."

He loved seeing her so happy, seeing her dreams finally com-ing true. He quickly corrected his thought: *their* dreams. Because ever since Austin had come into their lives, he'd finally caught Danae's vision for them as a couple, and now as a family.

He didn't think there was anything in the world that moved him more than hearing the patter of little feet, and that raspy voice hollering, "Dad's home!" every night when he walked in the door.

Things at work had finally slowed down a little and he felt like he could catch his breath. Thankfully, he still enjoyed his job, and the company made it worth his while. It was a good thing, now that there would be two more mouths to feed. Two more feet to shoe. Already, Austin was growing like kudzu. The twins' birth-day party at the inn had inspired Austin to make big plans for his fourth birthday, which wasn't until August. August 11, and the kid had talked about nothing else since. It was going to be a *long* summer waiting for that party.

He snagged a can of Coke and a bag of chips and motioned toward his man cave. "I'm going to check my e-mail before I hit the hay."

"OK. 'Night, babe." She tiptoed to receive his goodnight kiss and gave him one that seemed to promise more. "I'll check on Austin before I go to bed."

"I won't be long."

He grabbed his laptop and took it to the recliner. He had at least fifty unanswered e-mails, and he was tempted to delete them and pretend he'd never seen them. He threatened to do that every few months, but he never could go through with it.

He sorted a few he could handle quickly and started in on replies.

The phone broke the silence of the darkened house. He checked the clock on his laptop's toolbar and hurried to the kitchen to answer before it woke Danae.

It was almost twelve thirty. Either this was bad news or it was baby news. "Hello?" He answered cautiously, but couldn't keep the smile from his voice, suspecting it was baby news.

"Will you accept a collect call?" a mechanical voice said. Then Misty's voice speaking her own name formally.

"Yes," he said. "Yes, I'll accept."

"Dallas?" She was crying.

His heart slumped to his gut. "Misty. What is it? Is everything—"

"We've got a problem."

"Misty? What's wrong?" He braced himself against the counter, preparing for bad news.

"It's my sister." She dissolved in sobs again.

He didn't know what had happened to her sister, but he couldn't contain the relief he felt that this wasn't about the baby.

"She wants Austin. Charity wants him. To raise him. And . . . I don't know—I think maybe that would be best. Maybe . . ."

His heart seemed to stop beating. He couldn't get a breath. Finally he sucked in air and forced his voice to remain steady. "Misty? Why do you think that would be better? for Austin?"

"She's got kids. Oz would know his cousins."

He hadn't heard Misty call Austin by that nickname since the shelter.

"They're his blood cousins," she said. "And maybe—if I ever got out . . ."

What line had her sister been feeding her? *Oh, dear God! Give me the words!* "Misty. Listen, please. Let's . . . let's think this through. We told you we'd bring Austin to see you. We meant that. And if you want us to, we'll make sure he gets to spend time with his cousins. We would be more than willing to do that—happy, in fact. Danae could bring him any time. She won't have to work and we could—"

"I don't know. I've been talkin' everything through with Charity. She's changed. She's got her act together. She really does."

"Are you sure? You believe her, Misty? Because from what you told Danae, things weren't so hot with her." He couldn't afford to make her angry. And he felt like he was cheating. Hitting below the belt. But he'd never felt so desperate. They could *not* lose their boy. He leaned heavily against the counter, not sure his legs would hold him.

He tried another tack. "Austin is settling in here, Misty. Think about how hard it would be for him to have to make another adjustment. And can your sister afford another mouth to feed?" He couldn't even let himself think about losing Austin. And how could he ever tell Danae.

Part of him wanted to go wake her up. Maybe she would know what to say. How to handle Misty. Heaven knew he didn't have the words.

"I need to think about it. I can't just throw my boy away."

What? Where was this coming from? If he could have gotten his hands on this Charity right now, there might've been another murder. "How would that be throwing him away? He's thriving here. With us."

He heard noise and voices in the background. "I have to go. I'll call again as soon as I have it figured out."

"Misty, wait!" But the line was dead.

"What's going on?" Danae stood in front of him, the hem of her nightgown floating just above the wood floors.

He laid his phone on the counter and looked up at her. Her eyes widened in a way that told him he must look as awful as he felt. For a long moment, he toyed with the idea of lying to her. Telling her it was a wrong number. Or that he'd gotten bad news about their taxes. But he wasn't about to shatter the trust that had grown between them since that day he'd told her everything about his adoption.

He reached for her hand. "Let's go sit down, babe."

"Dallas? What's wrong? Tell me."

"It may be nothing," he said once they were seated side by side on the sofa in the living room. "Misty's sister might be contesting our guardianship. She wants Austin."

"What?" Danae shot off the couch. "That's crazy. Well, did you tell her she doesn't have a prayer? How did she get our number anyway?"

"It wasn't her I talked to. Her name's Charity."

"I don't care what her name is, she's not getting him. Who *did* you talk to?" She plopped back down beside him.

"It was Misty."

"Misty? Well, she surely set her sister straight."

He took her hand. "Misty is . . . reconsidering. I think Charity somehow convinced her that Austin should know his cousins— Charity's kids."

"You can't be serious. *They* can't be serious. Misty has never had a good word to say about her sister—or any of her family. Dallas, do something! They can't do this." She shot up again, and started pacing, then gave a little gasp, hands at her mouth. "What about the baby?"

He hadn't even thought of that. Losing Austin had been his only fear. But now the knot in his gut twisted. He couldn't remember, but he didn't think Misty had even mentioned the baby. "I don't think anything has changed there. She didn't say."

"But . . . if it's because she wants him to know his cousins, surely she'll want him to know his sister or brother too." Her voice was wooden. "We can let him visit his cousins. We can—"

"I told her that, Danae. I told her we'd do whatever it took. I told her how well he's doing here, and that we could give him things her sister never could."

"What did she say?"

He told her everything he could remember—except the fact that Misty had hung up on him.

He hauled himself off the couch and went to her, taking her in his arms. "Let's go to bed. There's nothing we can do about it tonight."

"Except pray." She slumped against him.

"And we'll do plenty of that. But we need to get some sleep. I'll call Carol first thing tomorrow and see what she knows about this."

Danae looked up at him, her expression dubious. "Carol didn't even know Misty was pregnant."

"I'll call everyone we've been dealing with. Every attorney, every social worker."

"And that guardian ad litem . . . what was her name?" Danae extricated herself from his arms and picked up his phone, scrolling through his contacts. "Surely *she* will see how ridiculous this is. She's supposed to be all about Austin's best interest."

"I just don't see how Misty could have changed her mind so drastically."

"Something got to her, Dallas. I don't know what her sister could have possibly said to change her mind, but I will fight for him. If it kills me, I will fight for Austin. For what's best for him."

"I know," he said. "*We* will fight it." But he had a sinking feeling in his gut. And his thoughts took him in crazy directions, plotting clandestine escapes out of the country, and delivering scathing diatribes to complete strangers laced with words he would never actually use. This wasn't conducive to prayer. He shook his head as if he could throw off the unwanted thoughts.

But twenty minutes later, they followed him to bed, growing more morbid and frightening with every minute that passed.

Morning finally came—after a miserable, sleepless night—and Danae hurried through her shower, wanting to be ready to leave the house at a moment's notice if they needed to. She had no idea what their options even were, but as she hovered near the door to Dallas's office just off the formal dining room, she tried to pray that God's will would be done.

Did God hear prayers when they were exactly the opposite of what the words expressed? She didn't know what God's will was, and frankly, right now she didn't care. She wanted *her* will. She wanted Austin. And the baby they'd been promised.

Dallas had started making calls around eight thirty this morning and had been on the phone constantly ever since. Between keeping Austin entertained and packing bags for all of them in case they had to go to St. Louis, she'd kept Dallas supplied with hot coffee and moral support. And—like now—she'd listened in on his end of a dozen different phone conversations. They'd decided that his masculine influence might be more persuasive, so while he did the talking, she riffled through the folders full of documents they'd acquired since Misty was taken into custody. Dallas had filled one legal pad with phone numbers and appointments, and another with hurried notes to Danae: *Carol Blye's number? or home study folder?*

"So, do you think we'll get to meet with the sister? with Charity?" He was talking to Carol, the social worker who'd handled Misty's interests in jail. He caught Danae's gaze, then rose and turned to look out the window that overlooked their street. "I see. Yes . . . yes, we can."

She thought she'd caught a spark of hope in his eyes, but maybe he was only pretending for her sake. She walked around his desk to stand beside him. She didn't like not being able to see his face.

"OK," Dallas said, his expression showing nothing now. "Yes, we'll be there."

He clicked off the phone and his cheeks puffed out with a sigh. "We're supposed to meet Carol at the jail tomorrow. She hasn't been able to talk to Misty, but she thinks the chances she'll talk to us are better if we can be there in person."

"OK. I'll call Mom and see if she can keep Austin."

He hesitated. "Carol wants us to bring Austin with us."

"What?" She felt the blood drain from her face. "You don't think they'll try to take him—" She couldn't make herself speak the words aloud.

"So help me, if they did . . ." He clenched his fists at his sides.

"They can't—legally—force us to bring him, can they?"

"I don't know. I haven't seen a court order."

"We could always drive back and get him—if it's a legal thing. I'm seriously afraid if we take him with us, we'll never see him again! Dallas?" Her voice rose an octave.

He shook his head, a deep frown creasing his forehead. "Yes, but I think we need to tiptoe pretty softly here."

"I don't care." She crumpled over the counter, but quickly recovered, new steel in her eyes. "We need time to prepare him, Dallas. He's not some pawn in a game."

"No, but he's not our son either, Danae."

30

At ten o'clock the next morning Carol Blye met them outside the entrance to the Justice Center where the jail was housed, and where Misty awaited her sentencing—and the birth of her baby.

The sun reflected off the many windows of the building, but the social worker's expression was anything but sunny. Dallas took Danae's hand and she braced herself for bad news.

"I'm sorry, Misty won't agree to talk with you," Carol said. She looked past them to the sidewalk. "Where's Austin?"

Danae held her breath.

Dallas scuffed the toe of his shoe on the sidewalk, but he met Carol's gaze. "We left him with Danae's parents. We didn't think he needed to be subjected to this conversation, and we didn't know who would watch him or—"

"We'll have to come up with a better explanation than that for Misty's sister." Carol's expression hardened. "Listen, I understand how hard this is for you guys, but just because you've been appointed Austin's guardians doesn't mean you can supersede the authorities where he is concerned. The last thing we want to do here is tick people off."

"Which authority requested that we bring him today?" There was challenge in Dallas's tone.

"I'm sorry. Leaving him at home was my idea," Danae said. "We—we can go back and get him if we need to." She felt a little guilty making it sound like a spur-of-the-moment offer when she and Dallas had premeditatedly decided on the tack they'd take.

"That's not the point," Carol said. "I'll handle the sister, but if we tell you to bring him next time, bring him."

They both nodded and apparently managed to look appropriately contrite, but Danae noticed Dallas didn't make any verbal commitments. She also noticed Carol hadn't exactly answered his question about which authority.

"So you're meeting with the sister today?" he asked.

Carol looked at her watch. "I'm supposed to meet with both of them in thirty minutes. Along with Dorothy Jessup—Austin's guardian ad litem. In fact"—she fished in her briefcase and came out with her phone—"I need to call Dorothy and let her know."

Carol set her briefcase against a light pole and strolled to the end of the walkway. They could just barely make out her end of the conversation, but Danae got the impression she wasn't exactly being forthright about what had happened.

Carol came back and resumed her place on the bench. "Well, we dodged a bullet. Let's sit down over here." She indicated a long bench in the sunshine.

Carol took one end while Danae and Dallas squeezed into the other corner.

The metal bench was cold, but the sun and Dallas's arm around her shoulders quickly warmed her. "So what happened? Did we do something to make Misty mad? I don't understand how she could change her mind so drastically almost overnight."

"I think she's somewhat in panic mode."

"So, what do we do now?" Dallas leaned away from Danae and unzipped his jacket before pulling her close again.

The social worker let out a sigh. "I don't agree with the choice of the sister to raise these kids and I—"

"Kids? Has she said for sure she wants the baby, too?" Danae asked, feeling panic rise in her throat.

"Charity hasn't been clear on that, but I don't think Misty would let Austin go to her if she thought it would separate the two kids." Carol frowned. "I think we have to assume the sister wants them both."

Danae slumped against Dallas, feeling utterly empty inside.

"Let's not despair yet." Carol leaned forward on the bench and held up a hand. "I think Misty is feeling a little desperate as the baby's birth draws near. Naturally, the birth is going to be very hard for her—it symbolizes the end to this . . . *reprieve* she's had. And losing another child. Once that baby is gone, she'll be sentenced, and she'll likely be sent to the penitentiary. I'm guessing that thinking of Austin somewhere familiar is comforting to her."

"But she told me point-blank she didn't want anyone in her family to have him! She called them 'lowlife perverts' at one point."

"Can you prove that, Danae? to a judge? Did anyone else hear that conversation?"

"It was at the shelter—where I met Misty." Danae closed her eyes, trying to remember the exact conversation. "I don't think anyone else was there. Or at least not where they would have heard her say it."

Carol shrugged. "It would be your word against hers. But if there's any truth to that label—lowlife pervert—it should come out in the home study."

"You mean she'll have to go through the same home study and everything we did?"

"Yes. And as you know, that can be a long process."

Despite everything, a frisson of hope went through her. At least that might buy them some time. "And what happens in the meantime? Until the sister gets cleared?"

"Could we keep Austin—and the baby—during that time?" The hope in Dallas's voice broke Danae's heart. Because she had an awful feeling what Carol's answer would be.

"You could possibly retain guardianship of Austin in the interim. That will certainly be my recommendation. And Dorothy will likely feel the same. I've worked with her before and she's very wise. And trustworthy. But a lot will depend on Misty."

"And she wouldn't even speak to us this morning." Danae closed her eyes. "Did we do something to make her mad?" she asked again. Carol hadn't answered that question to her satisfaction yet.

"No. Definitely not. This isn't about you two. It's about Misty coming to terms with losing her kids. She needs somebody to aim her anger at. And unfortunately, her sister has fueled the fire and made her question her decision."

"So what's next?" Dallas scooted from behind Danae and rose.

"We wait," Carol said. "I'll let you know what happens when I meet with the sister and if we need to reschedule the meeting with Dorothy. But"—she looked at each of them in turn—"You need to be prepared to bring Austin back. With all his things. I can't cover for you next time."

The sun had risen above the awning over the bench, putting them in the shadows. Danae shivered and rose to stand beside Dallas. He put an arm around her, drawing her close.

Carol gathered her briefcase and stood. "I'm sorry this has gone the way it has. Again, I'm not convinced the sister is the best place for Austin, but unfortunately, Misty's desire for her kids will carry a lot of weight with any judge—as it should," she added quickly.

"What do you think will happen?" Dallas asked.

The social worker shook her head. "I couldn't possibly predict. I think our best angle right now is the fact that Misty will likely want the two children to be placed together, and I'm not sure the sister has the means to take in both of them. She wouldn't have been so ambiguous otherwise. She works long hours and already gets government help with daycare for her own two children. We'll push hard on those issues."

Again, a glimmer of hope. And yet, if Austin had to be wrenched from them, Danae almost felt like the baby *should* go wherever Austin went. His brother or sister would be a comfort to him, and a link to Misty.

She'd been so desperate for what she and Dallas were losing, but now her heart broke for Austin. She remembered how pathetic he'd been that first night they came to the shelter. Frightened and pale and bleeding—and he'd at least had his mother then. If they forced him to go with Misty's sister, he would be completely alone, away from everything familiar.

Carol checked her watch. "I need to go sign in." She shook each of their hands. "Don't lose hope yet. I'll let you know as soon as I know anything. And stay by your phone in case things change."

Was that code for *in case you have to turn Austin over*?

How could they ever bear that? Her legs almost wouldn't hold her and she leaned heavily on Dallas, trying to draw strength from him. Strength he didn't look like he possessed in this moment.

<hr />

"Where did you guys go?" Austin's nose wrinkled in that funny way that had become as familiar to Dallas as his own breath.

"We were in St. Louis, buddy. Now hold still so I can zip your jacket." He gave Danae's mother a smile that must not quite have reached his face because Audrey returned it with a furrowed brow.

"Did everything go OK?" Audrey chirped, obviously trying to keep things light in front of Austin. But she wasn't going to let them get away without a report.

"Danae, can you help me with this jacket? I can't get the zipper to work right."

He turned Austin over to Danae, who knelt on the floor to finish zipping him up and then tie the strings on the hood under his little chin. Her voice was about as steady as the towers of building blocks Austin stacked, and he knew everything would come tumbling out in tears if she didn't get out of there.

"Why don't you go ahead and get Austin in the car," he told her. "I'll fill your mom in."

"Thanks babe." She stood and took Austin's hand. "Let's go, buddy. Can you tell Gram thank you?"

"Thanks, Gram."

"You're welcome, buddy. You come back any time."

"Tuesday." He bobbed his chin. "We *always* comes on Tuesday. Right, Gram?"

Dallas about lost it on that, but he managed to hold it together long enough to see Danae and Austin out the door. He closed the storm door behind them, and watched through the glass as Danae and Austin walked hand in hand to the SUV.

He turned to face Audrey, dreading repeating everything that had happened today.

Audrey looked as stricken as they'd felt when they first learned the news. "So you really could lose him?"

He shook his head. "I don't know. We're going to fight it, but there's only so much we can do at this point."

Her shoulders sagged. "I was afraid of this. How's Danae handling it? She was awfully quiet."

"She's just trying to be strong for Austin. But she's pretty shook-up. We just . . . we can't even imagine life without him now." He didn't dare trust his voice to say more.

"Me neither." Audrey put an arm around him. "Grant and I will be praying our hearts out."

"Thanks," he whispered. "We'll be right there with you."

"And that's the best thing any of us can do."

"I know. But . . . I've never felt so helpless."

"I know." She gave his shoulders a squeeze. "We just have to leave it in God's hands at this point."

He knew it was true, but he couldn't seem to open his own hands to release his grip.

31

Get your jammies on, buddy. It's already past bedtime."

If Danae hadn't had Austin to take care of, to make her laugh, and even to frustrate her at times, she wasn't sure how she would have survived these hours of waiting. They were torture. Still, it was a small comfort to know that her whole family, Dallas's brother, and as many friends as they felt comfortable sharing with were praying around the clock, storming heaven for grace.

Danae's fear was that God's grace to Austin might mean growing up somewhere besides with her and Dallas. She'd gone through a humbling moment this afternoon, praying desperately for God to work things out *her* way. She still couldn't help but believe that Austin was better off with Dallas and her than with the sister Misty'd had nothing good to say about.

But Danae had felt convicted of her own selfishness, and her judgmental attitude, believing that she and Dallas had an edge on Charity. Because of their money. Because of their beautiful home. Because of their college educations. Because of the upstanding families they'd been raised in.

She'd had to repent of that "holier-than-thou" attitude and put the whole situation in God's hands. Again and again. And every time the phone rang, her heart jumped into her throat and she had to pray all over again, *God, if it's better for Austin to be with someone else, then I trust you to do what's best. For him.*

She'd never prayed a prayer that cost her so much. But she meant it. She truly wanted God's best for Austin. She just had a hard time turning loose of the idea that she and Dallas *were* God's best for him. And she couldn't let herself think about what kind of God would have raised their hopes like this, only to dash them.

They hadn't heard from Carol all day. In some ways she thought no news was good news. And tucking Austin in now, she thought she could live with months of not knowing—if only he could stay here with them while they waited. But there were no guarantees.

And Misty's baby was due any day. If she gave birth before they settled things, and the baby went into foster care, it might be months before either she or Misty's sister gained custody of the baby or of Austin. So many unknowns.

"Does Poppa and Gram have any kids?" Austin peered up at her from beneath a mop of shaggy dark hair. They'd had to cancel a haircut appointment for him because of the meeting with Carol. Maybe she and Dallas could at least trim his bangs in the morning. She should have done it before baths tonight but—

"Do they?" Austin persisted.

She had to rewind to remember what his question had been. She hated how distracted this whole ordeal had made her.

"Sure, they have kids. I'm one of them. Didn't you know that?"

He wrinkled his nose. "*You're* not a kid!"

"Not now, but when I was a kid, Poppa and Gram were my mom and dad."

"How's come they're not still your mom and dad."

She laughed. "Well, they still are my mom and dad, but when I grew up I didn't live with them any more. I went off to college, and then I married Dallas and we got our own house to live in." This was hard to explain.

A frown creased his flawless face. "I'm not goin' off to college 'cause I'm always gonna live here, right?"

Oh, precious boy. She tried to make her voice light. "You're so smart, of course you'll go to college."

"Is there college at our town?"

"There is. Southeast Missouri State. You think you might want to go there?"

"Uh-huh . . . so's I could still live here."

She patted his tummy and tucked him in again, desperately needing to get out of here. "You've got a few years to worry about that, buddy. Let's get you through kindergarten first, OK?"

"Sadie goes to kindergarten."

"She sure does."

"But she's five."

"Yes she is. And when you're five you'll go to kindergarten."

"But you'll go with me, right?"

"I'll go with you the first day and drop you off but—" The phone rang downstairs and she stopped mid-sentence to listen. She heard Dallas's voice, but she couldn't make out what he was saying.

"One last tuck, buddy. You need to get to sleep." She gave the blankets a perfunctory tuck and reached for the lamp.

"But you didn't pray!"

She could hear Dallas, still on the phone. She was desperate to get downstairs and find out what was going on. But this was not a good night to skip prayers.

She lay across him and pulled him into a hug, saying a quick prayer. Maybe he'd only learned to use that bedtime prayer as a variation on the one-more-drink-of-water excuse. Still, it warmed her heart that he'd come to regard praying as an integral part of life.

A new—and frightening—thought struck her. What if that was the purpose of Austin having spent these days in their home? What if it was only so he could now take those prayers they'd shared with him into a home where prayer was unknown? Was she willing to sacrifice raising him, if it meant that someone who'd never known God might now have a chance?

She pushed herself off the bed. She didn't have the strength to think about that question now. "Goodnight, buddy. See you in the morning."

He closed his eyes and rolled onto his tummy so that his little rump stuck up in the air. She thought he was probably asleep before she reached the door.

Downstairs, Dallas was still on the phone, pacing the length of the kitchen. She touched his forearm and threw him a questioning look.

"Carol," he mouthed.

She couldn't tell from his demeanor if it was good news, but he didn't seem distressed. He talked for a few more minutes and she waited, every nerve on edge.

Finally he hung up and breathed out a sigh. "Charity is waffling on the baby."

"Oh, good," she breathed. *Thank you, God.* She immediately felt fickle and weak. What happened to "your will, not mine"?

"Carol thinks Charity knows she won't be able to take care of the baby, and that has Misty rethinking things." Dallas looked defeated.

"But that's good. Isn't it?"

"It is if she makes up her mind in time. But if this baby comes with things up in the air, we risk them going into foster care. Both of them."

She felt like she was at the top of the world's biggest roller coaster. And she was powerless to get off.

By Thursday, they still hadn't heard anything new. This limbo they were living in threatened to drive Dallas crazy. He'd gone back to work yesterday, and was in the office today—not that it meant he was getting any work done. He'd worked through the lunch hour though, and had at least managed to answer the most crucial e-mail.

His boss had been understanding, but since Thanksgiving he'd taken off more time than he had in all his previous years at the company combined. Was this just the way it was for parents?

He didn't know, but one thing he did know: he couldn't afford to lose his job.

Still, he'd asked Carol to call his cell phone rather than calling the house or Danae's cell. She had all she could do taking care of Austin and finishing up the final paperwork for family services. Carol had stressed that they needed to have everything in perfect order for the best chance that family services would allow them to remain in guardianship of Austin while decisions were made about the children's fate.

He cleared off his desk, tucked his phone into his pocket, and headed down to the conference room for a meeting. He'd never felt so disconnected from work. It troubled him a little, though he certainly had plenty of reasons to be distracted.

Halfway down the hall his phone chimed. He didn't recognize the number and almost ignored it, but something made him stop in the hallway and answer.

"Dallas?" It was Misty.

He turned and went back to his office, closing the door behind him. He'd just have to be late for his meeting. "Misty. Hi." He didn't even know what to say to her.

"Did they tell you? I . . . I had the baby."

"You did?" His pulse throbbed in his throat. "Is everything OK? Everything went all right?"

A too-long silence. "It's a boy."

"A boy. Wow. And he's OK? You're OK?" He felt like he was walking a tightrope strung over the Grand Canyon. He didn't dare look down.

Again silence—the longest pause of his life.

Finally, voice quavering, she said, "He's beautiful. And . . . perfect. He was born about eleven o'clock, I guess."

"This morning?"

"Yes, this morning." Muffled voices in the background, then Misty came back on. "The nurse says eleven thirty-two."

"Eleven thirty-two, huh? So he's just a couple hours old? And you're OK?" Why was she calling him? He didn't dare let himself wonder.

She sighed audibly into the phone. "It went fine. Easier than with Austin. Um . . . Hey, they won't let me talk but a few minutes, but I just wanted to say . . . I'm sorry."

Sorry? "I'm not sure what you mean."

"I'm . . . I'm so sorry. About everything. I kinda went a little crazy. That wasn't fair to you guys and—"

The awful sound of her sobs killed him.

"I'm sorry," she said again. "Tell Danae I'm so sorry."

"Misty? I . . . I'm not sure what you're saying. Is Charity taking the baby too?" *God, please! Not both of them.* How would Danae ever recover?

"No! No! Didn't they tell you? Didn't that social worker call you? Carol? She said she was calling you."

"No. We haven't heard from *anyone*. What's going on?"

"My sister . . . she flaked out. I shoulda known. I shoulda known," she said again. "I never should have changed it. I don't know why I let her jerk me around like that."

"So . . . ? Does that mean we . . . ?" He was afraid to voice the words. "You want us to have the baby?"

"As long as you'll take Austin too. I want them to be together. I told Charity that in the first place, but she—"

He had to sit down. Had to hang on to something before his knees gave out. He wasn't listening to Misty any more. He was thinking about this news—this amazing news—he had for Danae.

He swallowed a peculiar mixture of grief and joy. He wanted to ask her about the arrangements with the hospital. When they could come and pick up their son. But that would have been cruel. "Misty," he said instead. "Thank you. We're praying for you, Danae and I. Always. You get some rest, OK?"

"I have to go." Her voice was thready. "They're making me hang up now. I can't talk any more."

He couldn't talk either.

The line went dead but not before he heard her sobbing. It tore him up. It struck him that if they hadn't gone through the threat of losing Austin these last few days, he couldn't have begun to understand the depth of her agony. But he'd had a taste of that now, and it made the answers to their prayers all the more precious.

For a minute, he couldn't make his body obey his commands. He could only put his head in his hands and say *thank you* over and over. When he finally composed himself, he left a message with his secretary that he'd be out of the office until Monday. He turned off the lights, locked his door, and started for the elevator.

His cell phone buzzed in his pocket. He took it out and chuckled when he saw Carol Blye's name. "Hello?"

"Dallas, are you sitting down? Have I ever got good news for you."

32

Danae's car was in the garage when Dallas got home, but the house was quiet, and he was starting to become alarmed when she didn't respond to the sound of the back door. He glanced at the clock and realized it was nap time.

He took the stairs two at a time and found Danae napping, curled up on the end of Austin's bed. He knew she was soaking up every minute she might have left with her boy.

"Hey, babe," he whispered, not wanting to frighten her—or to wake Austin. He placed a hand on her cheek. "Danae? Wake up."

She stirred and opened her eyes, then looked past him at the clock on Austin's bedside table. "What's wrong? Why are you home so early?"

He put a finger over his mouth and held out a hand to her.

She eased off the bed, being careful not to disturb Austin. She followed him into the hall, pulling the door closed behind her.

"Come here," he said, still holding her hand.

"What is going on? Dallas?"

He led her to the kitchen where, if she screamed, Austin would be less likely to hear. He smiled at the thought.

He pulled her into his arms, cradling her head. The lump that came to his throat made him momentarily mute. "It's a boy," he finally choked out.

She pulled away, studying him. "What?"

"We have a baby boy, Danae. Misty called me at the office. Just a few minutes ago. We have a son, babe . . . Austin too—" His voice broke and he wrapped his arms around her, pulling her close, not wanting her to see his own tears.

"Oh, Dallas!" She fought against him, looking up at him with the most wonderful, incredulous expression. "Are you serious? What happened?"

He shrugged, unable to keep the smile from his face. "Charity flaked out. Misty's words."

"Oh, thank you, Jesus!" Danae dissolved in tears, then suddenly disentangled herself from his embrace. "What about the baby? When was he born? How much did he weigh? Is he OK? And you're sure it was Misty who called?"

"Whoa, whoa . . . One question at a time." He couldn't stop smiling.

It struck him that he was going to be in a world of hurt when Danae found out he hadn't thought to ask how much the baby weighed. Or how long he was. Or whether he had hair. Or a name.

"Dad?"

"Hey there!" Hearing Danae's voice, Grant smiled into the phone. Even after they were grown, it never got old hearing someone call you *Dad*. "How's my second favorite daughter? You're up awfully early."

She laughed at their ongoing joke. "Your second favorite daughter is doing pretty stinkin' well this morning . . . *Poppa!*"

"What's this about?" He held his breath. She sounded absolutely giddy.

"We have a baby, Dad! It's a boy. And he's ours. Misty changed her mind!"

"What? Oh, that's great, honey! I'm so happy for you. OK, so give me the details. Your mom is going to grill me. Hang on; let me grab a pen."

She gave a little growl. "Thanks to my hubby, I *have* almost no details about the baby. It's a boy, and he was born at eleven thirty-two this morning. That's all I know."

"Well, you know, that's all you really *need* to know."

"Dad, seriously?" Another growl. "Men!"

He laughed. Her joy was contagious. After all they'd been through, his heart was full for the way things had worked out. At least he hoped everything was worked out now. He wouldn't rest easy until they got the baby safely home.

Who was he kidding? He wouldn't rest easy ever again on this earth. Whoever said you quit worrying about your kids once they were safely married off hadn't had grandkids.

He shook off the thought. This was a time to celebrate. Prayers had been answered. Big prayers. "So when do you get to pick him up?"

"Tomorrow morning! We've got the car loaded, the car seat ready . . ." She sighed. "Oh, I hope I'm not forgetting anything! But anyway, is Mom going to be able to get away to go with us?"

They'd asked Audrey a couple of weeks ago—before the whole drama with Misty's sister almost derailed everything—if she would go to the hospital with them to watch Austin in the waiting room while they met the baby and let Misty say good-bye.

After that they planned to let Austin see Misty. Grant didn't like the idea. Didn't really think it was best for the boy. But they hadn't asked him. And—so help him—he would keep his mouth shut. "Your mom ran into Langhorne to get some groceries, but she'll be back any minute, and I think I can hold down the fort tomorrow so she can come with you."

Danae gave him the details. "Did you write it down, Daddy?"

"Yes, smarty-pants, I wrote it down. She'll be there, don't you worry."

"OK. I can't wait for you to meet him!"

He laughed. "I can't wait for *you* to meet him either!"

"Maybe you can come to Cape tomorrow after we get home and see him. We should be home by three or four."

"Well, if not then, I'll get there as soon as I can. We've got the rest of our lives to get to know him." He swallowed hard. "You did good, kiddo."

"Thanks, Dad."

He suddenly couldn't speak without turning into a puddle.

"You there, Daddy?"

"I . . . I'm here. My allergies are acting up." He cleared his throat loudly. "You know, kiddo, you may have gotten a late start with the babies, but you got the privilege of giving us our very first grandsons."

"Oh! I hadn't thought of that." She gave a weepy laugh. "Now *my* allergies are acting up."

"Not to mention, God made up for lost time by starting you out with a three-year-old."

Another little sob. "I'm hanging up, Daddy."

"Me too." Grant put the phone down and let his "allergies" have their way with him.

33

"Austin? Wake up, buddy." Danae shook his thin shoulders again.

"Can I play bideo games?"

She laughed. The boy wasn't even four years old, and they already had a fight on their hands when it came to those blasted electronics. "No, buddy. But you need to get up. Dad and I need to talk to you about something very important."

She went to open the "dinosaur teeth" curtains. April sun streamed in, bouncing off the pale blue walls, and matching her mood to perfection. She hadn't quit smiling since Dallas had awakened her from her nap. She didn't tell him, but she'd barely slept for a minute since she'd heard the news. They had a son!

And although she didn't think this baby could be any more a son to them than Austin seemed, still, there was something so precious and special about being able to meet this baby when he was mere hours old.

Dallas had gotten hold of the hospital, and everything was arranged for them to bring the baby home today. She didn't know how she could possibly wait until then.

Dallas appeared in the doorway. "Did you tell him?" he mouthed.

"Can I wear my Potamus Prime shirt, Dad?" They'd cracked up at his first mispronunciation of Optimus Prime and now would forever after picture the super villain as a hippo in metallic red and blue.

"Not today, buddy. We're going to the hospital." He turned to Danae. "Did you tell him?"

She laughed. "And you think *I'm* wound up? Of course, I didn't tell him. I wouldn't let you miss this."

They'd decided to keep the news about Austin seeing Misty very low-key. They'd talked about it several times over the past few weeks whenever they talked about the baby coming. Austin seemed pretty matter-of-fact about the prospect of seeing his mama again, but they were learning he was pretty matter-of-fact about everything. Well, except maybe bideo games. And Potamus Prime.

"Come here, Austin." She knelt in front of him. "Guess what happened last night?"

He broke away from her and riffled through a pile of toys in the corner of his room. "Potamus Prime. Potamus Prime."

"Hey, Austin. Get over here." She crawled over to him on hands and knees, capturing him and pulling him into her lap. "We can find your Optimus Prime later. Right now, Dad and I have something exciting to tell you."

She yielded the floor to Dallas with a smile, kicking herself that she hadn't thought to set up the video camera.

He sat cross-legged on the floor and leaned in until he was face-to-face with Austin. "You have a brother, buddy! Your baby brother was born last night."

"Our baby?" Austin pointed to his own chest.

"Yes! It's a boy! A brother!"

"Can he play with my Potamus Prime?"

Dallas fell over laughing, which instigated a wrestling match.

Apparently, it took more than a new baby brother to impress this boy.

"We'll be back to get you in just a few minutes, OK, buddy?" Dallas tried to look stern.

He felt bad leaving Audrey in the waiting room with a rather whiney Austin. The two-and-a-half-hour drive to St. Louis had not done his disposition any favors.

"You two go on," Audrey said, taking Austin's hand. "We'll be fine here."

"Austin, you be good for Gram." Danae eyed the elevator, understandably distracted.

"He will," Audrey said. "Now go. Meet your new son." She shooed them away.

Dallas caught up with Danae at the elevator, and pushed the button for the fourth floor. Misty wasn't on the maternity ward with the other mothers but had been assigned to a security floor, according to the receptionist.

The doors opened and they stepped into a stark white vestibule. He scanned the signs, looking for room numbers.

Danae nudged him, pointing to a sign high over the double doors to the left.

Psychiatric Ward.

Danae's brow furrowed. "Did they tell you she was on the psych ward?" she whispered.

He shook his head. "It's probably just for security. She sounded fine when I talked to her."

Danae grabbed his hand.

"You nervous?"

She nodded. "And excited."

He led the way down the only hallway that wasn't restricted, resisting the urge to look into the open doorways they passed. They went directly to the nurse's station. "We're here to see Misty Arato."

While the nurse made them each sign a clipboard, Danae explained, "We're adopting her son that was born yesterday."

"Yes. Are you just here to pick up the baby, or are you meeting the birth mother?"

"No," Danae said. "I mean, we know Misty. We're adopting her baby, but it's an open adoption."

"Her other son is down in the waiting room." Dallas put a hand at the small of Danae's back, sensing her tension. "We have permission to bring him up for a visit."

"I'm sorry, but Mrs. Arato is not allowed visitors."

Dallas leaned in and lowered his voice a notch. "Ma'am, we spoke with someone in the admin office two weeks ago. And Mrs. Arato's social worker confirmed just this morning that we could bring Austin to see her. She should be here in a few minutes."

"I'll have to check with security." The nurse dialed a number and repeated what they'd told her to the person on the other end. Without comment, she hung up and rolled her chair away from the desk. She glanced at Danae's bag and shook her head. "You'll have to leave that here."

Danae's eyes grew wide. "But . . . we have a gift in here for—"

"The patient is not allowed gifts."

"You don't understand," Dallas said. "It's not for the patient. We brought it for her to give her son. This is important."

Danae lifted the gift-wrapped soccer ball from her bag and showed the nurse. "It's just a little soccer ball. It has a lot of sentimental value. Please. It will come back home with us."

The nurse pursed her lips, studying the package. Finally she turned and motioned. "Leave your bag here. You can take the ball. Follow me."

They traipsed after her down a maze of hallways until they spotted a uniformed guard standing outside a room at the end of a shorter hallway.

The nurse spoke briefly to the armed security guard, who nodded and let them pass.

Misty was sitting up in the bed, and Dallas couldn't help noticing how pale and stressed she looked.

Beside him, Danae gave a little gasp. He followed her line of vision to the bed rails, where Misty's left wrist was shackled.

She gave an anemic wave with her free hand.

Danae hurried to her side and hugged her across the bed rail. Misty's gaze moved beyond her and past Dallas to the door, her features almost frightened looking. Dallas realized she was looking for Austin.

Tears streamed down Misty's cheeks unchecked. "I told them not to bring him up," she whispered.

"Why?" Danae took her hand and knelt to eye level with her. "Misty, Austin wants to see you."

She jerked her shackled arm, causing the cuff to clank against the metal railing.

That brought the security guard to the doorway. He left when Dallas motioned that everything was OK.

"Yeah," she said, her eyes narrowed. "I got to wear these right up until labor and delivery too."

"Oh, Misty. I'm so sorry. I wish I could have been with you."

"This might as well be jail. I don't want Austin seeing me like this."

Surely they could take the shackles off for a few minutes. His blood reaching a slow boil, Dallas whispered in Danae's ear. "I'll be right back."

He strode into the hallway where the guard was seated on a chair just outside the door. He jumped to his feet when he saw Dallas.

He made an effort to keep his voice steady. "Her three-year-old son is coming up to visit her in a few minutes. Could we please allow the woman the dignity of being able to hug him with both arms?"

"I'm sorry, sir. That's not my call. The prisoner is in the custody of the St. Louis County jail."

"And you are?"

"I'm with hospital security."

"But you have a way to unlock her cuffs, I assume?"

"Again, sir, that's not my call."

"Then who do I need to speak with to get her uncuffed? Just for five minutes. Please. Have a little mercy. Surely she's been humiliated enough."

"I'm sorry, sir. This is standard policy when the prisoner is serving life."

"What if there was a fire in the building? How would you get her out?"

The guard straightened and looked Dallas in the eye. "Sir, I'm not going to have this conversation with you. You may have your time with the prisoner—restrained—or I will have to ask that you leave the premises."

Still seething, he worked to rein in his emotions. It wouldn't help anybody if he got thrown out. But he was out of options. And he wasn't about to leave Danae to go through all this alone. He took a deep breath, composing himself before re-entering Misty's room.

"I'm sorry," he told Misty. "There's nothing they can do."

"Misty, please don't let this stop you from seeing Austin if you want to—" Danae stopped short. She picked up a corner of the bed sheet. "Here . . . What if we do this?" She worked quickly, camouflaging the shackles with the corner of the sheet and blanket.

Misty's smile didn't quite reach her eyes, but she nodded. "I do want to see him."

Carol Blye stepped into the room just then. "They're bringing the baby down now. Do you want Austin here for that?"

"Yes." Dallas and Danae spoke as one.

He sent up a prayer. "I'll go get him."

34

Growing more anxious with every tick of the clock, Danae waited for Dallas to bring Austin into the hospital room. Misty had the soccer ball tucked beside her, ready to give to him, but it was obvious she was nervous too.

They heard a commotion in the hallway and looked at each other, exchanging knowing smiles.

Misty laughed nervously. "I'd know those footsteps anywhere."

Danae nodded. Both of Austin's mothers recognized the patter of his little feet. She only prayed that Austin recognized Misty after almost five months.

He raced through the door ahead of Dallas, but Dallas scooped him up and carried him over to Misty's bed. "Say hi to your mama, buddy."

Danae watched his little face closely, certain she saw a spark of recognition.

Misty squeezed her eyelids together in an obvious attempt to hold back the flood of tears. "Hey, little man."

Austin scrunched his eyes up, mimicking her, and that broke the ice. He turned shy though . . . until he spotted the barely disguised soccer ball.

Danae had wrapped it by simply gathering tissue paper around it, and Austin couldn't keep his eyes off of it.

Dallas gradually slid Austin from his arms until the boy was sitting on the bed beside Misty.

Misty seemed to have forgotten anyone else was in the room, having eyes only for her son. She scooped up the ball with her free hand, holding it out to Austin. "Mama got you something, baby."

He gave her a look like she was being silly. "I'm not a baby."

"No . . . No, you're not," Misty said. "You're growin' so big I can hardly believe it."

He clutched the ball to his chest.

"You can take that . . . home with you."

He rewarded Misty with a smile, but it tore at Danae to see how shy and standoffish he was with her. She couldn't help wondering if he would have also been like that if Charity had ended up with him and *she'd* come to visit after five months. Why was she spoiling this time with such thoughts? She blinked them away.

"What do you say, Austin?" Dallas prompted.

"Tank you."

The door opened again and the nurse poked her head in. "We're bringing the baby in."

Danae's breath caught. She knew it was selfish, but she wished she could kick everyone out of the room except Dallas and Austin. She tried to remember CeeCee's story and to just savor every moment for exactly what it was.

Still, Missouri law required that the consent to adoption was not valid until the child was forty-eight hours old. Even though she knew Misty didn't really have the option to change her mind, after the whole mess with Charity, Danae would not breathe easy until eleven thirty-three tomorrow night, when every last one of those forty-eight hours had passed.

Another nurse entered, wheeling a Plexiglass bassinet in front of her. Carol took it from her and positioned the little crib beside Misty's bed. Danae caught her husband's eye and they both hurried to the baby. *Their* baby.

She'd waited so very long for him, and now he was here.

He had a fine down on his perfectly shaped head, and his skin was golden, not quite olive like Austin's, but Danae thought she saw a resemblance. His features were fine, like Misty's, and long pale eyelashes lay on the mounds of his cheeks. He was as perfect as any baby she'd ever laid eyes on. And she'd laid eyes on quite a few.

He was swaddled in a hospital blanket, and Danae could hardly wait to unwrap him and count his toes and fingers. She smiled to herself, remembering how Corinne and Landyn had been anxious to do the same thing with their newborns. Maybe there wasn't as much difference between birth mothers and adoptive mothers as she'd feared.

Dallas picked up the little blue card from inside the bassinet. "Danae, you were asking?" He consulted the card. "He weighed eight pounds, three ounces, and he was twenty-one inches long. Oh, and he's a boy."

She shot him a look that said, *You smart aleck!*

"Who gets to hold him first?" Carol asked, scooping the baby from the bassinet as if he were a football.

"Let Austin hold him first," Dallas said.

Danae could have kissed him right then and there. Sometimes she loved this man so much it hurt.

The sometimes dour social worker suddenly turned grandmotherly. "Are you ready to meet your little brother, Austin?" She brought the baby around to the side of the bed where Austin sat, and gently placed the tiny bundle on his usually wiggly lap. She kept one hand on the baby, but there was no need.

Austin held perfectly still, staring at his new brother with a look on his face that Danae didn't think she would forget as long as she lived. She was absolutely itching to get her hands on the baby, but she wouldn't have abbreviated this moment for anything.

"Did anyone bring a camera?" Carol asked.

"Oh!" Danae cast about the room, then deflated. "Mine is in my purse . . . at the nurse's station."

Dallas dug his phone from his pocket. "I've got it." He squatted down to get eye level with the two brothers and snapped several shots. "Misty, do you mind if I get some pictures of you with the boys?"

"Oh"—she put her free hand to her hair—"but I look a mess!" Still, she posed and smiled, and Danae was so grateful Dallas had thought to take the photo.

"What did you name the baby?" Carol asked, looking at Dallas and her.

They exchanged glances. They'd talked about names, but had agreed they wanted Misty's input too.

Dallas took a step closer to the bed. "Misty, did you have a name picked out for him?"

She looked surprised he would ask, then turned shy. "Well, I been calling him Tyler. It's a town in Texas. It seems to fit him. But . . . he's not mine to name. You can call him whatever you like." She gave Dallas a sly grin. "Long as it's not Bug Tussel"

They laughed.

"Tyler," Danae breathed.

Dallas looked at Danae, smiling. "I like it."

"Me too," she said. "If I can stand living with all these Texans. And Misty, we want to give him Morrison for a middle name if that's all right with you."

"Morrison? My name?"

"Of course. He has your blood in his veins. He's the most priceless gift you could ever give us."

"I was wantin' to ask you about giving Austin a second last name. Brooks . . . so he matches the rest of you, you know?"

Danae watched Dallas, saw his throat constrict before he replied, but there was a smile in his voice. "How about we trade you a Morrison for a Brooks?"

"That sounds like a deal," Misty said.

Danae tried her boys' names on for size. "Austin Morrison Brooks and Tyler Morrison Brooks. They sound like good names to grow into."

Misty stared for a long while at the two boys sitting on her hospital bed as if she were memorizing them. But instead of tears—for now anyway—there seemed to be peace in her eyes.

35

Dallas? Do you know where the receipt for the infant swing is?"

He appeared in the doorway to the kitchen. "It's not in the medical folder?"

"*Why* would it be in the medical folder?"

He shrugged. "Because it helps us keep our sanity?"

"Good point." She laughed. That was certainly true. Tyler loved the mechanical swing and it had bought them many extra minutes of peace over the last six weeks. "But are you serious?"

"Actually, I think I put a bunch of baby receipts in there the other day when I cleaned out that basket on the kitchen counter. I was going to sort them out later. Why do you need it?"

"There's a twenty dollar rebate for the swing that's about to expire, but I need a copy of the receipt to send it in."

"Oh." He had his head in the refrigerator, rummaging for an evening snack. "You want me to find it for you? Actually, I think that folder is in my nightstand drawer right now."

"No, I can get it. But there'd better be some of that salted caramel ice cream left when I get back down here."

No comment.

She swatted his backside on her way past. "Did you hear me?"

"I heard you. You want me to dish you up some?"

"Sure. I'll be back down in a minute." She trotted up the stairs, but slowed her steps in the hallway, desperate not to wake the boys. They'd both taken too-short naps this afternoon and she and Dallas had declared an early bath and bedtime for them. The days had grown longer and now, even though it was almost eight thirty, the remains of an early June sun filtered through the windows on the stairway landing.

She smiled at the thought of her boys asleep in their rooms. It felt like the most natural thing in the world to have those nurseries filled. She passed the door to Austin's room, but did a U-turn and came back to open it. Even though she'd checked the baby monitor just before coming up, she couldn't resist tiptoeing in to inhale his sweet baby shampoo scent and tuck him in one last time. She did the same with Tyler. She'd be up with him in a few hours for a two a.m. feeding—what had become her favorite time of the day.

Thank you, God. It was a prayer she whispered a dozen times every day. A prayer that had replaced four years of *Please, God.* She was still in awe of all that had happened in the space of a few months. Amazed at how two small boys could change their lives.

She found the folder in the drawer of Dallas's nightstand and sat cross-legged on the floor beside their bed, sorting through the receipts until she located the one she needed. She was about to close the folder when she noticed an invoice sticking out of the top of the folder. She tried to tamp it down, but discovered it was a legal-size sheet, taller than the folder. She removed it and folded it to fit. The familiar logo at the top of the page whisked her back in time. It was from the fertility clinic.

A strange rush of emotion filled her. She slipped the paper from the pile and studied it. The bill for their initial consultation with Dr. Gwinn, the fertility specialist. She smiled to herself. If he could only see them now.

As she smoothed the creases from the thin paper, her hand slid across the top where the date was printed: August 11. Her breath caught. Was that actually the date of her appointment? She remembered how hot it had been that day. Almost four years ago. They'd about baked in the parking lot, standing outside the building, trying to muster the courage to go inside.

But the significance of that date—August 11—made the tears come hot and fast.

Austin had been born that day! The very day they'd started fertility treatments. Their boy had entered the world, and God had answered their prayers for a child that day. Even as they'd walked into that appointment so full of hope and desperate prayers, God had already planned not just one, but two sons for them.

All those weeks and months and years when she'd thought it would never happen. When she thought God had forgotten their prayers, Austin had already been growing up.

And time was all that had stood between them and a dream that'd already been fulfilled. In God's perfect time.

"Happy Father's Day, Dad! Sorry we're late. Naps went long."

"Thanks, kiddo." Her dad strode down the front steps of the inn and met Danae on the sidewalk. "I appreciate your contribution." He pumped Dallas's hand. "Happy Father's Day, son. You waited a long time for this."

"It was worth the wait," Dallas said. "Happy Father's Day to you too."

They'd cancelled next week's Tuesday dinner in favor of celebrating together on this Father's Day Sunday.

It was Dallas's first, and Danae had played it up big, with his favorite breakfast, a homemade card from Austin, and a nice foot rub in his recliner after church. He'd sunk back into the chair, and sighed. "I could get used to this."

Of course, he'd given her *her* own first day in the sun on Mother's Day. It had been a year of firsts, and there was so much more yet to come.

Her dad gave Tyler a pat, and bent to ruffle Austin's hair. "What are you up to, Texas?"

Austin gave him a high five. "What're *you* up to, Missouri?"

Her dad had taken to calling Austin "Texas," so Dallas taught him a quick comeback, which her boy took great delight in delivering.

"Where's my girls?" Austin asked him.

Her dad gave a broad wink. "Sorry, Texas, the big girls aren't here yet. But the twins are in the backyard. Gram wants to eat outside again."

Austin made a dash for the porch.

"I'm on it." Dallas trotted after him.

Danae gave her dad a questioning look. "It's not like Jesse and Corinne to be late. You don't think they went to the hospital, do you?" Corinne's due date had been Friday, and her doctor planned to induce her if she wasn't in labor by Tuesday.

Dad shrugged. "We haven't heard anything. Here . . . let me take this one off your hands." He lifted little Tyler from her arms.

"Hang on. He needs his hat if you're going to be outside with him." She searched the diaper bag on her shoulder until she came up with the little baseball cap Chase and Landyn had given him.

She plopped it on his head, and they laughed as the hat fell over Tyler's nose and almost engulfed his entire head.

"That ought to do it," Dad said. He started bouncing the baby on his shoulder.

Danae pulled a burp rag from the bag. "If you're going to bounce him, you'll want this." She tucked it under Tyler's still-wobbly head.

Dad resumed bouncing and turned to follow Dallas and Austin to the backyard.

"Be sure you support his head," Danae called after him.

He turned back to her with a wink. "I think we'll be OK. I've done this a time or two."

She managed to look sheepish and waved at her boys before going inside.

Stepping into the house, the place she'd spent her own childhood, a rush of emotions washed over her. She'd spent so many years longing to fill a void, longing to fit in with her sisters, to give her parents grandchildren. She finally felt like God had made a home for her—for *them*—and had given them a full-blown family in a way she'd never expected.

No, it hadn't been an easy road. But when she looked back, she realized that if God had answered her prayers the way she'd so desperately hoped, she and Dallas would not have their precious boys.

She watched her father carry Tyler around the side of the house. Her boys would be a part of this amazing family. They would climb the same tree in the meadow that she had climbed as a little girl, and sit around the Whitman family table and create memories that would carry them through every storm. Her boys would be loved—and sometimes disciplined—by a whole crew of Whitmans. And they would learn, as she had, that they could take their deepest needs to a good and faithful God who would answer their prayers. In His own time, which was always perfect.

She was a slow learner. But she was discovering that sometimes life's greatest adventures—and greatest blessings—were found by taking another way home.

Group Discussion Guide

Keep in mind that discussion questions contain spoilers that may give away elements of the plot.

1. In *Another Way Home*, Danae—the second daughter of the Whitman family—and her husband, Dallas, have struggled with infertility for several years. She is growing depressed and even a little desperate, and it is beginning to take a toll on her marriage. Have you or anyone close to you struggled with infertility or secondary infertility (being unable to become pregnant again after giving birth to one or more children)? How did that struggle affect the marriage?

2. Another way that Danae's childlessness affected her was extreme jealousy of her friends and two sisters who had no trouble conceiving; in fact, her sisters experienced pregnancies that were unplanned, and initially, unwanted. Can you relate to the frustration and the sense of unfairness Danae felt? Have you ever been the object of a person's envy where some aspect of your life is concerned? Have you ever felt guilty for something that was beyond your control?

3. Dallas was adopted as an infant, but a humiliating experience as a teenager caused him to shut his heart to the possibility of Danae and him adopting a baby. Were you adopted, or have you adopted children, or had other close experiences with adoption? Are there prejudices against adopted children and adoptive parents? Why? What is the biblical perspective on adoption?

4. Danae decides she's tired of feeling sorry for herself, and when she hears of a women's shelter needing volunteers, she feels compelled to become involved. But her husband and her father are both concerned about the danger she might be putting herself in. Do you agree with the way Danae responded to those men's concerns? Have you ever felt torn

between obeying something you felt God was asking you to do, and heeding the concerns of people whose opinions you respect? How did you respond and what was the ultimate outcome? Have you ever been mistaken about something you thought God was calling you to do?

5. Danae, and to a lesser extent, Dallas, become involved in the life of Misty, one of the abused women at the shelter. They are especially drawn to her three-year-old son, Austin. Do you think they overstepped conventional boundaries in their level of involvement? If given a similar opportunity to babysit a child like Austin for a few days, would you agree to do so? Why or why not?

6. Did you see warning signs that Misty was planning to commit the crime she did? Were you sympathetic to her reasoning that she was protecting her son and herself by her actions? If Misty had confessed her plans to Danae or someone else at the center, what actions do you think they might have taken? What options did Misty have?

7. Once it became clear that Misty would likely go to jail for her crime, Dallas and Danae faced a huge decision, one for which they could not possibly see all the future repercussions. They made a decision, knowing that it might bring them great heartbreak in the future. What were the heartbreaking possibilities they faced? What was the best case scenario? Do you think they made the right decision? Do you think you would have decided the same way they did?

8. How did you feel about the entire Whitman family's involvement in the decisions about Austin? How much input should extended family have in an individual's or a family's decisions?

9. When Misty revealed that she was pregnant and desired for Dallas and Danae to raise her baby along with Austin, how did that affect their decision? Did it make it easier or more difficult? What new questions did Misty's revelation raise for the family?

10. Everything changed when Misty's sister decided she wanted Austin. What do you think Misty's reason was for changing her mind to allow Charity, her sister, to take Austin? Do you think there is merit to a child being raised by blood relatives instead of unrelated "strangers"?

11. After things worked themselves out, what do you think about Misty's decision to ask Dallas and Danae to legally adopt her infant, but not Austin, since Misty didn't want him feeling as if his mother had rejected him after *knowing* him? What challenges did this present for Dallas and Danae? What is your opinion about the children having an ongoing relationship with Misty? What are the advantages and challenges of open adoption?

12. What did you think about the mutual decision Misty and the Brookses made about the children's surname? How important is a name? How important is it to share a name with the family you live with? What kinds of issues might their decision bring about in the lives of Austin and his brother in years to come? How would you have handled this decision in Dallas and Danae's place? In Misty's place?

13. Misty decided to see Austin one last time since she could see him in the hospital, instead of in jail. What do you think about her decision? How difficult would a good-bye like that be? Do you see Misty as a hero, a villain, or something in-between?

14. What kind of issues do you think Austin might deal with as he grows up? How can the Whitman family help Dallas and Danae navigate the uncharted waters of raising two children in an open adoption when the birth mother is in prison for life?

15. How did the scene where Danae comes across the receipt from the fertility clinic make you feel? Has God ever given you such a glimpse of His perfect timing—only after the fact?

Want to learn more about Deborah Raney
and check out other great fiction from
Abingdon Press?

Check out our website at
www.AbingdonFiction.com
to read interviews with your favorite authors,
find tips for starting a reading group,
and stay posted on what new titles are on the horizon.

Be sure to visit Deborah online!
www.deborahraney.com

About the Author

DEBORAH RANEY dreamed of writing a book since the summer she read all of Laura Ingalls Wilder's Little House books and discovered that a little Kansas farm girl could, indeed, grow up to be a writer. After a happy twenty-year detour as a stay-at-home wife and mom, Deb began her writing career. Her first novel, *A Vow to Cherish*, was awarded a Silver Angel from Excellence in Media and inspired the acclaimed World Wide Pictures film of the same title. Since then, her books have won the RITA Award, the HOLT Medallion, the National Readers' Choice Award, as well as being a two-time Christy Award finalist. Deb enjoys speaking and teaching at writers' conferences across the country. She and her husband, Ken Raney, make their home in their native Kansas and, until a recent move to the city, enjoyed the small-town life that is the setting for many of Deb's novels. The Raneys enjoy gardening, antiquing, art museums, movies, and traveling to visit four grown children and a growing brood of grandchildren, all of whom live much too far away.

Deborah loves hearing from her readers. To e-mail her or to learn more about her books, please visit www.deborahraney.com.

We hope you enjoyed *Another Way Home*, the third book in Deborah Raney's Chicory Inn series. Here's a sample of the fourth book, *Close to Home*, which will be available in June 2016.

Chapter One

Can I bother you for a minute, Bree?"

Bree Whitman looked up from her desk to see Aaron Jakes standing in the doorway to her cubicle. Popping her earbuds out, she motioned to him. "Sure. What's up?" She tilted her computer screen downward so he'd know she was listening—and so she wouldn't be tempted not to.

"Do you mind coming down to my office for a minute?"

She laughed and stretched to peer over the half wall dividing the cubicles. His was two "doors" down. "This better be important if you're going to make me walk *all* the way over there."

"It's important."

She shot him a questioning look. Except for Wendy, the college girl who served as front-desk receptionist for all three companies officed in their complex, Bree and Aaron were the only two still in this wing.

Aaron had already turned and headed back to his cubicle.

She glanced at the clock on her computer. She needed to leave in fifteen minutes. She'd promised Audrey she'd stop at the bakery for some rolls on her way to Tuesday family dinner tonight, and she was supposed to pick up Grandma CeeCee in Langhorne on her way out to the Chicory Inn.

Sighing, she slid from behind her desk and went to Aaron's cubicle. She glanced across the office through the plate glass window that faced the street. The time-and-temperature sign on the bank across the street flashed from 101 degrees to 102. "Are we seriously in triple digits again?" She lifted her long brown hair off her neck, twisted it into a bun, and held it in place for a few seconds before letting it fall to her shoulders.

"Well, it is July," he said without looking up. Standing beside his desk, his expression said he was agitated by whatever was on his computer screen.

"Okay, so what's up?" she asked again, suddenly nervous about being alone in the office with him.

Aaron leaned over his desk and pulled up a spreadsheet on the computer, then pulled out his desk chair and stepped aside, indicating she should have a seat.

"What's this?" She sat down and looked at the screen. "Oh . . . the Broadhogan conference? I thought you had that all worked out."

He gave a low growl. "What doesn't kill you, makes you stronger, right? Isn't that the way the saying goes? *Please* tell me that's the way the saying goes."

"What'd they do now?" She rolled his desk chair closer to the screen and studied the logistics timeline he'd been working on for close to two weeks now.

Aaron put an arm on the desk and leaned in close enough that she could smell his woodsy aftershave. "I thought I finally had a workable schedule, and they sent it back *again*." He pointed over her shoulder at several highlighted changes he'd made in the spec book for the job.

This had to be at least the fourth time Aaron's proposal had been rejected. If Bree ran the company, they would have declined the job after the third try. But Cape Girardeau was a small town and Sallie Wilkes, their boss, couldn't afford to turn down work— or burn bridges. Even if they had to put in five times the hours on this event than any other conference they'd done in the history of the company. And that was saying a lot, given that Wilkes Event Planning had been in Cape for a quarter of a century.

Sallie often assigned Bree and Aaron to the same events because of their age. Barbara, one of the older employees, referred to them as the "hip young team." She and Aaron usually got handed the events at the college, the arts council, large weddings, or anything else that would draw a younger, more contemporary crowd. It made sense.

She and Aaron made a good team, too. Aaron was the more organized one—although you wouldn't have known it by his lackadaisical attitude toward this show—and he was good with the technical stuff. She shined when it came to the details—decorating and swag and signage.

Aaron pointed at the spreadsheet again. "Would you just look this over once more before I send it back? Please? Because if I have to redo it one more time, I will seriously just go flip burgers or get a job as a lifeguard or a nanny or something."

She laughed. "You'll do no such thing. Besides, you'd be a terrible nanny."

"Hey!"

She ignored him and studied the document, scrolling down the pages, and mentally walking through the event in her head as she'd learned to do. But it wasn't easy to concentrate with Aaron hanging over her shoulder, his warmth making her overheat, and his peppermint breath pleasantly distracting. "It looks good to me."

"That's what you said the last two times I had you look it over. Not that I'm blaming you," he added quickly. He patted her on the back and his hand lingered there a fraction of a second too long.

Aaron was a flirt. Not the obnoxious kind, but maybe the kind that wouldn't be so fun to be married to. In the past few weeks he'd definitely been turning on the charm when she was around. She hadn't done anything to encourage him. At least she didn't think she had.

She scooted the chair back, forcing him to step to one side. "If I were you, I'd just remind them that they pay us by the hour. That usually does the trick."

"Will do." He cleared his throat and glanced at his watch. "Hey, are you hungry? You wouldn't want to go get something to eat, would you?"

She cringed inwardly. Maybe his invitation meant nothing more than two coworkers grabbing a bite to eat, but it wasn't like him to be nervous, and he definitely seemed like there was a lot riding on her answer.

"Sorry . . . I've got plans already. But thanks." She liked Aaron. Maybe more than she wanted to admit. She did consider him a friend. But she wasn't ready for more than casual friendship. With Aaron or with anybody else of the male persuasion. Besides, it would be way too complicated to become involved with a coworker. To become involved with anyone.

"How about this weekend? Wasn't there a movie you wanted to see? We could—"

"Aaron . . ." She closed her eyes, scrambling for words that would let him down easy, realizing at the same time that she *wanted* to leave her options open. But that wasn't fair to him. Either she was interested or she wasn't. "I don't think I'm quite ready."

"Ready for what?"

Her face grew warm. "Maybe I'm misreading you. It . . . sounded like you were asking me on a date."

"And if I was?"

She rose and pushed the chair back up to his desk, stepping toward the doorway. "I don't think so. But . . . I'm flattered you asked. I really am."

He leaned against the desk, palms flat on the surface behind him, watching her with a sly smile. "And if I was just asking as a friend? Just popcorn and a movie with a friend from work?"

Why did he have to be so stinkin' good-looking? She felt reckless and a little out of control. But really, what harm could it do? He said just as friends. "Sure. I'd love to go to the movies with my friend Aaron."

He grinned. "Great! Just pick a day."

"Saturday?"

"It's a date."

She gave him a look. "No. It's not."

"My bad." He held his hands up like a shield, still grinning. "Poor choice of words. An early show, okay? We can do a matinee if you'd rather."

"Oh. That'd be good." Far less like a date. "I'll meet you at the theater, okay?" Even less like a date.

"Okay. I'll check movie times and text you and we can decide which movie. Does it matter which showing?"

"I'm free all afternoon." She was free the rest of her life. But he didn't need to know that.

Not yet. She turned and walked back to her cubicle, shut down her computer, and gathered her things. It wasn't until she was getting in her car that it hit her. She had a date Saturday.

No, Whitman. It's not a date. You're going to the movies with a friend.

Then why did she feel that same shivery anticipation she'd felt before her first real date with Tim?

There was a line at the bakery, and by the time she got the rolls and headed out to the inn, she was already fifteen minutes late and drenched in perspiration. Glancing in the rearview mirror, she frowned at her reflection. She'd gathered her stick-straight hair into a ponytail earlier, securing it with a rubber band she found in her glove compartment. She looked a mess, but Missouri in July was not conducive to any other hairstyle.

She looked at the clock and notched the cruise control up. Her in-laws knew not to wait supper on her. *In-laws.* Bree refused to think of them as her *former* in-laws, though technically, that's what Grant and Audrey were—now that Tim was gone.

Too often, she got off work late in the day, and she'd convinced Tim's family to never wait on her. The youngest grandkids couldn't be held off too long, and besides, the Whitmans' Tuesday night dinners were informal affairs. Pot luck, picnics even, whenever the weather was nice enough, with everyone just hanging out together, enjoying each other's company.

Now that Grant and Audrey had eight grandkids, things were usually geared around the little ones. And their bedtimes. She missed the early days when she and Tim would stay up with his brother and sisters—and later, their spouses—and play board games and card games around the kitchen table. In the old house—before it had become the Chicory Inn.

The refurbished bed and breakfast was gorgeous. Elegant yet cozy with its cream-painted woodwork and contemporary rugs and textiles. But sometimes she missed the old house—where Tim had first introduced her to his down-to-earth family. Or maybe it was just Tim she missed. He'd been gone by the time the restoration was finished on the inn. It seemed strange to think that Tim had never even seen the house where she spent so much time now.

In some ways, she knew his family better than he had. There were seven nieces and nephews he'd never even met. And changes. His parents were older; his grandmother was aging and—

CeeCee! She gasped and hit the brakes. She was supposed to pick up Tim's grandmother on her way out to the inn! She'd totally forgotten, and now she'd have to go back for CeeCee and be even later than she already was. *Good grief!* Had Aaron's little invitation flustered her that much?

She turned the Taurus around at the first field entrance she came to. The ditches were deep on both sides of the narrow county lane, and recent rains had washed the road out on either side of the culvert. She managed to make the turn, and as soon as she was back on the road, she called CeeCee's home phone. She hadn't yet figured out how to use the hands-free feature of her new car. Well, new to her anyway. The car was a 2013 model, but it was the newest car she'd ever owned—and the first vehicle she'd bought on her own.

She vowed to get the Bluetooth set up before the weekend. There was rarely much traffic on this state highway, but she didn't want to add an accident to her list of screw-ups tonight.

CeeCee's answering machine finally picked up on the sixth ring. *Oh dear.* She was probably sitting out on the front porch waiting. And had been for the past thirty minutes.

Speaking loud and slow, she left a message. "CeeCee, this is Bree. I'm running really late, but I'll be there in less than ten minutes. I'm so sorry I didn't call earlier."

She clicked off and called Audrey's cell phone. Thankfully, Audrey answered on the first ring.

Bree told her the same thing she'd told CeeCee, minus the loud and slow. Nor did she mention that she'd actually forgotten all about CeeCee and had to backtrack. "Has she called wondering where I am?"

"No," Audrey said. "But she wouldn't. You just take your time, sweet girl. She'll wait for you. It's not like she has a hot date or anything."

Bree laughed, then wrinkled her brow, watching herself frown in the rearview mirror. Did Audrey somehow know about Aaron? She wouldn't put it past her mother-in-law. Audrey was perceptive . . . sometimes *too* perceptive.

CeeCee wasn't waiting on the porch, and when she hadn't answered the doorbell after three rings, Bree used her key and let herself in. It was stifling in the little two-story house, but CeeCee always kept the thermostat at eighty, summer or winter. Still, considering CeeCee's age, she felt a touch of misgiving about what she might find. She walked through the rooms of the little house, calling CeeCee's name.

The door to the master bedroom was open. The shades were drawn and lamps turned off. But the lump in the bed was unmistakably CeeCee, tiny as the almost eighty-five-year-old woman was. It wasn't even seven o'clock yet. For a minute, Bree froze, thinking the worst.

But soft snoring came from the bed and Bree flipped on the light and went to the bedside, kneeling beside Tim's grandmother. "CeeCee?" She patted the crepey, thin arm that lay atop the quilt. "Are you feeling okay?"

A snuffle, and a start, and CeeCee sat up in bed, looking disoriented and weak.

"Are you okay?" Bree looked into the rheumy eyes, trying to determine if she was ill.

CeeCee threw back the covers and squinted at the clock. She was wearing a cotton nightgown. "Oh, no. Did I oversleep?"

"It's my fault," Bree said, not sure if CeeCee was confused or if she was referring to her nap. But surely she hadn't changed into a nightgown just to take a nap. "I'm late picking you up for our Tuesday dinner." She cast about the tidy room, looking for the outfit CeeCee had been wearing. "Can I get your clothes for you?"

CeeCee looked down at her nightgown. "Oh, I don't think I'll change."

Bree laughed, but CeeCee's expression said she wasn't kidding. Bree went to the closet and chose a pair of elastic-waisted pants and a colorful blouse she'd seen the woman wear often. "How about this?"

"I really think I'll just stay here. I'm pretty tired. I played bridge all afternoon, you know."

"Oh, but don't you want to go out to Grant and Audrey's for dinner? Everyone will be disappointed if you don't come."

"They'll get over it." She waved a frail hand and sank back onto the pillows. "Audrey said she'd do the dessert tonight anyway."

Was that what was bothering CeeCee? It was usually her job to furnish the dessert for Tuesday nights. But it wasn't like her to get her feelings hurt over something so petty. "Are you sure you feel okay? Have you eaten?"

"I'm just tired. Don't you worry about me. You go on and have a good time. Give them all my love." She sounded more like herself now.

But Bree was still worried. She said her good-byes but didn't feel quite right about leaving. She locked the door behind her, but in the driveway, she called Audrey again and told her how she'd found CeeCee.

"I wouldn't worry too much, honey. She did play bridge today, so maybe she's just worn out. And if she insisted, you can't force her to come."

"Well, if you're sure."

"Grant will check on her later tonight. You come on. We saved a plate for you."

"Okay."

Backing out of the driveway, she shot up a prayer for Tim's grandmother. If anything happened to her, she would never forgive herself. And none of this would have happened if she hadn't been daydreaming about that stupid movie date.

Chapter Two

She drove too fast and arrived out at the Chicory Inn just as they were clearing the table and dishing up dessert—Audrey's apple crisp and homemade ice cream. She held up the bags of rolls from the bakery and gave a sheepish smile. "Anybody want a roll?"

Audrey took them from her. "Don't worry about it. We had plenty to eat. I'll just put them in the freezer for next week. Unless you want one now?"

"Are you kidding? Forget my plate." She pointed to the apple crisp, which filled the kitchen with a tart, cinnamony scent. "This can be dinner for me."

"Don't be silly." Audrey gave her a one-armed hug and thrust a warm plate at her, a sampling of the supper she'd missed. "You eat. You're too skinny as it is. And don't you worry; I'll make sure there's apple crisp left for you."

"And ice cream," Bree said, taking the proffered plate but casting a suspicious eye on Tim's brother, Link, and three brothers-in-law who were standing at the counter snarfing apple crisp and looking as if they could easily put away a second bowl before she could put a dent in her plate.

Tim's three sisters came to her defense, ushering their husbands away from the counter. "You let us worry about them," Landyn said. "You eat, sis."

It warmed her heart when Tim's sisters included her, calling her "sis" the way they did with each other. "Thanks for having my back."

"You know we do," Danae said, laughing even as she shooed Dallas from the counter for the second time.

"Grant must have the kids?" Bree said over a mouthful of green bean casserole. "I haven't seen any of them. And where's that new baby?" Corinne and Jesse's new little girl—*four* for them now—had been born on Father's Day less than a month ago. Bree had only seen little Sasha twice. She was learning how quickly babies grew up and didn't want to miss holding this newest little one while she was still tiny.

"Sasha and Tyler are both sleeping upstairs," Corinne said. "Poppa has the other six playing some game he invented down in the meadow."

"Did Poppa get any apple crisp yet?" Bree asked, eyeing the dwindling supply.

Audrey popped her head around the corner. "Poppa had two servings before any of you got here. Don't you worry about him, Bree."

She gave an exaggerated *whew* and took a bite of Audrey's lasagna. The sisters started putting food back in the fridge and loading the dishwasher, and she hurried to finish eating so she could help. It seemed like too often she sailed in late and ate while the others did the work of cleaning up. They never seemed to resent her for it, but she sometimes worried they might.

They finished in the kitchen and Audrey shooed the young women to the family room. "I'll be there in a few minutes, but I want to start a breakfast casserole for tomorrow's guests."

Conversation among the sisters quickly turned to babies and marriage, and she felt herself curl up and withdraw a little. Tim's sisters were all three moms now that Danae and Dallas were raising the two little boys of an incarcerated woman. Since Tim's death, she'd swung between relief that he hadn't left her with a child to raise on her own, and grief that she'd never gotten to fulfill her dream of having his babies. At twenty-eight, and no prospects for a husband, she definitely saw her chances of ever having a family slipping away.

Some of her friends thought she was crazy to have kept such close ties to Tim's family. And maybe it was a little unusual. But it wasn't as if their marriage had ended in a messy divorce. Tim's family had kept her sane after he was killed in Afghanistan. They alone knew the man she mourned as well as she did. Knew he'd been a hero in so many ways—not just as a marine killed in the line of duty.

And as Audrey had told her more than once, the Whitman family's grief was doubled by the thought of losing Bree. "You'll never lose me," she'd promised Audrey. But they were words easily spoken in the throes of grief. And sometimes she wondered if it was a promise she could keep. If she got married again, how would any new husband feel about her keeping ties to her late husband's family? How would future parents-in-law feel about Bree's close relationship with Grant and Audrey?

Until recently, she'd been content to still be considered a part of the Whitman clan. To sit with Grant and Audrey and CeeCee in church most Sunday mornings, to feel that she fit in at their Tuesday night dinners, and that she was welcome—more than welcome—to come around any time she needed a dose of family. To feel close to Tim, the way she always had at the house on Chicory Lane.

But the winds were shifting. She felt it more each week. And she wasn't sure if it was her, or if it was Tim's family who was pulling away. If they were, it wasn't intentional. She knew that. But their lives had all gone forward, while more and more, she felt like the odd man out when the Whitmans gathered.

She loved this family with all her heart. She still considered them *her* family, and knew they loved her like their own daughter and sister. Yet with every new grandchild that entered the Whitman family, she felt her place—her *purpose*—in the family diminished. They were getting married, having babies. And she was stuck. Stuck in love with a man she could never have again. At least not on this side of heaven. She was in a holding pattern that would be painful to come out of, no matter how it came about.

Maybe that was why she'd agreed to go to the movies with Aaron. Maybe it was a way to ease into the—

"Isn't that right, Bree?"

She shook herself back to the conversation, racking her brain to remember what they'd been talking about. And drawing a blank. She laughed awkwardly. "I confess I wasn't paying attention."

"Are you okay?" Corinne's forehead furrowed with concern.

"I'm fine." Bree felt bad for making them worry. "Just thinking about some stuff at work." That wasn't exactly a lie. Aaron was at work.

"How's work going these days? I haven't heard you say for a while." Danae's sweet shifting of the conversation onto Bree only made her feel more guilty.

"It's good. We've been busy, so that's always good. Job security and all that. We've had a couple of finicky clients to deal with. But there's always that . . ." She was out of things to say, but they were all looking at her, waiting.

After an awkward moment, Danae jumped up. "I'll be right back. I'm going to check on Tyler."

"Would you make sure Sasha isn't crying?" Corinne asked. "I forgot to bring the monitor."

"I have an old one we don't use anymore," Landyn offered. "I'll bring it next time and we can just keep it here."

And they were off talking about babies and husbands again.

Bree waited until they were deep in conversation before slipping away.

She found Audrey in the kitchen. "I thought we were done in here. Can I help with something?"

"Oh, no." Audrey waved her away. "You go on and visit with the girls. I was just getting the kids something to drink. I'd rather they consume beverages with red food dye out on the lawn."

Bree laughed. "I can't blame you there. Here, let me help." She took the pitcher of what smelled like Hawaiian Punch from Audrey and filled little paper cups with cartoon characters on them. "Will Grant want something?"

"He'll want exactly what the kids are having. Just maybe in a bigger cup." She set a giant plastic St. Louis Cardinals cup on the counter, and Bree filled that too.

"Are they still down in the meadow?"

"Grant has them corralled on the deck. Do you mind taking the drinks out?" Audrey handed Bree a roll of paper towels. "You'll need these. I'll be right behind you with cookies."

"I'll let them know." She tucked the roll of towels under one arm, set the cups in the shallow tray Audrey provided and carefully carried it to the back door. Link opened it from the outside just as she got there. "Thanks, bro."

"Do you need help?" Tim's brother peered into the paper cups. "Who's the big one for?"

"Your dad. But there's more in the fridge if you want some. And cookies, according to your mom."

He looked sheepish. "Already had a couple of those."

"Link Whitman! Shame on you." She laughed. "I don't suppose you'll divulge their hiding place?"

"I'm not crazy." He grinned and opened the door wider while she passed.

Huckleberry, the family's chocolate Labrador, chose that moment to streak into the house at full speed.

Bree let out a little scream, balancing the tray of drinks for all she was worth.

Link grabbed the dog by the collar. "Huck! Come here, you crazy pooch!" He grabbed onto the panting dog with one hand and held open the door with a comical bow at the waist. "After you."

She gave Huckleberry the stink eye and blew out a sigh of relief. Link laughed, closing the door behind her.

Grant had rounded up the troops and had them sitting in a semi-circle on the floor of the deck. They smelled of sweat and grass and a hint of baby powder. She loved every one of them as if they were hers. She regretted so deeply that Tim had never laid eyes on his nephews or nieces—except for Sari, who'd been a baby when he left for Afghanistan.

Pushing the maudlin thoughts away, Bree carried the tray over to the oldest Pennington girls and handed them cups. They looked up at her with sweet smiles. Their skin had turned golden in the Missouri sun, but that couldn't hide the freckles sprinkled like sequins across each of their little noses.

Grant took his cup and helped her distribute the rest of the juice.

Within thirty seconds the first spill happened. One of Landyn's twins. Bree still had trouble telling Grace and Emma apart. Laughing, she unfurled a few feet of paper toweling and knelt to sop up the mess.

Grant picked up the little girl. "Don't cry, Em. There's more where that came from." He set her down and poured her a refill from his own cup. "See? All better."

The two-year-old smiled up at him, tipping the cup to her lips—completely upside down. Juice went everywhere again, which sent the other kids into an uproar of giggles—and Emma into louder wails.

Shaking with laughter—but silently, over Emma's head—Bree spun off another length of toweling and dried off the little girl. And Grant's shoes. Thank goodness the deck was already red-tinted wood. "I should have just let Huckleberry spill them all at once and get it over with."

Later, when the evening wound down, she found herself with Emma and Grace both on her lap, each toddler with an arm around Bree's neck, echoing their cousins' oohs and aahs as they all peered up into the summer sky, a full moon spotlighting the trail of a shooting star.

"Did you see it, Miss Bree?" Sadie's voice was full of wonder as she scooted over and tucked her hand in the crook of Bree's arm. "Did you? *I* saw it!"

"Me too. That was pretty cool, wasn't it? Keep watching. Maybe we'll see another one." The cicadas started up their evening song, drowning out the rest of nature's symphony.

How could she ever give this up? How could she ever let this family go? And yet, if she didn't, would she ever know the joy of having her own children, of knowing a love like she'd had with her Timothy? She couldn't go on feeling this . . . *stagnant* in her own life.

Sighing, she hugged the twins closer and squeezed her eyes shut to stave off the tears that threatened.

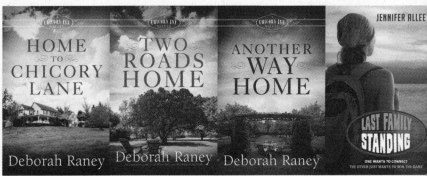
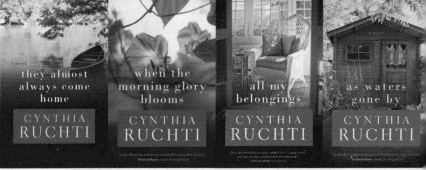

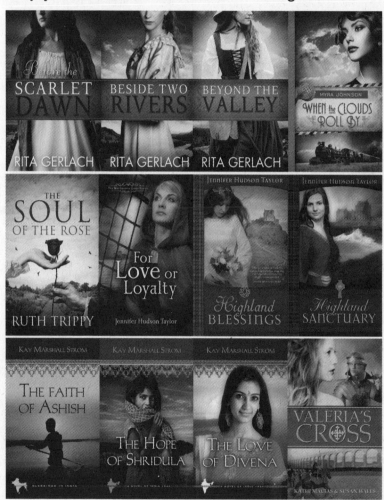

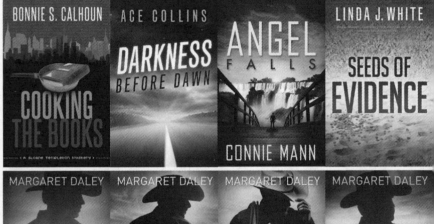

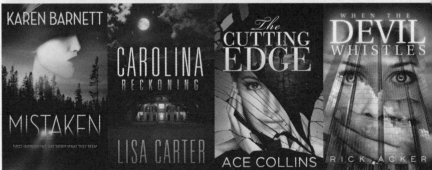

For other fine books, visit AbingdonPress.com